Nigh
Ti

CW01584256

'Another collection of first-rate tales from the second city.'

MARK BILLINGHAM
Multi-award winning & bestselling author

'A fresh collection of superb stories about the night and all that it brings, from children's bedtime, to shift work and the inevitable musings on love and life and death. Stuffed with talent and wonderful one-liners, this anthology is the best of the West Midlands and a showcase of who we are. I loved it.'

KIT DE WAAL
Award-winning author of *My Name is Leon*

'A highly imaginative collection of brilliant stories that beautifully capture the unique elements of place. The result is a fascinating and inventive narrative journey through the West Midlands.'

KERRY HADLEY-PRYCE
Prize-winning writer of *The Black Country*

'A dazzling band of searing tales, a perfect salute to the talent of the second city, and a sublime follow-up to Floodgate's first collection.'

JENNY LECOAT
New York Times bestselling author

‘Every piece in *Night Time Economy* is a gem – by turns powerful, uplifting, heartbreaking and funny, this anthology showcases the depth and breadth of writing talent to be found in the Midlands.'

ELIZABETH LEE
Author, *Cunning Women*

‘A compelling literary map of the nocturnal Midlands in all its rich and poetic variety. We see the snare of capitalism writ large here, blighted lives darkening with nightfall, but this is often offset by the human connections that the system can't break, and there's as much joy as despair in this innovative anthology. It brings out the best in some of our most talented writers, proving that short-form prose can illuminate the darkness as effectively as any creative medium.'

PAUL MCDONALD
Academic, comic novelist, & poet

‘It was a pleasure to read these short stories full of life. What sharp insights these authors have to share and with talent to burn. A delight.'

PAUL MCVEIGH
Award winning author & playwright

Night Time Economy

Edited by Garrie Fletcher
Peter Haynes
Nigel Proctor

FLOODGATE

First Floodgate Press paperback edition September 2024

www.floodgatepress.co.uk

Selection ©Garrie Fletcher, Peter Haynes and Nigel Proctor 2024

Introduction ©Garrie Fletcher

Stories ©Jamila Barry ©Sasha Butler ©Richard Lakin ©R.M.Francis ©Alan Beard ©Charlie Wilkinson ©Siobhan Maher ©Mez Packer ©James Brogden ©Catherine Lockhart ©Anjem Anwar ©Matthew Storer ©Patrick Boyden ©Helen Cross ©Liz Churchill ©Andy Howlett ©Taylor Burns ©Josh Allen ©Ian Whatley ©Alan Kane Fraser ©Sadie Kaye ©Kirsten Handley ©Zahira P. Latif ©Liz Kershaw ©Ben Waddington ©Lynne Voyce ©Cheryl Powell ©Esme Brown ©Nigel Proctor ©Chloe Sell ©Eleanor Trigg ©Tom Maguire

The rights of the contributors to be identified as the authors of this work has been asserted by them in accordance with the Copyright, Designs and Patents Act, 1988

Unless otherwise indicated, this collection is a work of fiction. Names, characters, places and incidents are either products of the author's imagination or are used fictitiously. Any resemblance to †actual events or locales or persons, living or dead, is entirely coincidental.

All rights reserved. No part of this book may be reproduced, stored in or introduced into a retrieval system, or transmitted, in any form, or by any means (electronic, mechanical, photocopying, recording or otherwise) without the prior permission of the publisher.

A catalogue record for this book is available from the British Library.

Paperback ISBN: 978-1-7394395-1-4

Typeset in Baskerville Neo & Monotype Grotesque

Cover design by Garrie Fletcher © Floodgate

Text design by Peter Burgess

Printed by ImprintDigital.com

Contents

I Am Midlander

Imagine you live in a country of over seventy-million people. A geographically small but densely populated country with such diversity that you only have to drive a few miles for accents and language to change. And imagine that you live in the heart of that country, in an area known as the Midlands – an area that is home to nearly eleven-million people, a million more than London, and yet culturally you are ignored.

The Midlands is large enough to be split into East, West and South and yet small enough, it would seem, to be ignored by most. The West Midlands is home to nearly 6 million souls, according to the 2021 census, but if you judged it purely on written work set here, you'd assume we were a few hundred thousand. Yet, as you'll soon discover, there are stories here, lives here, loves here.

At Floodgate, we know this. We know there's a rich seam of talent which stretches from Stoke down to Hereford, from Coventry to Oswestry. We know that inky gold flows forth from Stafford, Worcester, Solihull, Wolverhampton, Telford, Walsall, Birmingham and everywhere in between. We know there are stories of joy, despair, of urban struggle and triumph, of country folklore entwinned with modern myth and digital memes. We know it because we've read it, heard it, written it.

In these pages you will find work from established authors, emerging authors and some who thought they'd never be authors.

You will find the joy of communities coming together, of strong women fighting demons and battling against hardship, of people loving when it'd be easier to hate, of others breaking away when it'd be easier to stay, and stories about the spaces between worlds, about the shift from day to night, and the comfort and danger that brings.

Our Night Time Economy is one of humour in defeat, of power untapped, words unsaid then screamed, of obsession, lust, hope, redemption and joy. The stories within these pages are within us all and beat strongest within the hearts of the writers here because, like me, they are Midlanders.

Enjoy.

GARRIE FLETCHER

Flying

JAMILA BARRY

This is how I escaped from a Yoruba demon, true story. My name is Raina and I have a long history of bad decisions. Raina means queen, and I'm a proud woman. I like to say I raised myself, I came up from mud. I like to say my children are a reflection of me, and then bask in that reflected glow. I like to think I am the smartest person I know, but my life hasn't shown that. I just keep swerving left, left, left, like a broken compass that only shows the wrong directions. That year my bad decision was Taiwo, a Peckham rude boy with money.

This chapter in the Taiwo chronicles starts in Highcroft Hall, around two in the morning. Highcroft Hall was where Taiwo had his fancy apartment, all smooth bland interior and a mezzanine floor and a beige bathroom where a woman could be held hostage, hypothetically. Before the building was divided into so many overpriced flats with MDF walls, it had been what they used to call a lunatic asylum. And before that, it was a workhouse, purpose built in the eighteen hundreds. So, terrible things had always happened there.

Highcroft Hall in this reincarnation is gated, can you believe it? A gated community slapped down in the middle of Erdington's HMOs and care homes. You had to punch in a passcode to open the high wrought iron gates, then drive through the tunnel entrance, reaching the gardens and car park surrounding the building. I used to have bad dreams of being locked inside and that happened once. I also dreamed I would have to call the police, and that happened too.

But this night was calm, no drama. I had promised to stay the night, but a vaguely troubled feeling had grown over me and settled in my heart, snagging my breath and keeping me awake. I wanted to be at home, where nothing was luxurious and everything was falling apart, but I was safe. I wanted to be with my children, who were old enough to be alone, but I yearned for them anyway. By the middle of the night Taiwo was fed up and said he would drive me home, his feelings hurt by my spiritual absence.

Outside the world was silver and black, hushed and genteel, with a full moon watching over the rows of executive cars. We got into his Lexus – two doors, sunroof, red leather interior and pearlescent custom paint job. I hated that car; it was almost as terrible as the bathroom. Not all insentient objects are innocent, and I will tell you now, this car was a threat. However, my compass was broken and while I'd previously jumped out of that car for now, heady and heedless, I strapped in beside Taiwo and off we went.

We started, gliding through Erdington under darkly overhanging trees, past tall houses set well back from the quiet roads. Only a few people were out, and those were lurching pale faced addicts. Taiwo was building up speed, he was feeling rejected. Everyone who ever loved me has left me, he said early on, and I said – not me, never. He had been a surviving twin, left behind in Nigeria as a baby for unknowable reasons, raised in a boarding school, and I knew only my precious love could heal him. Now, to show his displeasure, he began to drive increasingly fast as we hit the Gravelly Hill Interchange. We rose up, Birmingham fell apart and lay out on either side of us. Aston was coming up to the right, a forest with only the treetops visible, a spire, the distant netting of the Villa stadium just showing underneath the clouds. To the left, the reservoir hid its secrets under the reflected streetlights. The Lexus picked up speed.

Part of me wanted to beg him to slow down, but my dark heart urged: faster, faster. We rushed on, the city blurring around us, swerving round cars foolish enough to share the road at this time. Once Taiwo braked for red lights and a walking duvet with two bright eyes and a ginger beard approached. The figure held back when he saw our faces through the darkened glass.

I haven't described Taiwo yet. He wasn't handsome, but he surrounded himself with beautiful things. As well as the asylum apartment and the car-of-bad-omen, he had a quadruple wardrobe stuffed with Italian tailoring and expensive, eccentric shoes. He had me, and whoever else, also. He had a winter coat of virgin wool and cashmere, softer than a baby's eyelashes. In his hallway he had shelves with fourteen pairs of Jordans, all red and black, all different, none of which he wore. He had a plush sofa which held the imprints of varied violations. He wore an Audemars Piguet (diamonds in the face), and he had a beautiful smile, with incredibly white teeth and gold canines. He said it was having his teeth whitened that brought his long career of fraud to a halt – he had used one stolen credit card too many for the procedure and the police had come for him while he was still in the dentist's chair.

Who knows, he had a lot of stories. Anyway, all I cared about was this – when he smiled in the dark, the golds would glint at me. It was like he was made of darkness, an absence of a man but for those little points of light, and it caused me to feel unspeakably, indescribably tender towards him. It would have me unmoored, unmanned, unwomaned, dizzy. I would hide his bite marks; I would smile back.

He wasn't a monster (he was a monster). The morning I lost our baby he carried me up to the mezzanine bed, wrapped me in blankets and hand fed me like I was a tiny bird. We pretended he'd never asked who the father was, never suggested I… but let's not remember that time. We would sleep in each other's arms, he would rub my feet as we watched cartoons together. He bought me white gold and diamond earrings and a diamond nose stud; its glitter would disturb my vision. Some nights he would show me his true face, a ruined child. Some mornings he would drive out so he could bring me coffee in bed. I know this doesn't explain why I stayed, any more than his beautiful teeth, but it's all I have.

By the time we reached Highgate there were more cars on the road, but there was no slowing now. I gripped the sides of my red leather seat and clenched my jaw and we were flying, past the ghostly white dome of the Central Mosque, past the empty football field and the wastelands grey in the moonlight, up the hill to the giant roundabout. When I was younger, I had witnessed a death there, someone hit by a car and flung into the air, leaving her clothes in a shredded heap long after the ambulance had left. Every exit of the roundabout was looped off with blue tape. I had been on my way home from work, anxious to get back to my children (a theme in my life) and I never could forget the woman who soared, her clothes left behind.

The way Taiwo was driving now was a threat, a punishment, an attempt on both our lives. He didn't speak and I couldn't speak and we careened up the Moseley road, veering round anything in our way, driving on the wrong side of the road up until the last second.

But then he stopped, at the wrong end of my street. He reached across me and opened my door, he said nothing. The road stretched out like a test… empty shops and quiet factories, then the lonely tunnel under the train tracks, a bridge of black bricks. Opposite my house was Trashy Barbers, where the Yemeni dealers spent their nights. They'd be in a line of parked cars, waiting for customers, some inside the shop, and occasionally, for amusement and exercise, they would fight on the road outside.

Why did this mean more than anything in our dramatic and volatile history? Why was this the moment I realised that you cannot make someone care for you, any more than you can stop them hurting you? But it was.

Alright, I said. I'll walk, but if anything happens, it's on you.

His face darkened, like a shutter pulled down. He snatched my door shut again and pressed the accelerator and we careened wildly to the end of the road.

WHY, he gritted out, WHY was I ALWAYS trying to make him feel guilty?

Trashy Barbers was locked, only a mattress left on the pavement hinted at the previous hours of revelry. I got out the car, leaving the door open and him calling behind me, and I ran into my house. Inside, the cats came running, thudding on the bare boards like tiny horses. A lamp was burning in the back room.

If this was a better story, I would have endured less shame, or left earlier, or never entertained him in the first place. If only I had taken one brave action or stood up for myself, even just once. But I'm just telling you how it was, and who I was that year.

Map of an Affair

SASHA BUTLER

Acocks Green

When he arrives it must be almost midnight. His phone died, he explained. She doesn't believe him but says nothing – Nokia brick, robust enough to smash windows, juice enough to power a man's social interactions for a week.

She'd been waiting on the railway bridge. Red brick built by men's bare hands over a century before. Beneath her, trains rumble on the tracks which scar across the city. Above, the crepuscular sky. Someone had lobbed a stained sofa cushion over their back fence and it had dropped down onto the no man's land before the tracks. A rat had shifted between a discarded takeaway. A baby shrieked. A siren catcalled. Life made its usual circular motions as she waited. So often she's waited for him. She'd smoked a cigarette, wondering how to tell him. Put her head back to the darkening sky to exhale.

He gestures to the house on the corner, where the bridge spills into an alley, which spills into a road of compacted semi-detached houses. More red brick, interspersed with peeling paint-black doors, parked cars, some rusted, metal bodies drooping upon slashed tyres.

Inside it stinks of marijuana. As usual, he takes her upstairs, pulling her hand in what she once would've termed affection, but now understands to be dominance and desire. She lets him.

He can have his cake and eat it, for the last time. This will only take eight minutes.

Before, he tells her to take off her clothes. He hasn't bothered undressing her for months.

During, she watches the floral lampshade that hangs at an angle from the only bulb dangling from the ceiling, like a girl falling out of a Broad Street nightclub.

After, they smoke his cigarettes in bed and other than her knee resting against his thigh they don't touch. The streetlights are on and the light drifting through the curtains is dulled, blurred, like the lo-fi music that carries from next door through the shared wall. She runs her eyes over his beard, neatly trimmed. He's still wearing the Cartier watch his wife bought him for his fortieth.

Eventually, cigs stubbed out, he turns to her as though they are real lovers, and says, 'I can't do this anymore.'

She stifles her surprise. The words she'd been intent on saying, spoken without her having to do anything. She shifts, propping her hand beneath her head, gripping her hair tightly. 'What's changed?'

'She's pregnant.'

She hates that, despite everything, her throat still tightens, as though choking on Birmingham's smog, back when the factories never stopped. He ignores her expression, swinging his legs from the bed, putting his feet on the floor.

'You've decided on fidelity?' she asks his back.

'Don't fuck about with me.'

'Isn't that all we do?'

His mind has never been a match for her. He sighs, as though he's the one who's hurt. As though he doesn't have all the cards in his hand. He pulls on his boxers, then his Levi's.

'Congratulations all the—'

'Please don't,' he says.

She closes her mouth, locates her underwear.

When they're dressed and sat on the bed like teenagers before their first kiss, he says, 'Money's on the side.'

'I hope you left me a parting tip.'

He leans in, holding her face in his hands. Is he trying to verbalise emotions that he doesn't have the words for? Remorse, adoration, sadness? Love? By now, she doesn't know.

Instead he kisses her forehead, wraps his arms about her shoulders, resting his chin on her head. She holds onto him, trying to build walls in her mind against the memories that are pushing through. She wants it to be over, for him to leave; she wants him to stay.

Sometimes you crave the things you know are bad for you. Because there is safety in familiarity, even when it's above you, kicking you down, foot in the ribs.

Then it's over. He leaves her in the post-sex gloom. He thumps down the stairs on those trainers which she'd always thought were ugly, even when he first bought them and pirouetted in her living room, huge grin on his face, when it was Christmas some years ago, when the fairy lights were on and the condensation on the windows fogged out the dusky street and she ate Bird's custard from a chipped bowl. Back when she believed that she would always love him.

BEFORE

Kings Heath

An RnB group are playing in the pub's upstairs room, and the volume makes her ears ring. Her friend is already downstairs buying pints at the bar, where the dark wood gleams in the electric lights, and she joins her, bored. Bored of the music and the jostling crowd and the man behind her with the hands that somehow kept finding her thigh where her mini skirt ends and her tights begin. Bored of not being able to reach that good level of fizzy, heady drunk, instead feeling lethargic, heavy, like a body in the canal.

Her friend introduces her to a man at the bar.

She slides her eyes over him: beardy, slim, probably a decade older, not really her type. But they talk, as the music upstairs bleeds through the ceiling, as her friend plies her and the beardy stranger with drinks. A graveyard of empty glasses surrounds them by the time last orders are called, and the dark summer sky presses at the embossed windows, trying to get in.

When he asks her what her name is – 'It's V,' she says, bare arm leaning on the bar – he says, 'What's your full name?'

'Just V.'

'Fine Just V, be an enigma.'

'Tell me yours.'

'Damon, but you can call me D.'

'Don't be stupid, Damon's cool.'

Later, he will tentatively run his forefinger up and down her bare arm, following the line of her veins which lead to her heart. Later still at the kebab shop, she'll tell him he's cool, not just his name, but him, in that hideous conversational patter that drunk people develop, talking in circles, explaining things that never needed explaining, and later still, when she's sobered up, she'll want to crawl inside herself, mortified.

When they first sleep together it's lazy, drunken, hazy. Their mouths smell of beer and slip over each other and they laugh about it. He tells her that he's married but that he's leaving her and that he'd like to see her, Just V, again sometime.

•

Lickey Hills

'So what would you want to do?'

They sit in his car in the car park. The land undulates before them, dropping away to Birmingham, which sprawls ahead, painting her glow upon the night sky. Orange-hues that last until dawn. Behind them, the road, the other side of the hills, are dark.

'Be a writer,' she says, tucking her hands beneath her armpits, as much to keep warm as it is to hold herself in embarrassment at admitting it. 'There's a course at UEA that I'd like to apply for.'

'When would you apply?'

'It's pretty steep. If I had enough money, then I would.'

'I want to read your stories.'

'All men say that.' She laughs. 'They never actually do.'

'Well I'm not all men am I?'

They grin at each other, then their grins slump. It's quiet but for wind-ruffled trees, owl hoots, insects crawling the undergrowth. No one else is here. They are hidden at the edge of the world.

'I'm sick of always meeting like this,' she whispers.

'I know, I know. I'll leave her.'

He strokes the side of her face with his thumb.

'UEA is East Anglia, right?'

A nod.

'Quite far away then.'

'I've not even applied.'

'But when you do,' he says leaning over the gear stick, his mouth almost touching hers, 'I'll come with you.'

Edgbaston

He pulls onto the drive. She's hidden in the back, lying beneath his coat so the neighbours won't see. He opens the car door for her as though he's a gentleman.

Inside his wife's coat hangs on a hook shaped like a dog's backside, with its tail high to keep the coats from falling. Gravity, wonderous in its certainty, when everything else is so uncertain.

The coat, the smell of the wife – perfume, burnt hair from curling tongs, hairspray – makes V's stomach twist to nausea.

What the fuck are we doing?

His Cartier watch on the bedside table – beside a pile of lightly thumbed books which she suspects have been placed there just to impress her (*Nineteen Eighty Four*, *Brave New World*, *The Alchemist*) – tells her it's 9pm. The wife will be out all evening; a friend's fortieth in Brindley Place. V imagines gold lights rippling on tar-black canals, a group of women in nice dresses bought from nice places smelling of nice things, a jazz group playing in the bandstand as revellers pass by, normal people on normal dates, sitting outside on terraces in the late summer evening, sipping cocktails.

She lies down on the mattress and realises she can't do it. Not here. Not when she can imagine the press of the other woman's body on the bedsheets, can almost feel the heat of her imprinted on its surface.

They fuck on the sofa instead, and then it's over, and she is crying, about the guilt of it and the cruelty of it and his lack of compassion for his wife and what that means for V, to love a man so lacking in empathy. It is all becoming too much, like a jug overfilled with water.

'I can't keep doing this,' she says, sitting on the sofa in her underwear, his shirt draped over her shoulders.

He frowns, naked in the kitchen, searching through the cupboards for something to eat.

'Why?'

'It's all wrong.' She pushes the heel of her palms into her eyes, rests her elbows on her knees.

'It's on my conscience, not yours. You shouldn't be worrying.'

'If you'd just leave her.'

The orchestral groan of the fridge renews, countering the silence.

'There's houmous on toast if you like? Then I'll take you home.'

Jewellery Quarter

He turns up at her flat, unexpected, uninvited, interrupting her writing, the unusually easy flow of her pen. He has come night crawling to her without even a ring on the phone.

His coat is wet and he has his work bag, has been working late, come straight from Colmore Row. Over the drone of dual carriageway, past ugly carparks, between the snare of streets and canals, his reflection bouncing on top of the smooth water. Past a few barges, with pansies on the roofs, painted navy and racing green, one appropriately named Nauti-boy. He is, and he hasn't got long; told the wife that he's tied up at work and will be home in a couple of hours. They'll have dinner together, and she'll light the candles and cook something flamboyant like a Thai green curry, homemade paste, homemade spring rolls, and they'll have a glass of Sauvignon and decompress after the day.

This time when they have sex he doesn't say much. He doesn't really kiss her. He tells her what he wants. She gives in, half despising herself, half driven on by a yearning to be wanted. Yearning for him to tell her that he's changed his mind. That he's going to call his wife and tell her he's not coming home.

This time, it might be different.

Before he leaves, he pulls out a fifty from his wallet and puts it on the chest in the hallway.

'What's that?' she asks, her voice not sounding like her own.

He slips on his wedding ring which he'd dropped in his suit

pocket. Murmurs of conversation sound from the apartment above, lives pressed together like sardines.

'If I pay you, you don't need to feel guilty anymore.'

'Pay me for what?'

He shrugs, a euphemism for sex.

When she doesn't respond he says, 'Being with me.'

'That's fucked up.'

'It's not. If I pay you then you're only here because you get paid. You're not hurting anyone.'

'But that's not true—'

'You didn't want it when we last saw each other. This way it's my choice. I still get to be with you and it's all on me.'

'So you'd rather pay me for sex than leave her? How gallant of you.'

It occurs to her that they have never met in the daylight. She has never seen his face by the glow of mid-afternoon sun. Always it's out of hours, it's in the bawdy evenings or sexy midnights or clandestine moments before dawn. The hours he can squeeze in around his other life.

'Sweetheart how can you hear that in what I'm saying? What I'm saying is that I want to make this work, I want you to feel good. I don't want you to worry. And I know you could do with the money.' He glances about the flat, the marked walls, the greying carpet by the front door. The unspoken ravine between their incomes coming into focus, like adjusting the dial on binoculars until the view is crystal. His judgement shrinks her back to childhood when she was awkward and bookish and insufficient. Never quite good enough for her parents, never quite good enough for friends. Always seeking a love bound by conditions. He checks the time. 'Think about it.'

•

She saves all of it. All her fuck money. And it begins a tectonic shift within her, how she feels about him. She starts to see the economic value of him. She does things to him just to keep him coming back with his wallet. Not because she enjoys him anymore. If he can use her, then she can use him. She starts to strain against herself, not liking who she is when she is with him. Reduced only to a body, her needs never met. She begins to rally against her passivity. Calculates how many more evenings with him she needs until she can leave.

Sometimes he likes to book rooms in hotels and pretend that they are strangers. He finds a room in Acocks Green and somehow it makes it easier for them both: a place that has no link to their real lives. She starts to pretend that she doesn't have a lover, and over time it stops being pretend. They always say the next time they'll meet. They stop texting in between. She's saved on his phone as Carl, in case he ever needs to call. He never does.

Sometimes during sex, when she squeezes his hips between her legs and waits for it to be over, she looks into his eyes and wonders: what have we done to ourselves? What have we done to each other?

After he leaves the dingy room in Acocks Green, she walks over the railway bridge. It's almost dawn, the birds chatter along the silvery tracks. Relief in her bones. Albatross lifting from her shoulders. She catches the first train home.

Every place she goes is a site of memory, bringing her back to him. The time when he first told her he loved her beneath an archway in Digbeth, broken glass crunching beneath their feet from someone else's lairy night; the restaurant in Moseley where he bought her dinner and the waiter presumed they were married; the traffic lights on the Hagley Road when they waited in his car for the lights to change and as they argued he admitted, 'I love you both. I can't leave her'; the Safeway where she'd bought a pregnancy test, terrified of a positive result, him waiting in the car park; the moonlit walk in Cannon Hill Park, when they'd broken in, climbing over the gates.

The city woven into the fabric of their love affair. A map directing to lust and love and longing and loss.

She deletes his number and cashes in the notes he paid her. She hands in her notice to the landlord. She accepts the offer for the writing course at UEA. She thinks about all the stories she's written, and how he never read any of them.

M42

It's a dewy morning and she's hitting seventy, car vibrating slightly. Birmingham at her back, the coast, the East of England ahead.

Phone rings, and she answers, balancing it between cheek and shoulder.

'Can I come over?' Damon asks. It surprises her: daylight slashes through the windscreen and he wants to see her.

'I'm not home,' she says.

'Later on, then.'

'I've moved out. I'm on my way to East Anglia.'

'Now?'

'Yes.'

'Fuck.'

'What?'

'I didn't think you'd actually do it. I didn't know you'd applied. They accepted you?'

'I was going to tell you when we last met.'

'Why didn't you?' He sounds as though he's been crying. In all the years, she's never seen him cry.

'You ended it before I could tell you. After that I didn't see the point.' She doesn't intend for it to sound cold. His heavy, uneven breathing intensifies. 'What is it?'

'She's left me.' A pause. 'I really fucking need you. I love you.'

She can feel it: the tug of the string that she could surrender to. That desire to be wanted, craving a devotion from him that he could never give. That age old yearning that has got her this far, and now has no place.

It's daylight now and her answer is clear. She presses her foot down on the accelerator, onwards towards the M6, heading out east.

The Chains

RICHARD LAKIN

I walk onto a stage the size of a picnic blanket, raise a fist, and shout 'Hello Cannock.' Laughs and jeers. 'If I was in Cannock,' – the neighbouring town – 'it'd be banjos, not dance music playing.' I point at a dated poster of my gurning face. 'As seen on TV. I'll be cutting the ribbons at World of Sofa on the ring road next Wednesday.'

I kept getting flashbacks of Talent Nights, Cheese and Chips, 'No denim' door policies, Aga-bleeding-doo and bottles of 20/20. Oh, I was back alright. My mistake was sacking my agent. She was about as much use as an ashtray on a motorbike. She was getting a percentage for making fun of my slide. But there was one thing Zara used to do and do well: she was one hell of a gatekeeper. I'd had a few stalkers and weird letters in my time and more nutters than you could shake a stick at. I was spared reading all those begging emails about kiddies with tubes sticking out of them or the horror story of the kennels that burned down. Back then I was doing stuff for Channel 4. I'd got that insurance ad with the parrot. There was talk of hosting a quiz show. One minute your face is everywhere, the next they're sick of the sight of it.

I ordered some grainy toast and some black coffee. My fifth of the day. Four over doctor's orders. I'd walked it, trying for more steps since I lost my licence. I was a shade under nineteen stone, whisper it. Nothing rock n' roll about an addiction to KitKat

Chunky. I'd made it to the high street without needing a fag or a sit down and sought refuge in one of those cafés you find in every town centre these days. You know, they'd got the loud photos of pie slices oozing gravy, quiche from the deep freeze and a full English. All of it was surrounded in the lurid oranges and sunshine yellows of a 1970s holiday brochure. Shift workers from Tesco and Screwfix were bolting down sausage, egg, chips and beans. A fella in a leather cowboy hat was using a fold of white bread like a squeegee to mop up bean juice.

I stared out at blockpaving glittering with frost. Plumes of a jogger's breath were frozen in bus headlights. Nightfall meant work and the little shot of adrenalin and knot in the gut it brought. It was why I'd only ever grazed before a gig. Folk with office jobs thought it must be a dream making an audience laugh (assuming that happened) and working an hour a day. But there was travelling and lugging bags about and trying to get paid. There was working nights when others were tucked up in their pyjamas. There was the ever-present self-doubt and smartarse twenty-somethings straight out of Uni touring on Daddy's allowance while pretending to respect your craft and experience while leapfrogging you. There was the fear and, if it went OK, there was that brief kick of warmth and adulation before you started worrying you'd got to do it all again tomorrow. My working life was immersed in fag ash, heckles, alcohol and painkillers.

I'd never played my hometown before. Little rule I had. I pinched the fold of skin between finger and thumb hard so it made me screw up my face. Zara called it 'centring.' People used to worry about the main act self-harming but these days they thought it was part of the show. I downed my coffee, folded a tenner in the menu. A copper bell above the door tinkled my departure.

I'd travelled enough to know it was like this all over – the march of the vape shops, the coffee chains, pasty providers, pizza slicers and phone-fixers. What was once Woolworths – and memories of scoffed pic n mix and seven-inch singles running along the wall – was a vast empty unit, its glass front fly-posted with long-gone circuses and monster truck rallies. I pulled up my hood as sleet streaked in from the marshes, white flecks in the darkness, and shuddered at memories of cross country runs through cowpats and ditchwater.

I'd have been about thirteen when Mr Jenkins told me to give this talk called Things That Keep Happening to Me. I started making notes in my rough book and it kind of spiralled and I couldn't stop. I told stories, did impressions of Greasy George the janitor and Nigel Shanahan's walk. I mimed Mr Gibbons doing the register.

I made some mental notes, worrying the high street was so quiet. There were signs for a Cultural Quarter that amounted to a few planters full of buddleia and fag ends. A silver deck chair was propped against an empty charity shop doorway. Café culture transplanted from Milan to the Midlands. I checked my phone, scrolling the RIP note on the local forum about Jenkins' death from cancer.

I ran through my intro in my head. The room at The Chains sat about seventy so I could've sold out four times over. I hoped they were paying more for the privilege of a small room. Perhaps a few would turn up to have a pop at the fella who escaped. They didn't like success in these parts.

Unlike the rest of town The Chains was heaving. Its pink neon lights reflected in a puddle. I stared down at a burger wrapper slicked to the cobbles and, for a second there was a glimpse of a shimmering star. I took a pint of lager into the back where they'd set aside a quiet room for me. There was a shuffle of feet and chairs scraping and ripples of laughter from upstairs but it didn't sound as if my warm-up was ripping up trees. Twenty minutes and there came a knock on the door. I waited a full thirty seconds on the stairs till the godawful dance music they were playing faded out. I pinched the skin at my thumb and shouted: 'Hello Cannock!'

I move things along with reminisces of pub crawls as a teenager and how the town's changed. 'You don't need a Tardis round here. You go for a pint at The Albion if you want to visit 1984.' We're into it now, so I throw in some of my stronger stuff. I remind them of the wishing well that used to be outside Tandy. It had a wire mesh to keep the winos from scooping coins. 'I want my money back. Yeah, I made a wish. Forty years later and I'm still waiting.' I pause, take a sip of lager. 'So much for modern surgery. They still can't safely remove two vertebrae and I still can't reach.' I bend right over at the waist, so my head's at belt level. 'You know I can almost get there. I can breathe on it, really. That's how close I am.' I tell a bloke in the third row – who's just the type to love it: Fred Perry polo, waxed greying hair cut in a fade – that he's got no such problems. 'Look at him. As flexible as a tomcat. Could suck a tennis ball through a hosepipe.' A woman beside him roars with laughter and I say, 'She knows.' They're having fun so I sip from my third lager. Everything's a little hazy around the edges, but that's more to do with the sweat and breath fug in this dank old building. I start on my bit on games lessons and how we had a teacher who used to be something in hurdling. 'He had this black tracksuit with red and yellow piping. He looked like a Mars bar working out.'

A guy's sitting at the bar, his back to me, hunched over a tall, thin glass. Don't know why he's here. You always get one. 'Our long jump pit was better known as the biggest cat litter tray in the county. Wasn't just for cats though. Word was Darren Parry used it too. He dropped the biggest length of cable I've ever seen. We thought an Alsatian had done it. A medical impossibility that should've secured him a slot in The Lancet.'

I finish off with the stuff I do about middle-class camping trips and the finale is the joy of train toilets. I bow as the lights fade. I can't get past the bar for cheers and handshakes so I have a few and stay and chat. I tell them I love the old place really. Tell them it feels real. And it does. I've had a connection here. They start asking direct questions but mean no harm. What happened to your breakfast show? Why don't you do TV anymore? I tell them it's like being a footballer and you drop down through the divisions and if you get a game you play. Glancing at my watch I tell them one last pre-Travelodge story about work experience in a condom factory when I see the guy from the bar sidle over from the corner. He emerges from the darkness, a warm, smeared shot glass in his hand. Tony Vernon. I was in his year at St Chad's. He had a backstory that dragged a black cloud into every room he entered. It's no surprise he drinks in The Chains; I doubt he's ever gone far.

He plonks himself down at the next table, so close he can bang elbows; no use pretending I haven't seen him. He spins his glass on the tabletop and without looking at me says, 'Darren died you know.' I guess Tony isn't popular, might even be known as bother in the bar as the others turn away and form a tighter circle around me at the table, chairs squealing as they're dragged on the sticky tiles. 'No, I didn't know,' I say.

'Making fun of the dead,' he mutters.

'If I stopped doing that I'd lose half my act.'

'I thought you'd forgotten us all now you're the big shot comedian.'

There are a few sighs and eyes rolling, but I give a shrug. It isn't the first time I've had to defend my profession and I should've guessed it'd happen here.

'Except you're no longer the bigshot these days, are you?'

'You're right,' I say, 'but it's been good to be back.'

'He's doing his bit fundraising for the hospice. More than you're doing,' a woman beside me says. St Gwen's is the hospice that cared for Mr Jenkins. It's on the tickets but it's the first time it's been said.

'He doesn't care about this place. Couldn't wait to get out.'

'Well, I've enjoyed everyone's company tonight,' I say and I mean it.

Tony turns up the collar of his coat and makes his way out. 'Always thought you were God's gift,' he shouts without turning back.

'He's bitter, that's all,' the woman who spoke up says.

'It's not his fault,' I say. They wait for me to elaborate but I don't.

'Why don't you come on for a drink with us?' the woman's partner says. 'We're staying out for a bit. You're more than welcome. Relive your past eh?'

I mention a few old haunts I remember; the kind of places where you queued after hours to pay two quid into an ice-cream tub on the door. One's now a Chinese restaurant and another has been turned into a care home.

'That sums up my life trajectory. Fast lane, Chow Mein, chronic pain.' It feels good to make them laugh without sticking to the script.

Tony strides off into the night, chin dipped into his collar. I raise a hand as he turns the corner. I think about going after Tony, buying him that drink, wanting him to laugh too. But Tony's a tough crowd to play. I choose the free drinks and the easy laughs instead.

Halieutic

R. M. FRANCIS

With thanks to Emma Purshouse

'Buckpool's Bramble tastes bitter this year,' Dad'd said. 'There's summat wrong with the yield.'

Me and Dad lived in the borderland between Pensnett and Brierley Hill – Brockmoor. Buckpool if you want to be specific, and people down our end like to be precise with these things. If you go too far up Commonside or Bromley, you're in another district. You wouldn't know unless you know. We're a hodgepodge of council estates, factories and dusky woodlands around here.

'Come on, mucker, if yo'm comin'.' Dad woke me with a gentle nudge on the shoulder.

'What time is it?' I asked, pulling back the duvet.

'Midnight.'

'Fuckin' hell.'

'Whatcha tongue. Yo' said yo' wanted to come.' Dad went to walk off. I saw he'd already got himself clobbered up in his waders and waterproof. He'd packed the trolley up before bed.

'I'm comin',' I called. I quickly jumped into my thermals and waterproofs.

We always used the back door and walked down the gulley between ours and Coren's terrace. Our street was a row of old miners' houses – redbrick two up two downs, narrow, cut away from the rest of the whirling estates of pebbledash semis colonised by

Irish Traveller families. Some people were funny about that, but me and Dad played darts with them in the Rose and Crown, and they give me my first gig doing groundwork when I turned sixteen. We pulled the gear down the road to the cut. By the canal bridge that led from domestic life into the nature reserve, all I could see was a grey mist and a hoary dew that framed Hawthorn, Rush and Arrowhead. I'd played army with Rowan and Tommy earlier that day and they showed me where they'd found a sack of drowned cats. Dad took my hand.

'Stay close,' he whispered. 'Stay off the shiny stuff.'

'What?'

'Kip on the path an' stay by me. Stay off the shiny stuff.'

As we crossed the bridge I looked to the left. The shiny stuff was the oily slick blackness of the cut water and its uncanny flickering currents set out against the light of the moon and stars. I'd never heard it called that before, but the phrase echoed through my life.

Dad pulled the fishing barrow and me along and down the tow path. His hands were huge, callused and muscular from years of working alloy and roofing. That'd fucked his knees and back up, but he never said anything. I could almost feel the mustard stains between index and middle finger. It was just me and him now. Mom had been sent down for robbing in Safeway.

'Er wor really fit for family anyroad,' Dad'd said. 'Her wor really fit for robbing. Her'd bin caught too many times and the judge said they'd run out of options.'

Even when she got out she'd been given an order to keep out of our lives. That was alright with us. It was usually the other way around, and lads from our end would end up been mothered and turn into proper fuckheads.

We got down to the old railway bridge. It always scared me. There was barely anything left of it. The trains used to run Brierley

Hill's Blue Bricks out to the world but that was long gone, and it was just a skeletal structure now. Rusted wrought iron and rotten timbers. Stood beneath, you'd look up and watch the night-time smoky dance of clouds in the sky. That made me feel weird. Just before this bridge was a fisherman's path. It led down to the pool.

'Stay close,' Dad said and squeezed my hand, pulling me up the slight incline from the cut and the side of the ruined bridge. Feet slipped slightly in the mud.

From here it was almost pitch black. The stench of dog shit, rotten lumber and pollen filled the air. The sounds of scurrying rodents and nocturnal birds scratching and clapping about made my heart quicken. All I could see was a thin cavern of black running down between two lines of trees. Everything was shadow lined – a different shade of lead. We walked on. We entered a different place. I'd heard Tommy talk about the thin places, and I'd heard Rowan tell him to shut his fuckin' gob. It was black, grill and ash, but as we walked, I noticed something.

Stay off the shiny stuff.

To our left was a shimmering. Two lines, in perfect parallel, that followed our route with a glisten, then the occasional flash of gold caught in the edge of my eyeline.

'Whass that?' I asked Dad.

'Can I come, Dad?' That was the eighth time I'd asked him. He slumped on the sofa watching the news and tutting to himself. A can of larger in one hand and a smouldering cigarette between his fingers.

'Yo' wo' gerrup,' he replied.

'I will. I promise,' I turned to him.

'Iss the only thing I've got to meself, lad.'

I stayed quiet and turned away. He kept watching the TV. I

looked along the shelf of the old fireplace – a few pictures of me, Dad's trophies, two packs of Lambert and Butler, and a pile of unopened letters. Dad worked two jobs and still managed to get me to and from school, and out to boxing on a Thursday, and he was captain of the darts team, but he always said that made him more work. He'd do this. He'd watch the news. He'd put me to bed, and once a month he'd go night fishing. It never seemed like a big deal back then. Kids, I suppose. And our generation too. How would we know what a bloke like that needed?

The weatherman had said it'd been an unusually cold and wet August and I remembered Mrs Bolton telling us about climate change. Dad tutted, sucked his teeth and took a drag of his fag.

'Get to bed now then,' he said.

'But Dad, iss Satdee!'

'Yo' wanna come wi' me, doh ya?'

'Dad?'

'Yo'm nearly eleven now, mate. I'll tek yo' out.'

I gave him a hug. He smelled of beer and smoke. I ran off to bed, grinning.

Stay off the shiny stuff.

I was scared but I couldn't say anything. The almost-luminous chalky colour amongst the shades of darkness shouldn't be there. They were out of time. They were out of place.

'Hang on,' Dad said, and he reached into the inside pocket of his jacket and pulled out a small torch.

The light beam punctured the shadowy trees and bushes as Dad shifted its direction with swift swipes.

'Yo' see?' he said.

'Holy fuck,' I said. Dad clipped the back of my head with his hand. 'Soz.'

'Thin places, they call them,' Dad said.

'I know,' I replied. 'Tommy told me about it.'

'Oh yeah?'

'Yeah, wharr'is it?'

Dad moved the light across the floor of the woodland. In the thicket of nettles and weeds were long, wet stretches of metal, cloaked in mosses and lichen.

'Thass the old railway line. It used to move the wares from the brickworks up there.'

He shifted the torch up and to the sides, illuminating the marble of whites, reds and browns of birch trees growing out through the sleepers and rails. I took a sharp inhale and cold night air tightened my throat. I stared at the parallel lines of iron that ran through this newly natured place. I stared at the ripped-white of the birch trunks – ashen alien limbs. I wanted to touch. I gripped Dad's hand and he gripped back. He pulled me on, and we took another narrow desire line down to the water. I kept looking over my shoulder and searching for the odd sounds of the fidgeting creatures in their nightshifting.

I watched Dad who didn't need any light to fix hook to reel, reel to rod, and cast off. He unfolded two chairs and we sat.

'Weird ay it?' he said.

'What?' I asked.

'That. The perfect line of those seven silver birch trees popping out through the old tracks.'

'It is, ar.'

'They say things about silver birch, yo' know.'

'What?'

'The gypsies do. They say things about new beginnings, doh they.'

He lit another cigarette and passed me the thermos. He pulled the reel delicately with his index finger and placed it back down on its stand. I watched him take long drags of his cigarette and blow the fumes out into the moist air – thick plumes of faded white clouded the darkness then dissipated above our heads. I could taste the dew settling on the grasses. I could make out the different densities of mist across the black pool. The almost silence was punctuated by the almost rhythmic snap scuttles of nocturnal creatures. As the clouds shifted across moon and stars, little glimmers of shining shapes appeared in the surrounding woods – I couldn't make out if it was a wet rock or an animal's eye. We were surrounded by the still stench of the pool, the end of summer seedling of wildflower, and the mud caked earth.

'Wharr'else do they say, Dad?' I asked.

'Eh?'

'About the silver birch?'

'Oh, I dunno, lad. Iss saft supposition ay it.'

'I s'pose.'

He turned his head away from the spot in the pool where the float plopped against the inertia of the surface. I didn't look back. I just felt his gaze for a few seconds and then my peripheral vision caught him turn away again.

'Yo'm alright, ay yo?' Dad asked.

'Yeah, I'm fine.' I said.

'Not too cold?'

'Nah, I'm sound.'

'An' … yo'm alright properly ay yo'?' His big hand lifted from the rod and landed on my forearm.

'Yeah, fine. Sound.'

'Sound,' he said, and removed his hand.

•

Dad showed me how to set down the equipment and pack it up. He was precise. Everything had its order. Everything had its place. The sun was just starting to rise and the greys had started to turn a strange amber and indigo.

'We day catch nothing,' I said as we started back up the fisherman's path.

'It doh matter,' Dad replied.

The morning light was starting to dawn-strike the woods. The thin place looked less *thin*. We walked to the left of the old railway line, pierced by the seven silver birches. Dad held my hand and pulled the trolley with the other. We were just getting up to the decaying bridge and the cut again when he stopped.

'Look,' he said. He crouched and pointed into the trees.

I followed his finger out to a small dingle just ahead of us. The morning sun hadn't reached it. Four creatures, dog-sized, black and white, were just sniffing at the ground before burrowing down into a crack in the soils. One adult and three infant badgers. The small ones went down first and just as the adult went to follow, it looked back and around. It looked at me and Dad and sniffed at the air. It seemed to shrug then it disappeared.

'How about that for a catch?' Dad said.

'No one'll believe us,' I said.

'No one expects the truth from a fisherman anyroad.' He smiled and raised his eyebrow like he did when he cracked a joke. I laughed, but I didn't know what he meant really.

We slipped the line down to the tow path again and strolled up to towards home.

I pulled a few brambles from the bushes as we walked and offered one to Dad. He shook his head.

'Buckpool's Bramble tastes bitter this year,' he said. 'There's summat wrong with the yield.'

The Broken Areas

ALAN BEARD

She stood in front of a house that looked bombed, at a quiet junction. She led him through a garden of nettles, then through a wavering 'V' of knocked out bricks, to fuck amongst the rubble on a coat laid down.

After, she got her clothes together, accepted a lit fag from him. She talked about going home, a flat nearby, a whisky before turning in, pulling back her hair as she gave him details. She said she could see the silver discs of Selfridges through one window. Through the murk he saw her ears, tiny and concise, her fingers bringing the cigarette up and down to her mouth, the purse of her lips as she exhaled. A turning car lit her up briefly like a white flame and he asked could he come back with her, all the money he had, and she agreed to one last fuck there, in the warm, seeing as he had eighty quid in his hand, but that was it.

She took him down afterwards, in the silver lift, saw him out. He didn't know where he was in the city, tufts of grass outside the closed-up building, pavement and tarmac scuffed with broken areas. He thought to lay down on it, like it was the frayed carpet of her flat, as if the warm cat might come and curl up by him, near enough to hear it purr.

He lay on the damp concrete, faint light breaking, birds singing, and imagined the earth, the world beneath the concrete, the huge weight of it suspended in space and slowly, slowly revolving. The trees in the street were feathery, the buildings soft like rubber in the dawn, he thought about getting up but didn't want to before she'd opened the curtains and seen him there.

The Era of Endless Street

CHARLIE WILKINSON

For days now, the hours of daylight have been a perpetual dusk, the sun shrouded, only a suggestion of damaged radiance to the west, where the sky browns to the colour of an apple core. It is as if someone has been slowly stripping every inch of luminescence out of the world.

'You can walk it from here,' the taxi driver says, angling his head to where Ian Gant is sitting, cold and hunched on the back seat of the cab.

'Can't you take me? My suitcase is heavy.'

'Sorry, mate. It's difficult turning round down there. Not the easiest place to get out of, Endless Street, if you know what I mean.'

'But surely…'

'See that church there. Take the first turning on your left and Warren Lodge is on your right.'

'Not lodge… house. The Warren Guest House is where I want to go.'

'So you said. I heard you quite clear enough, mate,' the driver replies, getting out of the car and going around to the boot.

Then Gant is standing next to his suitcase on the pavement. The glow in the west is being gathered into the approaching dark; ferrous browns, substitutes for a sunset, are fading above the outer suburbs of the city. Although the main road is wide, there is no traffic. At intervals along the street, which are lined with shuttered warehouses, the relics of businesses that closed decades ago, lampposts emit a yellow, brumous light. The road is slick with recent rain, its gleam tarry, as if he might risk sticking to it. In the distance, the illuminated dome of a Sikh temple is peeled down to onion-gloss. Although he's been told that The Warren Guest House is close by, he'd like to check the driver's directions. He's tired, reluctant to risk walking in the wrong direction. The church on the corner is Victorian, its red brick the colour of dried blood. When researching The Warren online, its location was first given as Lozells, then Smethwick and finally Hockley, as if it were an area with no fixed position. Indeed, it has a forgotten air, suggesting it has slipped over an edge where no council or parish is prepared to claim it.

A notice board outside the church, which might once have provided his location, has been painted over. The graveyard is overgrown with nettles and limp dead grass. The Warren Guest House proves to be a two-storey building with a white façade and what looks like the rusting remains of a Regency wrought-iron balcony, which tilts slightly at one extremity. It's hard to be sure whether this is an original feature of the building or something that's been kept after the demolition of a period property. There's a livid light on in an annexe and over the door a sign saying 'Reception'. Inside, a man with a beard is sitting behind a desk. Behind him, CCTV screens give Gant a preview of the Warren's interior: slanting corridors viewed from above, empty staircases and closed doors that imply they've been sealed up for ever. The office floor is littered with defunct computer equipment. Gant hands over his reservation and the man gives him a card with two codes on it.

'What time is the front door locked?' Gant asks, as they step outside.

'No worries. Man always in there. He is … how you say… janitor?'

After taking him to his room, the receptionist strides off without a word. Gant tries the code four or five times. He normally has no problem with keypads, but something appears to be faulty with this one or he's doing something wrong. As he's twisting the latch first one way and then the other, a second man materialises soundlessly beside him. He's lean, swarthy, with loose skin hanging from his cheekbones.

'Here, let me,' he says.

He passes him the card and watches intently as the man keys in the code. The door swings open at once; an austere space, uncarpeted, a double bed, cream-coloured walls with pictures; a window covered by a beige blind. He turns to thank his rescuer but is only in time to see him slipping sinuously round the far end of the corridor, his feet hardly skimming the ground. Is this the janitor or another guest?

Inside, there's a wardrobe with no coat hangers; no point in unpacking since there's nowhere to put his clothes. He flings his suitcase on the thin duvet. The room is cheap and he hadn't expected much, but even so he'd not anticipated this: no coffee, tea, a kettle or towels. He puts his hand on the radiator: cold. At least there's a television. He picks up the remote and presses the power button: no electrical crackle, the screen a blank, depthless grey-black. It's been three months since he lost his job, bettered by unsalaried, inanimate objects, their greater command of algorithms, their untiring capacity for toil. This is his final trip to his native city before poverty renders further extravagance, however carefully costed, impossible. He might as well explore the neighbourhood. There must be a pub or a cheap restaurant nearby.

Outside, it's dark and chilly: wraiths of his white breath blooming and dispersing as he walks towards the main road. He's surprised to see the church on the corner lit up, the windows a grubby gold, the interior radiance half occluded by grime. Someone must be in there, cleaning the brass perhaps, although the building has every appearance of being deconsecrated. He makes his way through the lych gate and up to the main door. It's locked. With the flat of his hand, he pounds on the wooden door, and then listens. He's unable to detect even faint sounds of movement, the scrape of a chair or the sound of footsteps on the flagstones from within; yet he's certain there are people inside. He senses their presence, their silence as a mode of arcane concentration – the magnetism of many minds drawn together, intent on a hidden task. His hand is raised, to beat on the door again but louder, when there's a voice behind him.

'Not yet. You're not ready.'

He swings round. A figure just outside the porch, looking in his direction, but in the shadow-strewn light its face appears unformed, as though a nylon stocking has been pulled down tightly over it.

'What do you mean?'

But already the man is moving off, weaving his way through the gravestones, his gait agile and gliding in a way that reminds him of the janitor. A moment later, he's slipped over the wall of the cemetery and onto the road. Gant runs out. Then he spots what might be the man illuminated for a few seconds by a lamppost before he vanishes, submerged by distance and the dark. Gant walks on up the road; he's gone no more than a hundred yards before the streetlights go out.

He's up and down all night. Famished after his failure to find a pub or restaurant, he's drunk pint after pint of water as a way of assuaging his hunger. The cold is such that he's had to put on his socks and spread his overcoat on top of a covering that is as close to diaphanous as a duvet can be. As he tries to create an island of warmth in his glaciated bed, he hears, seemingly every five minutes, footsteps ascending, and sometimes descending, the staircase.

How many bedrooms are there above? There must be far more guests on that level than on the ground floor. And someone is prowling around. Whenever Gant pads out to the bathroom, he glimpses a flitting, elusive figure, usually at the far end of the corner – or just discernible, fading into the shadows near the top of the stairwell.

Yet he must have been sleeping, if only fitfully, for his watch tells him it's a quarter past four. He's hungry. Perhaps there will be something in the communal kitchen, although an earlier search revealed nothing except tea bags and a half pint of rancid milk. He's almost level with the bottom of the staircase when he glances up. There's a warm light, a gold-bronze lustre which can only come from the upstairs landing. It's possible that there is a second kitchen up there. The stairs are carpeted, a relief from the ice-chill of linoleum on his feet. At the top of the landing, corridors stretch both ways in a manner that appears incompatible with the outside of the building. There are no room numbers on the doors. After the cold of the ground floor, the hum of central heating seems in itself a form of welcome; the lighting fills the space with a hospitable glow, a memory of brass and copper, snug corners close to log fires.

As he takes the left turn and steps along the corridor, he makes no sound on the carpet. He tries one of the doors, but it's shut fast. Even when he rattles the handle, there's no response from inside. Just as he's about to return, he notices a double door, steel but with wide panes of glass built in at eye level. Inside, there are rows of people seated in pairs on opposite sides of small tables. They are silent, some with their hands over their ears, others lean back very slightly, but all are rapt with concentration. They are playing some kind of board game that Gant is unable to identify; the pieces not unlike chessmen, but variously coloured and carved into outlandish shapes. As they move them around the boards, their actions are deft but slightly slower than normal, as though performed in a trance of attention. He notices that on every occasion a piece is lifted it lights up for an instant before being set down. Some of the colours are ones that he finds it difficult to name, even though they are distantly familiar, as though recalled from a reverie or, an experience before birth, an interstitial space.

A hand on his shoulder, resting with a light touch but minatory in its implications. Then the voice again: 'Not yet. Don't you understand?'

Gant does not understand why he fails to swing round at once. By the time he glances behind him, the janitor, or someone like him, is shimmying off, the edges of his body somehow indistinct, as if he's about to merge with the light at the far end of the corridor.

The next morning he awakes, shivering. Outside, the dawn is pale blue-grey, a few of the less amorphous clouds drifting like ice floes. The Warren Guest House has the cheapest rooms that he's ever seen on a booking site, but surely an adequate level of heating over winter is a basic necessity. He scrambles into his clothes and makes his way round to reception. Inside, there are now around eight people. All heavily bearded, they're seated in an unsmiling row behind a desk. The largest and most imperiously hirsute of them is wearing a round smoking hat decorated with multicoloured hieroglyphs. Gant senses but cannot articulate a subliminal correlation to the carved pieces in the unidentified game. There is no sound in the room. On the wall next to them, the CCTV screens flicker through their repertoire of corridors, staircases and anterooms.

'Would it be possible to have some heating in room four? I can't tell you how cold it was in there last night.'

Every eye is looking at him levelly; their faces illegible, as if fixed in the amber light. Just as he's about to repeat his question, the receptionist from the previous afternoon stands up as if about to accompany him outside, but the man in the cap tugs his sleeve and pulls him back down.

'Ask janitor,' he says.

'And where will I find him?'

'Janitor next door. You speak with him.'

'I'd also like something to eat. Can you recommend a place nearby?'

This time there's an exchange of glances. The receptionist coughs and then lowers his head. Again, it's the man in the hat who answers: 'No food.'

'Look, I've fully grasped the fact that you don't serve meals here. I'm merely asking to you to recommend a cafe… or even a take-away… nearby.'

'No food outside.'

'So how am I supposed to eat?'

'Food here. But not yet. Ask janitor.'

Gant hears his own involuntary gasp of exasperation; then registers himself raising his hands upward – as if imploring an absent deity to reassert itself. 'Considering that you don't even serve breakfast, you might at least have some…'

'You eat here. But later,' the man reiterates, raising his voice very slightly.

Now that their leader has spoken with commanding finality, the others lose interest. Gant shuts the door a shade too firmly as he leaves. To his surprise, he finds he's shaking with rage. For a moment, he considers booming back inside, issuing ultimatums, threats to report them to various authorities, but he's no sooner put his hand on the doorknob when he stops. There's something threatening about them – even when they're sitting down. What would they be like if they stood up?

There is another option, he decides. This time instead of walking in the direction of the church and the main road, he will walk down Endless Street. It has every appearance of being a residential area, but after a while he must surely come to a junction, a shop, perhaps a pub or a restaurant. If he postpones his excursion for now, something will be open eventually.

Two hours later, he sets out. Often, around mid-morning, there's an interval of what now passes for brightness, the dark-grey drear breaking up for a while, the sun leavening behind an almost white cloud, even a patch of blue, something half forgotten, yet hoarded at the back of the memory; the light in the trees lining the street ethereal, as if on loan from a far place. The red-brick, semi-detached houses, with their pitched roofs and bow windows on the ground floor, are of a design prevalent in the city. Most have tiny front gardens and privet hedges. There are none of the stylistic flourishes to be found in the more upmarket suburbs. They seem, if not exactly alike, to be remarkable similar. As he progresses, he keeps his eye out for a turning or even a footpath that might lead to a green space. But there is nothing, only the repetition of the same architectural features. The road curves gently to his right, the camber's incline consistent – he is going neither up nor downhill.

How long has he been walking for? he asks himself. He wishes that he'd taken note of the exact time he'd left. He stops, and for the first time notices that every front door is identically painted in midnight blue. Every door handle and letter box has the same brassy gleam. The only change is the quality of the light, the shadows staining a pavement, a slow but perceptible darkening. Perhaps he should knock on one of the doors, ask someone for directions to the nearest pub, café or convenience store. That he's not seen a single pedestrian – no one walking the dog or an old lady with a carrier bag back on her way to the shops – is perplexing. And though there are cars parked on the verge, no traffic, not even a bicyclist, has passed in either direction. He moves towards a wooden gate, but after closing it, glances up at the house: the curtains on the top storey are drawn, as they are on the neighbouring properties on either side. Everyone is asleep.

The next morning, after he returns from the bathroom, he senses that someone has been, albeit briefly, in his room. Seconds later, he spots the glow of a small red light below the television screen: his duvet has been straightened and there's a remote control on his pillow. He presses play and the janitor appears. Below his shoulders, the lines of his jacket, collar and tie are sharply delineated, but his features are out of focus, as if suspended at the moment the fog thins. Gant changes from channel to channel – always the same face fills the screen. The janitor begins to speak; he is, he says in a soft tone that Gant has not heard before, going to explain the rules of a game. It is advisable, strongly advisable in fact, to listen with care.

That evening, the receptionist arrives and takes Gant to the upstairs room, where his opponent for the night is waiting and the carved figures are laid out of the board. There are no introductions, and the other man, with an oatmeal face, thin hair and a mouse-coloured tweed jacket and tie does not meet his eye.

They play, for hour after hour. At first, Gant surprises himself by winning, but as he begins to tire in the small hours, his opponent rallies, pulling off victory after victory, at first narrow but then increasingly conclusive.

Slowly dawn, cloud-filtered, seeps into the room and as the carved pieces are picked up and placed on the board their glow is less bright. A few minutes later, the janitor's voice on an intercom tells them to make their final move of the night. Gant is taken to a warm bedroom on the same floor as the games room. His suitcase stands upright beside his bed; food in a plastic dish has been placed on a side-table next to a water carafe, but now he no longer has any appetite. He drifts off, sleeps dreamlessly, but when he wakes up he is disorientated. His watch has stopped. Unable to discern whether it's day or night, he gets up and draws open the curtain: a blank wall, but what is on the other side? More curtains, he suspects, but this time set into the window frame.

As he gets dressed, he tells himself that now is the time for explanations. He half expects to find the front door closed, but it is open. The light has the texture of almost evening. There are sprigs of occasional mizzle in the air. The sky is broken clouds rushing, shadows alternating with pale slivers of sunlight that jitter on the bonnets of cars and the rain-slick forecourt. There is a sense of a vast supply of darkness being held in reserve. Gant walks round to reception. Three men with beards are lined up against the wall and drinking from earth-brown mugs. A faint fragrance of coffee is overlaid with the smell of unwashed bodies.

'I'm grateful for the upgrade in my accommodation, but I demand to know exactly what I've let myself in for. I booked for two nights and I've been here for three – or is it four weeks. Are you charging my debit card? I think you should know that I have very limited resources. I'm unemployed…'

'You employed,' the man in the smoking cap replies.

'What do you mean?'

'You work for Warren Company. Night programmer.'

'Not in a job I applied for. And as far I'm aware, I'm certainly not being paid.'

'You paid in…how you say?' the man asks his squatting neighbour.

'In kind… you eat, drink, have room with heating.'

'Warren Company very good,' the man in the cap continues. 'I starving, now eat; first no roof, now roof. Is simple.'

'Well, that's fine for you, but not for me. I'm leaving here today. Please inform the management of my decision.'

'You tell janitor. Not our problem.'

'You try leaving already,' the second man puts in. 'Now you back here.'

By the time he crosses the forecourt, the hour has skipped straight over dusk and onto night. Above him, the sky is an almost impermeable black with only a few last points of brilliance. Somewhere, the mill is grinding out the last sea-salt sparkle of stars. The janitor is in the lobby to intercept him.

'You're working over the road tonight.'

'In the church?'

'It's owned by The Warren now.'

The doors of houses further along are opening; men are streaming out, some of whom he recognises from the room upstairs. As Gant makes his way towards the church, the man in the tweed jacket falls in beside him.

'It's safe to talk until we get there,' he says. 'What do you make of the janitor? I saw you talking to him just now.'

'I've met people I prefer. He appears to be in charge here.'

'Some say he's more apparent than real.'

'What do you mean by that?'

'He's a projection ...sent up from below. It's seems likely that all the houses in this street have cellars and basements. The company's not called The Warren for nothing. The real bosses are burrowed in below.

'And so the janitor is what, precisely?'

'No more than an image of a quasi-humanoid. A kind of ambulating interface if you like.'

Inside, the church has been stripped back to bare stone painted white. The tables for the board games are laid out in rows as if for an examination. They sit down opposite each other; the echo of the last footstep fades. Silence, somehow reverent, as though in mourning for what was present before the absence. The boards are wider than on the previous occasion; there are more pieces, an increase in complexity. Time limits are introduced to speed up play. Gant is unsure what the outcome will be. Does it matter if he wins or loses?

Over the following weeks, from snatches of conversation, sometimes overheard, he pieces together a mosaic of theories, not the whole picture but fragments of competing schemata: (1) They are part of a research project aimed at finding methods of calming and occupying a skilled work force made redundant by the rise of artificial intelligence. (2) They are the subjects of a psychological investigation monitoring behaviour in captivity. (3) They're trialling a new board game to find an appropriate level before it is released onto the mass market. (4) They are being trained as adepts of a cult that is exploring new forms of ritualistic behaviour.

On the second day, his partner changes. As soon as the game begins, the man seems to slip into a trance; he is not even looking at the board; then his opening gambit is made without the use of his hands. The piece slides so silently, so smoothly, across the board that it is as if it is being cushioned by an imperceptible current. Glancing around, Gant realises that his new opponent is not alone in possessing this gift. On the table nearest to them, a piece is trembling in mid-air – held by an unseen hand, a mind waiting to make its next move.

Day after day, he walks through the dusk to the church. How many months has he been working for the Warren Company, Gant wonders, as he ambles alongside the man in the tweed jacket, whose name he always forgets to ask. Although everyone he's met since his arrival, apart from the employees in reception, has previously worked, before being made redundant by high tech industries, no use is made of their specific skills. Here progress is solely measured by increased proficiency in the game, those who have acquired psychokinetic skills being especially valued.

'Have you noticed how the days are getting shorter?' his companion asks. 'I've been getting up every few hours. And it's nearly always night or late evening. Perhaps there's an hour or so of proper daylight but not much more.'

'I don't know what to make of that. We're in the grip of some kind of fundamental shift in geography; it's as if we've moved into the polar night. But where's the ice, where's the snow? And I can't understand why we're here at all?'

'I've come to believe that every move we make in the game is recorded, just as the keystrokes on computers could be captured by malware. We are information, suppliers of infinite angles and permutations; quite probably sources of pyscho-kinetic ability to be harvested, energies that were not previously well understood. And as to where we are, you tell me?'

'Somewhere near Smethwick, Lozells, perhaps Hockley. That's what I thought.'

'Handsworth?'

'Possibly. Anyway, wherever we are, I don't want to stay here much longer.'

It's a week, perhaps two, before Gant makes his move. He picks a time in the middle of what had once been day, a moment when the workers were asleep, and even the janitor might have returned to the basement should whatever keeps him visible need to be rewired. The receptionists, or at least some of them, would be awake, but this was no great matter; when had they ever tried to prevent him from leaving?

It's colder outside. The day-night sky is black but with an adamantine sheen. The heavens are free of cloud cover and yet there is not a single star in evidence; it is as if they have been liquefied, spread over the firmament, laminating it with the gloss of forgotten sunshine. The Manichees believed that the light of our universe is being removed and reconstituted in heaven. He senses himself as sentient in a third space situated between substance and eternity.

The last time he walked down Endless Street, hoping to find food and hospitality, there'd been not one fork in the road, not a single lane or alley to elsewhere. And then he'd found himself coming back along the same stretch of the street that he left hours before, back to the front door of the Warren, the view of church on the corner. This time he'd go in the other direction; follow in reverse the route the taxi driver had taken until he arrived at the Jewellery Quarter. From there, he had enough money to take a bus home.

As he strides past the church, he notices the windows are not lit up. Inside, the boards are waiting for the game to resume, its flow of information expressed as geometric patterns, the recurrence of strategies embodied in time and space. Then he's on the main road, moving swiftly past shuttered warehouses, derelict manufactories, the blind-eyed shops shut for decades, the dim shapes of buddleia triumphant on crumbling walls; even the drug dealers and rough sleepers, cocooned with their shivering dreams, absent; no petrol-scent in the air of the still city. Then, about twenty yards in front of him, a man zigzagging along the pavement, lit up for a while by a streetlamp before dodging back into the shadows. It's hard to know whether he's drunk or has been driven to exhaustion. There's no sound, no singing, swearing or shouting, just the slap and scrape of his footsteps.

'Excuse me,' says Gant, quickening his pace. What harm can come from speaking to him; he's harmless – surely? 'I'm trying to reach the Jewellery Quarter. If I just keep straight on, I think…'

The man stops, silhouetted by the lamplight behind him. 'Straight on? What are you talking about?' He sounds angry, his voice slurred, though more from tiredness than drink. 'There's no such thing as "straight on", not any longer.'

'Well, I've been walking… *straight on*. For a mile or more.'

Silence – as if Gant's response is being cogitated on, every aspect of his statement considered – then: 'Granted, you may have seemed to be heading in that direction, but you're not. Otherwise,' he adds, stepping into the road and moving away, without waiting for a reply, 'I'd have reached there long ago, wouldn't I?'

With nothing to be gained from pursuing the conversation, Gant plods on. The shops and factories give way to a residential area: red-brick houses with front gardens, the curtains drawn tight across the windows on the upper storey. The road is curving gently now. At regular intervals, there are trees on the pavement. He tries to tell himself that returning to The Warren is impossible, an ultimate negation of geography. And then he understands. He is alive in the era of Endless Street, where everything is only information collected: the repetition of our actions, the hours spent playing the nameless game, the accumulation of decisions to move this piece here and that one there, before we head off, our data preserved in the undying dark.

Night Work

SIOBHAN MAHER

April

Our walk to the park passes a house, the middle child of a terraced trio set right on the pavement. Two strips of packing tape hold a handwritten note to the front window, printed with deliberate capitals: SHIFT WORKER. SLEEPING. DO NOT RING BELL. The final four words are underlined twice, each stroke scored in a different ink.

The first time I spotted the sign, I laughed. Those passive aggressive stops pressed onto the page, those underlines, a tally of interruption. The noise I made, a single bark of mirth, made you laugh too. We continued up the road like that — me, bent over the pram handle, huffing *ha-ha*, and you in state, trilling with delight.

We are not so jovial this morning. What the baby books call soothingly a *sleep regression* has you gripped in some unseen witching hour torment. For four nights now you have woken howling. I feel your devastation viscerally, without hope of knowing its cause. When held to me your cries judder still, so we sit that way most of the night. Come daylight we are emptied by our shared and personal ordeals. But yet, we are awake.

I imagine the shift worker now as we trundle past their home. I picture them scrawling those lines on the note, desperately begging with rollerball and biro that their night-time labours be rewarded with rest.

Once upon a time I dealt in their kind. A manager would call with some new job or project and I would rustle up a troupe of contractors. I added my eight-and-a-half percent to their rate and did not mind that I had to call them after hours, as your daddy cooked a late dinner. I ate with the laptop open on my knee, feet pulled up on the sofa, still in my work tights. It cannot have been only six months. Sometimes I see the names of my clients on hand dryers and supermarket scales and feel a tug towards them.

My sense of time is distorted, or maybe my sense of place. For I have dropped out of my world and found myself in theirs. You and I work through the night, a tandem production line of feeding, growing, shitting, cleaning. There is no currency in this economy, no hourly rate. Your KPIs are monitored, charted in a red book, but I am unfairly recompensed for my efforts. Perhaps it is the worthlessness of these hours but morning grants me no rest. However fruitful your night, you call out from your cot as early as an office worker, not fooled by the blackout blind. You feel the call of day and rise diligent to meet it. I feel sick sometimes, dizzy with fatigue, dreading the hours that stretch ahead.

I lean my weight on the pram, stabled with your small, solid body and the tools of this new trade. The wide gates of Mary Stevens Park welcome us in, lead us onto tree-shaded paths, smooth under our wheels. I push the pram in laps around the bandstand until your eyes flutter shut. We pass the plaque, a pledge in memory of a dead wife and something clogs my chest when I read its inscription.

More capital letters, cast here in bronze: A PLACE OF REST FOR THE WEARY.

May

I gather myself into tights and skirt suit, the sturdiest clothes I have worn in months. I am contained in buttons and waistbands, given human form by their shape. My hastily dried hair springs into frizz as we pull into the station. You are Daddy's today. You stare at me from the backseat as I leave you.

There is another mother on the train, wrangling a toddler into its pram. I smile at her, give her the glance of camaraderie and then remember my own comrade-in-arms is missing. The crisis of identity triggered by your arrival is not, it seems, assuaged by your absence. I feel fraudulent in every way. Perhaps a 'keep in touch' day is to re-anchor to yourself as much as to the world.

The train sways from D to B, houses becoming factories as the postcodes change. Back gardens with red-and-yellow swing sets give way to graffiti-iced railway arches and sky-scraping glass.

It is Thursday, so the office is alive with a familiar spirit. Thursday nights are team drinks. In three hours, maybe four, they will exit onto Colmore Row and head into the city. I am told this evening is not the usual Old Joint Stock or Troc jaunt. Targets have been hit and management is paying. Tonight, the teams will decamp to Orelle and get *messy*.

To skip a Thursday night is an act of truancy. It is in the dark and the drink that friendships grow, the better to sustain the grind of our office. This is how management likes us – a slightly wayward pack, driven by grit and energy. If the night spills into the morning, even better.

A story is told of my team leader, two years or so before my time. He rocked up one Friday morning, Thursday still in his veins, and closed our branch's biggest deal. Legend has him standing on his desk, phone cord pulled straight, gesticulating as he delivered a daring persuasion. Tongue furred, perhaps, but slick. It is all very Wall Street and has become company canon. Such mythology grants Thursday nights a veil of great importance, despite such a performance never happening since. Get smashed, get friendly. Get fearless.

Come! The team implores me. But I am already drunk, slurring slightly as I speak with my manager. The softened folds of my brain cannot keep pace in either banter or business. It is, I sense, not so attractive to be this insensible on a Thursday afternoon. I am teetotal but swooning, inebriated by broken nights. The intoxication of a sleep-starved brain is neither witty nor bold. There is no water-cooler fodder in my after-dark activities. It is solely with you, my lone drinking companion, that a bond is formed.

My manager ignores my muddied speech and rambling review of your progress. Interested only in my plans for next month, he wants to be sure I am still returning. He wonders, too, if I am *coming for drinks tonight?* He glazes when I demur, expounding your bedtime routine and nocturnal vigour.

Whether he is dismissive or disappointed, I am too tired to tell.

June

I leave work at five-thirty to the moment. I use the bathroom at four: not so early anyone clocks my preparations, not so late I need to go before I leave. I wash my coffee cup too, preferring to be thirsty than add a minute to my exit. When the sales floor clock shows half five, I jam my jacket on and start to my feet.

Two weeks into my return, most of the team have bored of giving me a nightly round of applause. One will usually bid *farewell, part-timer* as I head, alone, to the door. Andy has Solitaire open under his Outlook, Zara is browsing the Outnet sale, but they remain at their desks and do not suffer the slackers' shame of leaving on time.

With a brisk trot across the Snow Hill concourse, I make the quarter to train, muscling onto a carriage already packed full at Moor Street. I get a seat at Cradley, just long enough rest before the jogging walk to your nursery. The staff greet me and coo to you, *Hello, Mom. Mommy's here!* The address that made me bristle in maternity now fills me with joy. My exertion-damp armpits grow cold under my suit and a cough threatens my dried-up throat, but yes – I am Mom.

You are the first to arrive and the last to leave. What is exemplary in my office embarrasses me here. I sling my bag into the pram so I can lift you onto my hip, steering the drunken buggy with one hand as I press you close with the other. We chatter as we walk, in our respective babble, practically nose to nose. I remember all over again what the first flush of love feels like.

The evening stint begins with milk and stories. When your daddy gets home we tag-team bedtime and feeding ourselves. You sleep through now but not without squeezing us for every minute of our evening, as if to make up for your abandonment by day. Your meandering bedtime is tortuous and beatific in turns. I am spent by the time sleep finally settles but miss you the moment you drift off.

With you unconscious, I pull up my emails. Someone starts a round-robin at nine, a nonchalant *just before I head off*... I could reply but cannot give the impression I am not managing my workload. There is a subtle line between grafting and struggling. I save a response in my drafts.

What once was a handful of after hours phone calls is now another shift, stretching into midnight, often beyond. Tonight, I draft a job ad – lingering briefly on the boards for myself – and research the exhibitors at next week's expo. I book a grocery delivery and message, one week late, a watchful friend. Some nights

I sit on the sofa staring or scrolling, clawing myself an hour alone. Your daddy hauls himself into bed the moment you are down but I choose peace at the expense of rest.

Anyway, these hours of industry are so familiar to me now.

She Knows Jazz

MEZ PACKER

It doesn't take much for your friends to persuade you – *Come on, Ricky Boy, one for the road* – and you head to The Dog, back in the precinct. The place is rammed after hours. Choking fag-air and hot condensation dripping down from the ceiling. But you're young, there's live music and imported American beer, and you're that high you can tolerate anything.

You drink your beer straight from the bottle and lean back at the bar, facing the stage. You've practised disdain in the mirror. This James Dean pose, this sulk-face, in this outfit. Leather box jacket, ripped jeans, beaten up high-tops. Fringe flopping into your eyes as you nod to the beat while your friends slink around the place, winking at girls.

One girl, you notice, displays an equal contempt as she elbows her way to the bar. Her hip grazes your thigh as she slots in beside you, clutching a tenner. You pretend not to see her, take a lingering chug on your beer but cut her a glance from the edge of your eye. She smells scorched, volcanic, a blistering hotbox of trouble. You stand tall, flick your fringe, but she doesn't turn or even blink. She orders a drink.

No purse or handbag, she pays with the note and pockets the change. Brunette, gamine, retro clothes, white T-shirt – no bra – skinny black trousers. Delicious, unwinnable. It's an effort not to keep licking your lips.

On the floor, you spot a train ticket (is it a ticket?) and seize the moment. 'Hey! You dropped something,' you say.

She cups an ear, wearily.

'There.' You point to the floor with your nose. 'Your ticket.'

'Not mine,' she says without looking and pushes her way back through the crowd with her drink.

Frenchie (you've named her already) is with a small group of chaps at the back. Serious, toe-tapping types who look as if they've got Miles Davis tattooed on their dicks. Pork pie hats, goatees, one with a ring on his thumb! A couple of moon-eyed girls stand jiggling beside them. But the girls can't keep time, can't dig the band's rhythm and anyway, the men are all looking at Frenchie. Running their tongues over their teeth as if they can already taste the volcano.

She knows jazz. You can tell by the way she drums out the nifty five-four with her fingers. You move closer. Lean against the wall, sweep your fringe from your face, and keep time with the tiniest nods of your head and she spots you, raises an eyebrow, and smiles with one side of her mouth.

It gives you the courage to offer your hand. 'Wanna dance?'

Frenchie wrinkles her nose, but she doesn't say no.

That's when your pals return – rowdy with booze – and your best chum drops his arm on your shoulder and slurs something into your ear. You can smell the rum on his breath as he leads you away, and Frenchie cranes after you, as if to catch what he's saying, and for a proud-chested moment, you know you have her attention.

It's half an hour before you cut loose from your pals. Frenchie's not on the dancefloor, not at the bar. You wait in the corridor next to the toilets trying to act cooler than cool, but ten minutes pass and you realise she must have gone elsewhere. You push outside, scan the late-night crowd that's spilled into the precinct and the people look ghostly, silvered in lamplight. Breath billowing, spectral, in the frozen night air. But Frenchie's not there.

Squad cars sail past on the ring road. Sirens roar. The night flashes blue and the air's laced with sulphur and hashish. Two women totter past on stilettos and double over outside M&S, laughing like demons. One of them squats by the phone box and hoiks up her skirt.

'Shield me, Babs, shield me,' she says, as hot piss steams over the flagstones.

You walk on; past the couples sucking one another in doorways, past lads stuffing mouthfuls of chips, past a staggering woman who asks for a light and then asks if you'll take her home for the night. And there in the distance, heading towards the cathedral through Broadgate, you see her. Walking alone. Flat shoes, head down, fists pushed deep in her pockets as if she's slipping away from the scene of a crime.

'Hey!' you shout. 'Wait!'

She turns, folds her arms, cathedral spire rising behind her.

You catch up, breathless. 'You can't leave without telling me your name.'

'My name doesn't matter.'

'Fine. Okay. Then give me your number.'

In your bedsit, drinking Bushmills, tea lights twinkling, Coltrane on the turntable, Frenchie runs her fingertips along the spines of your albums, mouthing the names – Mingus, Getz, Brubeck, Monk – before joining you on the sofa where she rewards your audacity with a kiss. A kiss with narrative. A kiss that starts out blasé but soon promises more than you'd hoped.

But she hesitates; pulls away. 'Wait here. I need the bathroom.'

'As if I'm going anywhere,' you say.

While she's gone you turn down the music. Bite your thumbnail. Wipe a finger of dust off the mantlepiece. Minutes pass. Is she laughing in there? Is she crying? Girls cry, you think, but surely not Frenchie. You hear the flush. Change the album to *Kind of Blue*. Top up her whiskey, top yours up, too. Finally, she appears in the doorway and except for the candlelight's rippling dance on her skin, she is naked.

'Sweet Jesus,' you whisper.

She holds up one finger. 'This once,' she says, 'and no more.'

'Yes of course.' You are shaking.

Frenchie is unpredictable; pushes you off when you're in your flow. Desire burgeons, flip flops, somersaults. She just *has* to smoke, she says, and she lights up and straddles you, smoke coiling around her. Contemptuous again. Beyond that, she deliberately drags a sharp nail over your belly and for a moment you imagine she might disembowel you and you brace and squeeze your eyes shut. But instead, she holds the cigarette tip too close to your nipple. The heat of it. The smell of singed hair. A spasm of fear.

'Woah,' you say, and she laughs and squashes the smouldering butt in the ashtray. Leans forward, kisses you hard on your lips and your chin, and her mouth travels down, over your trunk, further down, right to your root. And your mask slips. Your pose, your affected disdain, borrowed style: bottled beer, James Dean frown – they mean nothing to her, or to you anymore. And you know you have met your match because Frenchie's not carefree, she is careless and hot as the earth's molten core.

•

Later, coiled in your sheets, smoking a joint, she mocks the unforgivable gaps in your album collection. Where's Lucky Thompson? Where's Milton Marsh? She knows jazz, and her knowledge exposes your own self-regard, and it stings, and you tell her straight what your chum said about her back in the pub: *Steer clear of that one, Ricky boy. She's a succubus.*

You get up on one elbow, intrigued to see how she'll respond to the slight.

'Really? A succubus!' she says. 'Is that right?'

Immediately, she takes your face in her hands, and it feels as if she might gouge you or snap something vital. But she kisses you, vehemently. The taste of burnt liquorish spliff on her lips and her tongue, searing your mouth with her mouth. You can't pull away. You want to be burnt and bruised by her. You want to be shaken and moved by her and the shock of renewed desire sends you reeling, and she could do anything, anything, anything. But she releases her grip and sighs and rises up off the bed and glides back to the bathroom.

When she returns, she is dressed again, and she comes to you and touches your forehead with her fingertips. You could weep. You feel almost penitent.

'Please don't go. Teach me what you know about jazz.'

'But I'm a succubus. I'll hurt you if I stay.'

'Honestly, I don't mind,' you say. Frenchie half-smiles, again, and walks out the door.

Succubus, you say to yourself in her wake and resolve to look the word up in the morning.

Last Service of the Night

JAMES BROGDEN

The Ferryman of the Dead gets on my tram at Wolverhampton St George's.

I don't actually see him climb aboard, mind you. It's the end of my shift and I'm on my way to the office to hand in my card reader and do my numbers. Dave the driver switched everything off, locked his cab and went home, and I did my usual last check down the length of the tram for any lost property, so there's no way anyone could have been hiding on board waiting for me to leave. I wouldn't even have noticed him at all except that I've been stupid enough to leave my own coat behind and it's when I go back for it that I see him: sitting there on one of the seats at the very back, in the dark. Not moving. Not doing anything. Just sitting. Like he's waiting for something.

The only light is coming from the depot building a little way off so I can't make out any features but my first instinct is that it's some homeless bloke or a junkie who – don't ask me how – managed to sneak aboard without either me or Dave noticing and is planning to spend the night. I do not want to be the person responsible for the mess that the cleaning crew will find in the morning.

I should call security, I know, but then I'll have to explain how I let him get past me in the first place. I've been working on trains and buses my whole life and I've had all sorts of altercations. I've been threatened with knives, needles and all manner of body fluids. I've had to peel some folk out of their own vomit and do CPR on others while waiting for an ambulance, so even though yes, I should really call security, I decide that I can handle one bloke on his own.

As it turns out, I am woefully wrong about this.

I open the external door control panel, swipe my card, open the door and climb up.

'Right you, off!' I order but he doesn't shift. He just turns his head slightly to look at me.

'Well now,' he murmurs. 'Here's a thing.' Closer to, he looks to be about middle-aged, clean-shaven, dressed in a dark jacket, smart jeans and boots. Not your typical junkie ensemble, I think, and start to wonder if maybe I've made the wrong call here, but I'm committed now and have no choice: I square up to him.

'Get off this tram right now or I'm calling security!'

He doesn't seem bothered in the slightest. 'You can actually see me, can't you?'

'See you? I'll do more than bloody see you, mate! I'll—'

That's when all the lights come back on.

I stare around in confusion.

I hear the heavy whine of the engine starting up again.

'Right,' says the dark man. 'As interesting as this is, I think it's you who should get off now. The driver's arrived.'

'What the hell are you talking about?'

'The driver of this special service.' He nods towards the front. The lights are still off in the driver's cab but I can see that the seat is occupied and just about make out the gleam from a very bald head. It's definitely not Dave. 'He's on a very strict schedule. He won't wait to let you off and once that door closes again, you'll be with us to the end of the line and that's not somewhere I think you want to be.'

It's when I see that he's got an accomplice that I realise what's going on. 'Wait – you're stealing a *tram?*'

He laughs like this is the funniest thing he's heard in his life, literally throws his head back and guffaws, and I can see all of his teeth, very bright and sharp. Eventually he subsides. 'Oh my,' he gasps, wiping his eyes. 'Oh that's good. *Stealing*. You're good. I like you.' While I'm watching him gather himself together, utterly dumbfounded, the doors make their little electronic *pip-pipping* noise and close and the tram sets off. 'Yes, I like you,' he repeats. 'It's such a shame, really.'

I go straight back up to the other end of the tram and knock on the glass of the driver's cab. All the lights are off in there and I still can't see his face, only the dome of his bald head and the track ahead unrolling itself underneath us through the windscreen. 'Oy!' I shout. 'You want to stop this right now! I'm calling the police!'

I take out my phone and try to do exactly that, but there's no signal, none at all, on any network, and despite what you see on the TV you can't make a 999 call without a signal of some sort. This cannot – *should* not – be happening. We're in the middle of a city, for God's sake.

'Don't worry,' says the man at the back. 'I'm not going to steal it. I just have to pick up a few special passengers, that's all. I think you might actually be of some use after all.'

'What kind of use?' I shout back. 'Whatever it is you're up to I'm not going to help you do it!'

We stop at Pipers Row. Both platforms on either side are empty under the lights, the shadows hard and sharp-edged. I wait for the doors to hiss open so that I can make a run for it but they remain firmly closed. Nevertheless, the pre-recorded woman's voice says, 'This tram terminates at Edgbaston Village. The next stop is the

Royal,' and the pre-recorded man's voice replies, 'Please stand clear of the doors.'

They'll still be saying that to each other after the people that made their voices are long dead. There was that woman in London whose husband did the recorded announcements for the Underground and for twenty years after he died, she'd go and sit on the platform just to hear his voice again, until one day they changed it for a robot. There was an outcry, they put him back and for all I know she still goes there to this day.

Ghosts, all around us, all the time, even on the train home.

Looking back down the tram I can see five of those scrolling yellow LED signs that say, 'The next stop is the Royal. This train terminates at Edgbaston Village,' all in a line to where that bloke sits smiling on his own.

The driver's dashboard has two CCTV screens, one either side, so that he can see back along the length of the tram and make sure that no idiot passenger gets himself stuck in the doors. I remember one time this woman with a load of shopping bags came running up just as the doors were closing, absolutely dead set on getting aboard – she slung her bags on first as the doors were closing but she was too slow to get in after them and the doors closed on the strap of her handbag. Well, the doors are programmed to open again if something over a certain size gets jammed in them but the strap of a handbag basically isn't even there as far as the sensors are concerned. The driver (who, to be honest, was not doing his job properly) saw the green 'doors locked' light and drove off but the shopper had the strap wrapped around her wrist and couldn't untangle herself. She got dragged screaming off the platform and along the track for twenty yards before I could hit the alarm. She lost two fingers and all the skin off one side of her head.

As awful as that was, in retrospect it's tame compared to some of things I see tonight.

We should be slowing down as we approach the Royal but for some reason we seem to be going at the same speed. I peer over the driver's shoulder and sure enough, the speedo shows a steady 33mph. We sweep straight past the next platform and a dozen faces gaping with astonishment. I turn as we pass and see those scrolling LED signs change.

This tram terminates at Edgbaston Village

This tram terminates at Edgbaston

This tram terminates

This tram terminates

This tram terminates

And then:

This tram is not in service

2

We zoom through Priestfield and The Crescent and mercifully begin to slow as we approach Bilston. Here the platforms are staggered because the track runs through a narrow brick cutting and the southbound platform is about a hundred yards further on than the northbound one. But we go straight through that platform too, under the dual carriageway and slow to a stop right where there should be a big patch of wasteland on the left, scrubby bushes and trees growing over where Bilston Central Railway Station used to be, before it was demolished in the 70s.

I say *should be* because the station house is there again. Big, Victorian-era brick and stone but no lights in any of the windows. It's not a hallucination, it's bloody *there*. I can tell because the streetlights from the other side of the track are throwing shadows in the tall archways all along the front and on the faces of the five men standing on the platform, waiting to board.

They're miners, it looks like, but from a long time ago if their clothes are anything to judge by – big hobnail boots, baggy trousers and braces up over their bare shoulders. They're naked to the waist, worm-pale flesh streaked with black. If they're feeling the cold they don't show it, though I suspect that the cold is the least of their problems. Maybe it was an explosion or a pit collapse, I don't know, but their injuries… what I do know is that they must be dead because nothing living could have sustained such damage and still be standing.

The little illuminated circles by the doors light up and the woman's voice says, 'Stand clear, doors opening.'

The dead men shuffle forward.

Either they're dead or I'm going mad – it doesn't matter because I'm going to make a run for it as soon as those doors open. I edge closer to the door furthest away from where it looks like they're going to get on.

'I wouldn't do that if I were you,' says the smiling man from the back of the tram.

His voice is calm but at the same time it feels like being slapped. I spin.

'Why?' I demand. 'What's going to happen if I do? What's happening here, anyway?'

'You're needed,' he replies, as if that's any kind of an answer. 'I said that you could be of use after all. You're the Conductor.'

'What the fuck is that supposed to mean?' I'm trying very hard not to shout. If I start shouting it'll turn into screaming and I might just not be able to stop.

'It means that although most of the stops along our route are in, shall we say, *other* places, there are going to be several platforms where there will be living, breathing people who will want to get on. Your job is to make sure that doesn't happen.'

'I don't understand!'

'For doing this without incident,' he continues patiently, as if talking to a child, 'you will be allowed to get off before our final stop. Anybody else who gets on…' He shrugs and indicates the outside, where the dead miners have climbed down from the platform and are waiting patiently just on the other side of the glass doors. The light from inside the tram spills over them and I can clearly see their burns, their splintered bones, the sheen of viscera. 'They will have to accompany us to the end of the line.'

'And just where is that exactly?'

'Oh, I think you know. Every transport line in every city in the world has a service like this. The Silverpilen in Stockholm. The Kisaragi Express in Himamatsu. The Mineola of Astor Place in New York. Old, new, steam, diesel, electric – I've ridden them all, and guided many souls to their final rest.'

'But who even are you? Are you…' I swallow, can't say it.

He smiles and nods but not like a yes-nod, more the nod of someone who's been asked this question countless times.

'Not in the way I think you mean,' he replies. 'In my own way I'm a conductor, just like you. You are entirely free to get off – I can't stop you – but as I say, if you do then someone's going to get on who shouldn't and tomorrow you're going to wake up to some very unpleasant news of their fate. I'll look after my people, you look after yours.'

I mean, when he puts it like that what choice do I have, really?

Then the doors open and the dead start to climb aboard.

3

I keep telling myself: just imagine they're ordinary passengers, just all with season tickets that you don't have to check.

But it's not easy.

We pause on the bridge over Black Lake, which used to be part of Ridgacre Canal before it got cut off from the waterways network. A young woman in a dripping wet dress climbs out of it through a thicket of reedmace, carrying a small, wrapped bundle clutched tightly to her chest. There's no platform here so I help her aboard. She thanks me in the tiniest whisper and moves to sit as far away as she can from the miners. She is solid – drenched and ice-cold, but as real as my own hands.

At Winson Green a family of gypsies come trudging up the Hockley Brook from Black Patch Park where Charlie Chaplin was born – mom, pop, and seven little-uns, all big-bellied with starvation and dressed in rags. As soon as they get aboard, the kids start running around and squealing, having a great time. The adults are all silent and withdrawn, wrapped up in themselves, but the kiddies either don't know that they're dead – or don't care.

And everywhere that we stop to pick up one of the dark man's special passengers, the city is different too. Older. In some places huge chimneys of blackened brick rear against the night sky, belching smoke. In others we pause impossibly between rows of back-to-back slums that haven't existed for a hundred years. At one point there is a carpark by the track, and old sodium-yellow street lights reflect from hubcaps and wing mirrors that my dad would have known.

As we approach Jewellery Quarter I start to get nervous, on account of how the station is sandwiched between two cemeteries – Key Hill and Brookfields – and I actually catch myself thinking, *I hope there's going to be enough space in this thing because overcrowding can be dangerous*. I laugh so hard at the irony that the dark man raises an eyebrow at me.

'Something funny, Conductor?' he asks.

I get myself under control. I don't like the way my laugh sounds. Too much like screaming. 'It's a Health and Safety thing,' I reply. 'You wouldn't understand.'

Anyway, it turns out that we trundle on through Jewellery Quarter without stopping. I suppose that everybody in a cemetery is at rest, if you think about it, so it's not that surprising we don't have passengers here.

'There is something I'm trying to understand, though,' I add, amazing myself even as I say it.

'Go on.'

'Your people,' I say. I'm trying to phrase this delicately because they're standing all around me. 'Some of them look like they've been, uh, *waiting* for quite a lot longer than others. So why now? Why tonight? Why didn't you come for them years ago?'

The dark man nods and I feel oddly happy that he likes my question, as if I've pleased a strict old uncle. 'I'm here for the ones that missed the connections they should have caught. The terms *years ago* and *tonight* have no meaning for them, or me, or the driver,' he replies. 'They only have meaning for the living world, whose perspective is necessarily quite linear.'

'Riiiight,' I say. 'But why tonight? Why *this* night?'

'Would it make more sense to you if this was Hallowe'en? Or Dia de Muertos? Or Hanal Pixan? Or are you just asking 'Why me'? Because I don't have answers for you there, brother. You and I, we don't write the timetable, we just work it.'

We nearly make it through the city centre before it all unravels.

At Grand Central there's a chap in an old steam-engine driver's uniform with a badge that says his name is Walter, just above the bullet hole that killed him. Horse-drawn hansom cabs trot past as he climbs aboard. At Town Hall, where sandbags fill the arches and anti-aircraft searchlights sweep the sky, there's an ARP warden and a woman with immaculate victory rolls, both killed in the Birmingham Blitz. Then at Five Ways we stop for a young lad dressed in his Friday night best: pointy shoes, spray-on jeans so tight you can tell his religion, and a huge blood stain on the front of his white shirt from the stab wound from whatever stupid drunken fight got him killed. He's not the problem. It's the idiot who comes running in from the opposite direction, who's seen his ride home about to leave but hasn't clocked the *Not in Service* sign, who jumps in through the closing doors at the other end of the tram before I can stop him.

He whoops and looks around with a grin.

Then his face changes.

Now up until this point we've passed plenty of ordinary people who have been able to see in through the windows and mostly they've just looked pissed off that I'm not going to let them on – they certainly haven't started screaming and pointing in such a way as to suggest that they've seen all the dead folk inside. I don't understand why this is. I just put it down to *him* looking after *his* people.

But that's just what this idiot does because he's inside now, isn't he?

And he can see them – all of them.

At first, he thinks it's a joke. Or some kind of weird historical re-enactment costume party. Then, when he can't dispute the evidence of his staring eyes, he starts yelling and screaming, demanding to be let off, stabbing at the emergency door release buttons (which of course don't work) and thumping on the windows. I try to calm him, honestly, I do. He stinks of booze and I know that any second his fear is going to turn violent and he'll try to take it out on someone, and that better be me because I dread to think what'll happen to him if he attacks the dead.

I suppose this is *me* looking after *my* people.

Like I said at the start, I've been on trains and buses all my life and I've had to deal with my fair share of passengers turning shirty. I've been sent on all sorts of customer service and conflict resolution courses but if there's one thing I've learned, it's that there's nothing quite so effective as a good pre-emptive strike.

So I hit him.

In the face.

Hard.

I mean what's he going to do – call the police? It could get nasty but it doesn't. He collapses into one of the seats looking stunned at me with blood pouring out of his nose.

'Why did you…?' he tries to say but it sounds like 'Bye did joo…?' Then he goes white as a sheet, leans forward and I manage to jump clear as he pukes all over his shoes.

I hear one of the dead people tut disapprovingly.

Still, I can't help feeling sorry for the lad. I pick my way through the crowded carriage to the dark man. 'This can't be right!' I protest. 'He's done nothing wrong!'

He nods that little nod again – he's heard all this before too. He gestures around at his passengers. 'Do you imagine that notions of right and wrong had much to do with what happened to them?'

'But it's not his fault! You can't do this!'

'And again, what makes you imagine that I am in charge? I told you, it's not the likes of you or I that make the decisions. It's the driver you want to talk to. But I should let you know, he's never been known to change his mind about a passenger.'

I push and shove my way through to the front, to the driver's cab, and only then do I allow myself to see what must have been there all along – or maybe the Ferryman of the Dead finally permits me to see it, the way he doesn't let ordinary folks see in. Maybe it's his way of helping me to understand but I really wish he hadn't because there are still nights I wake up screaming at the memory.

The driver's head is still turned away from me but I realise now that what I've been mistaking for a bald scalp is actually the polished bone of a naked skull and I can see the reflection of his face on the inside of the windscreen.

The hollow eye sockets.

The grinning teeth.

We're slowing for Edgbaston Village, the end of the line, where the doors are going to open one last time, though this isn't its last stop. It will carry on past the big concrete barriers where the rails finish and take the Ferryman's passengers where they need to go, along with anyone else left aboard. I look at the lad, curled up in his seat, covered in puke and blood and the snot of his own sobbing, staring around at the other passengers with white and terrified eyes. Fuck this, I think. Fuck whatever sick game this is. I go over to the lad, bunch my fist in the front of his hoodie, haul him to his feet and drag him over to the door.

'Conductor?' calls the Ferryman.

I ignore him.

'Take his place if you like, but don't try to take him with you, or you'll both die.'

The tram rolls to a stop, the doors make their little blipping noises and open, and I stand on the threshold with the young man slumped against me blubbering, 'Please… please…'

And I know what I have to do.

4

The Ferryman was right, of course. Over the following days the story of the missing young man appeared in the local news but no sign of him was ever found. The last sight of him was on CCTV coming out of a club and running for the tram stop at Five Ways, only no tram can be seen on the footage and after that he just disappears. Nobody asked me about it for the simple reason there was no duty rota with my name on it.

I can't even remember how I got home.

That non-existent shift was my last. There's not much of a job for ticket inspectors who won't go out of their doors after dark. I can't even drive anymore and when I go walking, I keep away from railway tracks. You never know when you're going to see that commuter train with the extra carriage – the one that's dark and closed while the rest are crowded like cattle trucks.

Or the bus with the *Not in Service* sign, empty but all lit up inside.

Or the taxi just idling in a side road, where you wouldn't expect there to be many fares.

You'll see them, all right, but it'd be better not to.

Best to just walk, I reckon. There's no rush.

The last service of the night will come for you soon.

Village of Rainbows

CATHERINE LOCKHART

It was shaping up to be a perfect May Bank Holiday. Ash and Jas had so far squeezed every ounce of colour and joy they could from Birmingham Pride, and they knew there was still more to come. They had revelled in the fun of Friday night's free community event at the Smithfield site in Digbeth, and they had joined hands in the flickering stillness of the candlelit vigil; united by the flames of their community.

Saturday, they had spent their afternoon watching the parade make its way through the streets in all its multi-coloured, musical glory, and they had eaten lunch in Victoria Square, perched on the edge of the fountain.

Then, they had walked the same streets that the parade had traversed hours earlier, the remains of confetti beneath their feet, until they reached the Hippodrome Theatre, the gateway, almost, to their slice of the city. Here, they basked in the last of the day's spring sun at the street party, wandering the market stalls, and watching local talent perform on stage.

Later that evening, they had chosen to take a short break, heading home for a quick outfit change before returning to their rainbow village for 'warm-up' drinks at Missing Bar

Birmingham's queer village had been there for them like a silent, supportive third friend through all their ups and downs. They had healed heartbreak singing karaoke in The Village and spent warm August evenings drinking hazy summer cocktails in the garden of The Loft. Jas had fleetingly thought she'd fallen in love at The Fox and quickly fell out of love again over gin and tonics at Glamourous. They had danced their doubts and stresses away at The Nightingale and listened to stories of times gone by over drinks at Missing Bar. They had toasted life's wins at Sidewalk, and watched more drag performances than they could count at almost every club and bar in the area from Eden Bar with its botanical exterior to The Missing's Studio 48.

Tonight, Jas hoped, as they left Missing and headed towards The Nightingale, would be just as beautiful; a shimmering swirl of moments that would eventually blur beautifully into the memories of all those other nights they had shared here.

'Rhinestone Rhino, has more of a ring to it than Rhinestone Cowboy, don't you think?' Ash pointed out, neck craned upward, towards the diamond-encrusted, disco-ball rhino that stood proudly on the rooftop above them, at the junction of Hurst Street and Bromsgrove Street. The darkened sky was a backdrop to the rhino's personal party. Streetlights refracted in the shards of broken mirror that covered the surface of the animal.

'Apparently they gave it a heart,' Ash continued, eyes still fixed on the rooftop as he recalled a story he'd been told less than a week earlier, 'put a memory stick inside it with music, photos, videos, and stories. Do you think it's true?'

'Does it matter? Sometimes the myth is more magical than the truth, right?' Jas responded, shifting impatiently from foot to foot. She hadn't spent hours choosing her outfit, doing her hair, and touching up her make-up – glittering eyelids designed to catch the light inside the club just right – to spend most of her night outside on the cold, grubby pavement listening to another story in the Ash series of LGBTQ+ history. It wasn't so much that she found them boring, but more that she felt like there was a time and place for them.

'Besides, we're in the heart of the village ourselves, the stories and the music are all around us.' She twirled as if demonstrating.

'This is the 'Gay Age'!' She laughed, gesturing to the glowing neon sign below the rhino, which should read 'Gay Village', but four of the lights were out, resulting in this somewhat humorous error in the signage.

'The Gay Age', Jas really liked the sound of that; The Golden Age, the Gilded Age, the Gay Age, an era that gives rise to rainbows and re-defining gender, to confetti and colour, to queer liberation, and to freedom.

Jas was giddy and just a little tipsy. This weekend marked her first Birmingham Pride living in the city. She remembered her first experience of Pride vividly; arriving in the village had felt like arriving home, to somewhere she felt she belonged among the pockets of queer joy and friendship all around her. Living in the city meant that she didn't need to rush off to catch the last train home anymore. Her opportunities had been opened wide, and she was keen not to waste a second.

Ash got the not-so-subtle hint and moved on silently, continuing along Hurst Street with Jas trailing just behind. They passed the front of Sidewalk, and at the corner, they turned down Kent Street where they joined the queue of people waiting outside The Nightingale Club, or as they fondly knew it, 'The Gale'.

The pair felt as though they knew The Gale intimately, as if time had got them well acquainted. They loved its dark walls that were adorned with colourful, fluorescent murals; each telling a different story. They knew the faces and names of the resident DJs, drag performers, dancers, bar staff, and door staff that made them feel like part of the family. And they would argue fervently with anyone who called the club *Gales* or *Nightingales*, because they believed that to be inherently wrong.

Ash was doing just that when the pair reached the front of the queue.

'I'm just saying,' he argued with the group of strangers behind them, 'The full name is *The Nightingale*. There isn't an *S* in sight, so it can't be *Gales*, it has to be *The Gale*.'

'Come on,' Jas laughed, dragging her friend into the club before he launched into full lecture mode.

The air inside was veiled in a lingering fog emitted from the dry ice smoke machine, and they had to weave their way through a dense sea of people to reach the bar where they ordered drinks before making their way to the dance floor.

The floor, like that of many clubs, was slightly sticky from spilt drinks but they didn't care because it reverberated with a bass that buzzed through their bodies, calling them to dance. They became part of the heat and swell of the unchoreographed crowd; bodies moving together like a wave in time to the music.

Jas soon became so swept up by the beat that she almost didn't notice Ash had left her until she turned to say some witty aside she soon forgot, and found the space beside her decidedly Ash-free. Craning her neck, she spotted him kissing a perfectly beautiful stranger in a dim corner of the club. As he moved back towards her, blushing sheepishly and trailed closely behind by the beautiful stranger, she locked eyes with a woman just to the left of her friend.

The woman was vaguely familiar, Jas couldn't quite place where she knew her from but assumed that they had passed once or twice before, somewhere in the village. It could have been the Dutch courage of alcohol or the buzz of music shivering through her body, but Jas felt compelled to move towards her, to move into this woman's orbit.

Jas had never been a person who used apps to meet people; she simply couldn't be bothered to make endless small talk. She had instead long-hoped for some kind of meet-cute, perhaps in a queer bookshop or at an art gallery but catching a woman's eye in a gay bar during Pride weekend certainly made for a good Sapphic romance story opening. Only time would tell whether what she felt was love or lust, but Jas knew that the ending to her night was about to change.

She moved across the club, trying to silently communicate her intentions with Ash as she grew closer to him and to the woman. Ash followed her line of sight and quickly understood the message, grinning mischievously at his friend in response.

'Hey, I think I've seen you around.' Jas was forced to shout to be heard over the throbbing music.

'Yeah, I thought I recognised you,' the woman shouted back. 'I'm Lola.'

'I'm Jas,' she replied, edging closer to Lola to be heard.

Without exchanging many more words, Jas and Lola began to communicate in new ways; in dance and the shared heat of bodies pressed close together, and in kisses with hands soft in the smalls of backs and the napes of necks.

Glowing with sweat, they headed out onto the balcony smoking area for a breath of fresh, cool night air – laughing together at the irony of it – before returning to the centre of it all. Brought together as a newly-formed group of four – Jas, Lola, Ash, and the stranger whose name Jas never caught – sang until their voices became hoarse, danced until their feet ached, and drank until everything was just a little fuzzy and blurred at the edges.

Around 3am, Ash and Jas almost fell out of the club, arm in arm, laughing. Lola – her fingers entwined with Jas's – following them. The beautiful stranger had vanished into the darkness hours earlier, and Ash was content in the knowledge that, even if he never saw him again, he had shared a beautiful night with a beautiful person.

After the loud throbbing of music playing inside, the streets outside felt serenely quiet; traffic still rumbled along the roads, and there were other late-night revellers around, but there was something peaceful about the lamp-lit darkness.

Giggling and chatting with a deepness that only close friends can conjure, Ash and Jas wandered slowly home, trying – where they could – to involve Lola in their conversation.

Despite the state of the world right now, Jas felt oddly safe in the darkness, hand in hand with another woman, even though she knew that as a queer woman, she shouldn't. She'd heard the stories: of words and more thrown from cars, of stalking shadows in the underpasses, tales that made her shudder. The thought didn't stop her from gripping Lola's hand tighter and pulling Ash closer to her side, but this village of rainbows felt like it belonged to her, to all of them, like a protective bubble, its iridescent oil-spill colours caught in the moonlight.

The village was always there from sunrise to sunset but night-time was when it truly seemed to come to life. It became a place that called to her, and she came running, eager to be a character in the stories that would one day be told about this place to those who came after her.

Jas had spent so many years not knowing her true, authentic self that she often felt like she had missed out on many of the seemingly simple experiences that most of her other friends had already lived through during their university days. She felt a rush of joy whenever she realised that coming out had given her the chance to 'catch-up'; to dance without feeling self-conscious, to flirt unabashedly, and to experience, perhaps, the start of a romance.

She was still daydreaming, or rather nightdreaming, when they arrived home, at Dorothy Towers. Their apartment was housed in a tall block of flats, a tower of windows, many of which were still softly lit.

Cleveland Tower was one of two residential tower blocks on Holloway Head, which, as a pair, were formally known as The Sentinels. That isn't what most people called them though. Dorothy Towers, Fairy Towers, the Pearly Gates, these incredibly normal, almost dull-looking buildings had gained their various aliases from the people who had once lived here and the stories held behind each door. The Pearly Gates, was perhaps the most morbid amongst the pseudonyms, referring to the buildings' history during the height of the HIV crisis, and the gay men who had lived their final days within those walls. Dorothy or Fairy Towers, gave a more camp suggestion of the towers' history; provoking memories of the many 'friends of Dorothy' who graced their hallowed halls.

Upon moving into their new apartment in Dorothy Towers, Ash had been keen to learn everything there was to know about their history and that of the wider Gay Village, and would take any opportunity to sit in a quiet corner of one of the bars to listen to countless tales from the older, more storied members of the community.

Jas, however – while maintaining an interest in those who had paved the way for her to be her authentically queer self – was more impressed by the tower's proximity to that neon nightlife she sought out so voraciously. The apartment's crowning glory for Jas, though, was the balcony, from which she could admire the lit-up skyline of Birmingham by night; toy-sized taxis crawling by on the streets way below, their headlights roving, and buildings climbing their way to skyscraper-status.

In the autumn, when the weather prevented her from going outside, she would stand with the doors open, the distinctly earthy scent of rain creeping to her as raindrops bounced on the balcony. She admired the way drifts of rain looked when they were caught in the slanting light of streetlamps.

Gentle summer nights were her favourite though. She would drag a chair outside, inhaling and exhaling cigarette smoke in clouds that would temporarily fog her view, letting the crisp, late-night air prickle the skin on her bare arms. She would sit there until she felt herself become part of the city's darkness, and she would watch the deepest hues of night soften into the rosy-pink dawn of a new day.

As she bid Ash goodnight, her hand still holding onto Lola's, Jas knew that she wanted to share that beauty with Lola. Grabbing a blanket from the back of the sofa, she wrapped them both in its embrace as they stepped out onto the balcony. Huddled together for warmth in the cold of twilight, the two of them watched the world go by and spoke softly about their dreams for the future before finding their way to the bedroom and slipping beneath the sheets.

Lola was the first to fall asleep, and Jas studied the way her hair pooled on the pillow, and her glitter-speckled skin twinkled with every tiny movement. As she drifted off, Jas dreamed of dancing beneath a sky of glitter balls, inside the rhinestone rhino, and of becoming one of the many stories planted in its heart.

The Jalebi Man

ANJEM ANWAR

The air was filled with sweet anticipation, the sky a deep crimson and burnt orange hue. The last bit of light gently filtered through the kitchen window before the sun disappeared for the night. Kasim stood patiently over a pan of bubbling oil, his hands deftly squeezing his icing bag filled with sugary syrup, to form his beautiful jalebis.

The aroma stirred up a rich tapestry of memories. Carefree walks home from school, when a stop at the Halwai was a must. A shared bag of sticky, sweet jalebis, a treat to be savoured on the way. Jalebis, mithai, and samosas adorning tables during Eid parties or the grandeur of wedding banquets. The sun's warmth as they raced through the dusty streets or the thrill of chasing carts in a playful rush. And the exhilaration of kite flying season, a time of competitive spirit and ruthless kite cutting.

An angry oil spatter broke him out of his daydream, diverting his attention back to the task. Kasim was running behind tonight and needed to quicken his pace, but he knew from years of experience that cooking and baking were not to be rushed. They required patience, love, and care. The success of a dish depended on subtle choices, such as the time taken to caramelise your onions slowly. Or perhaps, the love you showed your dough as you worked it after the second or third prove – the soft, pliable texture under your hands. Or maybe, the patience to perfect your bake so that it was enticing to savour with both your eyes and mouth, the golden-brown colour and the delicate, flaky layers.

He placed his last batch on the counter to cool. Then, reaching out, he clicked on his mirror-patterned lamp from Pakistan. The sun had set now and Max wandered in, indicating his impatience to leave the house.

He had adopted Max when he was a tiny little labrador, a little ball of black fur. Max was a creature of routine and he enjoyed his night-time adventures with Kasim across Birmingham. They were like Batman and Robin, saving the city from dull treats with their jalebis, one customer at a time, their bond growing stronger with each adventure.

It was warm and could easily be mistaken for a summer evening, even in the middle of September. Max meandered in and out of Kasim's legs as Kasim began to pack the wicker basket that would be strapped to the back of his bike. Finally, he grabbed Max's body harness and coaxed him into it.

Old Joe sat majestically in the distance, towering over Birmingham University's campus. It chimed seven times as Kasim and Max exited their overgrown back garden onto the street. The roads were quiet as they made their way down Dads Lane; a few pedestrians bumbled along and lethargic traffic gently littered their route. Max sniffed yearningly at Dads Lane Fish Bar, imagining the succulent taste of battered fish and fried potatoes. The chip shop was bustling, as usual, a stream of customers making their way in and out in an orderly fashion, their mouths watering as they grabbed their paper-wrapped goodies and headed back home to feast.

'So, I thought we'd visit Mrs Green first,' he informed Max, trying to distract him while almost half expecting a reply. However,

Max just stared at him with his coffee-coloured eyes and panted. Kasim laughed and reminded himself that Max was just a dog, no matter how blurred that line of intelligence and self-awareness felt at times.

He cycled on, Max running alongside him, towards Pershore Road. Crossing heavy traffic, Karim paused at the bottom of Milner Road. He took a deep breath to steady himself for the ride uphill, to Mrs Green's house.

Kasim had always been fascinated by Mrs Green's house, which sat in a tiny cul-de-sac off Milner Road. Her front garden felt like an erratic jumble sale of stone angels, available in every shape or size. He wouldn't have been surprised to find Mrs Green standing in her Sunday best as she haggled with a customer over the price of one of her angels.

As they reached her drive, he rested his bike carefully on her moss-covered wall. He grabbed his Jalebi package and untied Max from the bike.

Kasim knocked on the door and waited whilst the angels lining the living room window stared at him. Remembering an old Dr Who episode, he wondered if they would move if he looked away.

He had known Mrs Green for a few years now, with her short frame, thick mane of grey hair, quirky dress sense and equally quirky personality. They met because of Max's unwitting curiosity, that usually led to chaos. It had been a beautiful spring day and Mrs Green had sat elegantly amongst the dog walkers, students, children, and optimistic sunbathers, painting in Selly Park. As she had taken out her much-deserved sandwich for a spot of lunch, the wind carried its scent to Max – who had bounded over to her, knocking down most of her art supplies. Kasim apologised profusely but Mrs Green had been too enamoured by Max to care.

That adoration for Max, mixed with a bit of loneliness, had kept Kasim and Mrs Green in each other's lives.

Mrs Green was a creature of habit, and her usual order consisted of jalebis covered in pistachio sauce and a scattering of chopped pistachios. There were times when she could afford to pay him in full, or they would trade, usually for her apple crumble. She made apple crumble just how Kasim liked it. The apples in small chunks and the buttery crumble made up a large portion of the bake. There was a delightful hit of cinnamon after each bite.

Kasim waited patiently, surprised that Mrs Green hadn't answered her door. He knocked gently again, disappointment bubbling deep inside him as there was still no answer. He always enjoyed his weekly interactions with Mrs Green, her take on the world and, of course, any juicy gossip littering the streets of Selly Oak.

Kasim sighed deeply and carefully placed his parcel behind one of the many flowerpots lining her doorstep. He linked Max's harness to his bike and manoeuvred it from the grove, willing his dismay to dissipate.

Turning right, he resumed his uphill trudge towards Warwards Lane. As they reached Sameena's house, which sat in the middle of the hill, her neighbour's dogs exchanged greetings with Max. Warily, Kasim placed his bike along the brick wall, worried it might glide backwards into the mouth of Warwards Lane. Two hyper toddlers, waving and banging on their living room window, interrupted his thoughts.

'It's The Jalebi Man!'

Kasim stuck out his tongue at them. The two girls giggled and cackled in response.

Kasim had first met Sameena and her girls whilst he'd been out walking Max. The girls had run up to him as they'd walked past the play area in Selly Park. Max had been delighted by the attention and the girls had given him a stroke and lots of fuss. So it continued until the greetings and exchanges became longer, allowing for more in-depth conversations.

Sameena had told him she was a pharmacist working part-time in Bearwood. Kasim shared how he worked as a para-legal in Birmingham City Centre and the jubilation he felt when making jalebis. A freebie to sample his magic at creating the perfect jalebi with a thick layer of chocolate hazelnut spread and chopped nuts had resulted in a paid standing order.

Sameena's husband opened the door, looking flustered, 'Hi Kasim, I wasn't expecting you, and Sameena isn't in.'

Kasim tried to hide his sadness at her absence, but his face betrayed his emotions, 'Oh, will she be back soon? I'm just dropping off her usual parcel.'

'Mate. I'm not sure, and I assumed she would have told you she wasn't in.'

Kasim tried to think back to their last conversation. Had he done something to upset her? It was very unusual for Mrs Green and Sameena to ghost him. Before he could lose himself further in his thoughts, the girls asked if he'd made them anything.

Plastering a smile onto his face, he turned to the girls and replied, 'Of course! Pink jalebis with sprinkles and the best bit, they're my treat!!'

'Pink jalebis!

'Sprinkles!'

'We should call him The *Pink* Jalebi Man!'

The girls giggled as if sharing a private joke and Kasim laughed, a full belly laugh, momentarily released from his misery.

As Kasim reattached Max's harness to his bike, he hoped he hadn't done anything to damage his friendships. He was grateful how meeting Sameena had made him aware of all the South Asian hot spots. He knew to go to Stratford Road in Sparkhill to get fresh fruits and vegetables and which halal butcher was the best on that stretch. He had found a piece of home amongst the tantalising scents, vibrant colours, and stores filled with miscellaneous goods imported from Pakistan.

If he fancied a takeout, he knew to venture down Ladypool Road in Balsall Heath. He had first experienced it at night with Sameena and her husband. If he closed his eyes, he could be in Lahore at night – narrow streets filled with people looking to feast their bellies on delicacies and delights. During hot summer nights, Kasim often wandered along Ladypool Road, grazing on samosas, pink falooda and mango lassi.

They crossed the road and cut through Selly Park, giving Max both time to explore and to relieve himself.

Leaving the park, they turned left and walked past the array of shops that had popped up along Raddlebarn Road. A hubbub of students outside the Greek takeaway, the beautiful aesthetic of the hairdressers, and an ode to hipsters everywhere – an old-fashioned barber and a beautifully curated vintage store.

Kasim came to a halt just opposite the florist. 'Come on, Max. Our next stop is infinity and beyond!' Kasim chuckled at his joke.

Max stared at him in confusion.

Their next drop was at Mohsin's house – who had the personality of Buzz Lightyear with a hint of Johnny Bravo's vanity. Mohsin was known for his boundless energy – forever running marathons, leading exercise groups at the local leisure centre and jogging through Selly Park. They'd met through Sameena and her glowing recommendation of his jalebi making magic. Kasim had risen to Mohsin's challenge of a 'healthier version' of a jalebi by making him high protein dark chocolate bark topped with nuts, seeds, and strands of wavy jalebi pieces.

Kasim knocked on Mohsin's door. It seemed empty, and there were no lights on. He waited patiently as anxious thoughts began to intrude aggressively in his mind. Why was no one in? This was a part of their weekly routine. Had they decided they no longer wanted to see him? Were they all out together somewhere, avoiding him? He'd worked hard to build a family in this little place he called home. Feeling frustrated, Kasim slid his parcel carefully through Mohsin's letterbox and continued his journey along Raddlebarn Road towards the top of Heeley Road.

The road was lined with identical houses, with *To Let* signs sticking out of them like oblong horns. This road was his biggest seller. He made his way down, stopping at several houses filled with students – drunk, high, or just plain hungry. Kasim filled their hungry palms and mouths with pink jalebis finished with strawberry icing and rose petals, jalebis filled with chocolate orange, white chocolate bark filled with marshmallows and thick pieces of jalebis, and jalebis layered with Biscoff dust.

Having finished their delivery run, Max and Kasim crossed the road to Selly Oak train station. The platform was quieter than usual, and the small group of students on the opposite platform were probably heading into Birmingham city centre for the night.

Their final jalebi stop was Bournville to see Roger and Kasim could do with seeing a friendly face after his night of missed connections.

Roger was a dear friend whom he had known the longest. When Kasim had first moved to Birmingham, he would take Max on walks along the canals over the weekend. The reason was two-fold: one was to cure his ever-growing loneliness and the other was a need to explore his surroundings. Kasim had always enjoyed looking at canal boats – so he stood examining one with its whimsical design of a painted forest in lavender, cerulean, and silver hues. He was surprised to see the head of a dog, almost the spitting image of Max, poking his head out of the canal boat. The dogs had barked at each other as if to accuse the other of imitation, resulting in Roger popping out to investigate the commotion. They had introduced themselves and marvelled at nature's attempt at self-plagiarism.

After that, they would politely bid the other good morning as Kasim walked past while Max and Rolio exchanged pleasantries in the only way that dogs can.

One morning, neither the dog nor his owner was visible. Kasim and Max thought they must have stepped out and continued on, unperturbed. However, the same thing happened the following morning and then the next.

On the fourth morning, Kasim stood nervously next to Roger's canal boat until he dared to get him and Max aboard. He tentatively knocked on the door, bravery nearly escaping him like air from an errant balloon.

A puffy-eyed Roger opened the door and when Kasim asked if everything was okay, he was informed that Rolio had passed a few days ago. Kasim offered his condolences and sat and listened to Roger as he shared his fondest memories of his beloved dog.

And when it had gotten all too much for Roger's broken heart, he had sat silently with him.

In that stillness, a friendship had been born out of shared sorrow and human compassion. The polite greetings evolved to having coffee together or sharing lunch on the boat, or Roger walking Max on occasion. The canal boat became Kasim and Max's second home, filled with laughter, friendship, anecdotes, and a shared adoration of all things dog.

A rumbling sound indicated the train's arrival. Kasim and Max got on and stood in the open space by the door, listening to the train's hum and the chatter from passengers. Within a few minutes, the intercom alerted them of their imminent arrival at Bournville Station. They made their way off the platform and to the side, down towards the canal.

To Kasim's surprise, as they approached the canal boat, lights twinkled off it like fireflies. A small wooden table had been placed on the path. A faint hum of jazz filled the air. Hesitating momentarily, Kasim wondered if he had forgotten that Roger was entertaining company.

While he stood in his indecision, Roger spotted him hovering and called him over. 'Kas, why are you standing there like a lemon?'

'The lights, I thought I'd forgotten that you were having company over tonight.'

'No, no. Now come here, Kas, I want to show you something.'

Intrigued, Kasim hurried along the path. Roger motioned for him to stop as he reached the boat's edge. 'Do you trust me?' asked Roger sincerely.

Kasim, surprised by his question, answered him as honestly as he could, 'I do, Roger, but I've not had a great evening. What's going on?'

'We've got a surprise for you!' shouted Mohsin and Sameena, jumping out from inside the canal boat. Kasim looked bewildered and shocked as Mrs Green followed them out and Roger handed him a blindfold.

'Will someone just tell me what's going on? I thought all of you were avoiding me because I'd offended you guys!'

'Of course not, you numpty! We love you,' scolded Mrs Green, giving a hug. 'Humour us, sweetheart, put on the blindfold.'

As Kasim placed the blindfold over his eyes, the others excitedly chattered around him as they carefully guided him further along the path.

'You know you talked about selling your stuff at the Halloween fair?'

'The fair we haven't organised yet.'

'But we will.'

'And how you've been asked to make stuff for weddings?'

'And we know there're loads of events in Brum that would love your jalebis. Well…'

Kasim felt the blindfold loosen, and as he blinked, he saw it: a handcart decorated in mustard gold, emerald green and luminescent white.

'It isn't exactly a shop,' said Mrs Green.

'But it's a step in the right direction,' said Sameena.

'We'd still need *our* weekly deliveries,' said Mohsin.

Kasim stood there, overwhelmed by their kindness and generosity – his voice drowned by a sea of emotion.

'Group hug,' Mohsin shouted.

'Thank you so much. This means a lot. It's honestly perfect,' Kasim replied finally, unable to articulate his gratitude gracefully. 'This is the kindest thing anyone has ever done for me.'

The others milled around together, telling Kasim about the months of work that had gone into making the cart. As he stood there, taking in this life he had created and reflecting on his gratitude, Sameena interrupted his thoughts.

'Oh, I forgot to ask. Do you like the name?' asked Sameena, 'My girls suggested it.'

Kasim laughed, his heart filled with joy, 'I love it!' he declared.

The name on the sweet cart read: *The Jalebi Man*.

The Trees

MATTHEW STORER

From the week after the attack, until the day of his arrest, every night Ed would go out to count the trees.

He'd set off after work – seven, eight at night – returning to the Hockley Street flat well after midnight. He might head over to Chinatown or to Digbeth. Or down Corporation Street, out under the sterile concrete of the expressway.

Some nights he'd venture further.

Edgbaston.

Moseley.

The Sabbathlands of Aston.

He made notes as he walked. Detailed scribblings: species, size, identifying characteristics. When his route overlapped with previous outings, he'd re-read the messy pages, struggling to decipher increasingly frantic handwriting.

Sycamore, willow.

Ash, oak, lime.

It was several weeks before Ed realised what he was doing was madness. A survey of a city's trees – and practically that was what he was doing – required more discipline. He needed to approach it scientifically. A clear methodology was in order, a fixed route every night. Change could then be accurately observed, monitored regularly over time.

But where should he trial his improved approach? Well, that was obvious. The city centre. The brutalist, bomb-damaged, degenerated, regenerated, re-regenerated, neglected, beautiful centre.

Goodbye chaos. Hello order.

So every night Ed would go out to count the trees.

Up Newhall Hill, left on Colmore Row, then right, past the Cathedral – Burne-Jones's beautiful windows – straight though Pigeon Park, the kids beatboxing by the obelisk. There's the Joint Stock – designed by Bruce Chatwin's grandfather no less.

At Temple Row cut down Needless Alley – what a name – and stroll along New Street. Past the old Kardomah Café, where Emmy Bridgwater used to go. Inside, a beautiful mosaic covers the first-floor wall. Head past the Pizza Hut that was the Tavern in the Town – pause quietly for a moment there – and keeping the Bullring's bull on your right, head towards St Martin's. Press on up Digbeth High Street, over the hidden river. Resist the urge to detour into the Anchor or the Big Bull's Head. Instead take a left at the Custard Factory, past the trendy bars around Gibb Street and Heath Mill Lane.

Now you're onto Fazeley Street. Walk the long stretch out into Eastside and its park. Up Queensway, Steelhouse Lane, past the police station, the courts, the hospital, then out again under the ring road. Into what's left of the Gun Quarter. The Bull and The Gunmakers are here but don't stop, though you should. Go on down Henrietta Street, past The Hen and Chickens – no time for curry, not tonight – and there's The Wolf. From here it's two minutes to St Paul's Square. You're pretty much home.

Ed had researched these streets. Some years before, he'd planned a walking tour – the forgotten history and culture of his celestial city. He'd got as far as advertising it in The Hockley Flyer when Covid had arrived and – as with work-life balance, sensible politics, and, oh, thousands of innocent people – the idea had died a death.

That all felt a long time ago now. These days Ed no longer had time to think about old buildings, the dead citizens associated with them.

He was too busy counting trees.

They were driving home, coming off the motorway one sun-dappled September evening. The city skyline spread out before them, a picnic of light.

'Don't you think there's more than there used to be?' Rosie had said.

'Eh?'

'Trees. Never used to be so many.'

Generally, Ed's inclination was to be dismissive of Rose's random outbursts. It wasn't sensible to encourage her. He was driving. He needed to concentrate.

'Every city has trees dotted around,' he said.

'Dotted around? It's pretty much jungle!'

'I'm driving, Rose. Do you want us to crash?'

'There's definitely more than there used to be.'

'Whatever,' he'd said. But as they drove he couldn't help looking, across the city's warehouses, factories, its soot-covered chimneys.

She was right.

Trees.

Lots of trees.

That was the Sunday. The following Tuesday work blew up, as it often did. An urgent bulk brochure order came in at three, another at four. Cue bedlam. From then on it was work all hours: early mornings, late evenings. Relentless. He barely saw Rose. He could tell she was annoyed, but what exactly could he do?

'You'll keel over,' she said, 'if you go on like this.'

She was right, again. A fortnight later – work showing no sign of easing – he finally made it out for an evening. A Saturday night gig at the Institute: Ash.

The room was hot. During 'Petrol' Ed started to feel faint. Hands clammy, heart racing. As the song ended, he felt a tightness. Sharp as a knife, chest tightening like a clamp.

I'm dying, he whimpered.

One ambulance ride later it proved a false alarm. A panic attack. Too much stress. He felt foolish but the doctor was sympathetic. She signed him off work for a fortnight.

'Do try to relax,' she said.

Of course he should relax. That was obvious. But some things are easier said than done. The days after his attack Ed felt anxious just going outside during the working day. He was convinced someone in HR would spot him, get him sacked. That was their job, wasn't it? To try and catch you out.

This was the anxiety talking but what difference did that make?

Absolutely none.

He fell into a routine. He'd sleep late, potter around the flat, then when evening fell, he'd walk. Looking for trees. It was surprising how many there were. Take St Philip's Square. Obviously there were trees there – it was a park – but if you'd asked him before, he'd have said eight, ten max. Now he counted.

Thirty-eight.

Same with St Paul's. He'd have said twenty.

Eighty-five.

He found his nightly surveys distracted from his stress, his mind benefitting from the change of focus. When he went back to work – 'I'm absolutely fine, I don't understand all the fuss…' – it seemed sensible to keep the walks going. Rosie wasn't so sure.

Forthright as ever, she said as much.

'Don't you see,' he replied, 'this is the only thing keeping me sane?'

He had no choice. So neither did she.

Every night Ed went out to count the trees.

At first his return to work went off without drama. Colleagues recognised he was fragile and for a while cut him some slack. It didn't last long though. Each day new orders came in. Soon there was a backlog. His workload increased as a result, his stress level rising by the hour. Only when he walked out each evening did his anxieties dissipate, like exhaust fumes, into the night air.

On his walks he found the city's greenery more widespread than he'd previously thought. Of course there were hold-outs – much of the Jewellery Quarter was treeless, Digbeth too – but elsewhere trees had taken root in the most unlikely places. The Methodist Hall tower on Corporation Street was now a miniature sky forest, whilst in Union Passage a tree grew from a first-floor gutter.

One night after completing his usual circuit he'd kept going. He'd ended up by the Hagley Road. Silhouetted in the dark, the Two Towers: Perrott's Folly, Edgbaston Waterworks. Ed recalled Tolkien's Ents. Walking trees. He tried to picture Treebeard creeping through sleeping Birmingham. Ridiculous. Yet the fact remained: trees were everywhere. Not in ones and twos either. Mature specimens grew all the way down New Street. How could that be? It was only pedestrianised in the Nineties. They'd never plant trees that large. But saplings wouldn't have had time to grow that high. It made no sense.

Thoughts like these occupied his waking hours. Through the day, into the night. Every evening now he was staying out longer. Unsurprisingly, his relationship with Rosie was suffering as a result. She didn't understand, she said. He was doing a very good impression of a crazy person. Just what exactly did he think he was doing?

He didn't know. He just knew he couldn't help it.

One day he fell asleep at work. At his desk. When he woke, he'd briefly thought no-one had noticed. Then he saw the email. From his boss, Cherry. It was headed 'Sleeping Beauty'. Could he see her in her office please, straightaway?

He kept his job. Just. Cherry had, in the past, experienced mental health issues herself. She was inclined to be sympathetic. To a point. This was his final warning. If it happened again? He was dead wood.

And that was that. He'd survived. But no sooner than he finished work the anxiety blew up again. What had he been thinking? He couldn't afford to lose his job. Not with rising inflation, not with his utility bills. Birmingham was bust, its council tax ballooning. What had he done? Was he mad?

No matter what he tried, he couldn't get calm. Once more panic gripped him. It wasn't as scary this time – not now he knew what he was dealing with – but it was still unpleasant. Extremely unpleasant.

Count the trees, he thought. Count the trees. He was hyperventilating. Hands shaking, he took his notebook. He slowly circled the cathedral.

Count the trees.

He counted.

There were thirty-nine.

Thirty-nine?

He counted again. It wasn't easy to keep track in the gloom. How many times had he counted these trees? Surely enough to be confident in his numbers. Something was awry. His head pounded. His routine was meant to bring order, calm but with every step his anxiety increased. He felt his heart expand, ready to explode.

Deep breaths. Please. Come on.

The air was warm, clammy. He sat down but it didn't help. He felt he might pass out. Best keep walking.

There were new trees on New Street.

A sapling on Digbeth High Street. It was clearly part of the eternally ongoing road improvement works, but so what? It was there. That was all that mattered.

He staggered on, past Digbeth's derelict factories, its old pubs, the cleared development bombsites. Trees everywhere. What had they come for? What were they after?

It was obvious, wasn't it? The council was screwed, everyone knew it. Libraries shutting, bins overflowing. Only that week he'd almost stepped on a used syringe on Colmore Row. The whole city was going to the dogs.

Not that it was just Birmingham.

London was an island for the rich these days, trees sculptured to death.

Sculpture culture.

Yet elsewhere, there wasn't enough money to maintain the roads. And hadn't a council up north chopped down its trees? Shameful that was. Then, to top it all, an incompetent government, unable to make a decent decision on anything.

A total shambles. Everywhere you looked, humanity abdicating its responsibilities. Was it really any surprise the trees had decided enough was enough?

Crazy thoughts. But that didn't matter. They briefly diverted Ed's brain from its anxiety. That was the important thing. And it worked. Somewhere between Digbeth and Eastside he began to calm down. It wasn't that there were fewer trees here, if anything there were more – guerrilla trees, taking advantage of vacant lots, derelict warehouses, fenced off building sites – but they stayed in the shadows. They let him pass.

It was almost five in the morning when he got home. By then he was feeling a little calmer. A logical explanation was vaguely discernible. He'd been fending off a panic attack. He'd been agitated. He'd got himself confused. That was all.

There was a note on the kitchen table. Lined paper ripped from a notebook, weighed down with Rosie's door key. He read the loving words, words she'd clearly agonised over. Were they teardrops making the ink run?

As he read, he recalled those playground ways of saying goodbye: I'm gonna make like a banana and split.

Yeah?

I'm gonna make like a tree and leave.

He couldn't sleep. He knew he should call Rose but knew too he would never get the words right. One thought shouting over everything now: out in the night the trees are moving. Creeping in from their strongholds in the shires, taking a silent stranglehold over the city. His city, dreaming itself into a nightmare.

Because roots can grow through concrete, can destroy walls.

Ed imagined a city deserted: windows smashed, branches protruding. Trees on Old Joe, the Rotunda, the BT Tower. A birch emerging from the Council House dome, a woodland of willows in the Town Hall. Tropical jungles beneath the Bullring's greenhouse glass. The Dale End and Jewellery Quarter car parks, the Birdcage – each transformed to hanging gardens, green waterfalls that would surely dwarf their Babylonian predecessor. The library's mesh overtaken by ivy, the Cadbury factory overrun by beech forest.

A metropolis reclaimed: the world's first true green city.

Ed called in sick. All day he lay on his bed. Eyes wide, sweating. He ate nothing, drank only black coffee.

That long afternoon slowly several things became clear. He mustn't panic but a slow revolution was underway. The strategy was one of stealth. This takeover would be slow. Decades might pass before it culminated. So there was still time. But he was one man. He needed allies.

And that wouldn't be easy. Clear-cut evidence had to be gathered and that was down to him.

Once again, when night fell, Ed headed out to count the trees.

Perhaps, beneath the noise, Ed's overwrought brain still hoped logic would return. If that was the case, it would be disappointed. Not only did the increased tree numbers in St Philip's remain, there were now eighty-eight in St Paul's Square and three new saplings on Digbeth High Street.

Ed saw now how the trees had advanced so stealthily: the canals.

Who gave any thought to them? But those stagnant monuments, liquid relics of the Industrial Revolution, were green arteries, running inwards. Bringing trees into the city in their hundreds.

That must be it.

But how did the trees move in from there? Under cover of darkness, of course. Even the most distracted shopper would notice oaks wandering down New Street. But how, exactly? As he walked, Ed tried to find a plausible theory.

Wind- blown seeds.

Accelerated growth, bamboo-style.

Roots burrowing unseen, emerging in new places as if always there.

None felt likely.

But there was another scenario.

Not all of these intruders were surreptitiously creeping in.

Young trees arrived every day in broad daylight, ferried in as part of the planning requirements for the myriad of towers and townhouses rapidly gentrifying Digbeth and the Gun Quarter. Like the wooden horse at Troy, the enemy was being welcomed with open arms.

Why on earth would we do that?

In the early hours, by a Hockley car park, Ed worked it out.

Mind control.

Incredible. Somehow – God knows how – the trees were influencing people's thoughts. Making them think they needed greenery in their lives. Encouraging people to plant saplings, unwittingly boxing themselves in as they did.

Ed could see this wooden army was relentless, implacable. And it was growing all the time. Its assault was slow but inexorable as the tide. And it would not stop, would never stop, not until Birmingham's citizens were completely surrounded – at the mercy of the trees.

He walked all night. Once again on the verge of panic, where possible he stuck to streets with minimal foliage. He'd thought he had time. He was wrong. There was no time at all. How long before they identified him as a threat? Weeks? Days?

By morning he was at his kitchen table, on the phone. He tried the council's parks department first. He was on hold for almost an hour before hanging up.

Next he tried the police. He explained that yes, this was an emergency, a most definite emergency. The switchboard operator didn't seem to understand the urgency. In her defence, Ed was probably not as clear as he could have been. He'd not slept for days.

'Ring 101,' she said.

He did. They at least listened this time, a long silence following every comment he made. They'd send someone around, they said. But it might be a while. They hoped he'd understand. They were busy with real human criminals.

It was clear the authorities weren't going to help. There was only one other person he could think of to call. Thankfully she answered. He explained everything. Even talking quickly, it took a while.

'Well?' he finally asked. 'Will you help me, or what?'

Silence. For a moment he thought he'd been cut off. Then he heard a sniff. Rose was crying.

'Oh Edward,' she whispered, 'I think you need help. I just don't think I'm the one to help you.'

He hung up.

He was on his own.

Alright.

He made another coffee.

Time to work out a plan.

By early afternoon he was back in town. He'd driven in from the B&Q in Erdington. Leaving the car at the Bullring, he walked up to New Street. As usual, the preachers were out by Waterstones. He ignored them, walking straight to the nearest tree. There, with his newly acquired chainsaw, he began to cut it down.

No-one tried to stop him. A few shoppers shouted pointlessly but he could hardly hear them over the noise. Who was really going to stop a man with a chainsaw?

It was an impressive piece of kit, making quick work of its task. He was four trees down, well into his fifth, by the time the police finally arrived.

•

The hospital room is light and airy, overlooking a tarmacked courtyard where the patients exercise. No trees are in sight, no green of any kind. Olive, Ed's favourite nurse, has made it clear there are none anywhere nearby. Nothing to worry about, she says. He's perfectly safe here. They'll look after him for as long as is necessary.

'How long will that be?

He's asked this question more than once. The answer is always the same.

'Just as long as is necessary.'

It's pleasant here. Ed's feeling a lot better. It's true he gets anxious now and then, worrying the trees are still out there, but when he does Olive calls the duty doctor, who gives him a special shot. Ed sleeps a lot these days. They don't mind him sleeping – which is nice – but sometimes he feels guilty. He knows he should be doing something. Contributing to society.

Doing something about the trees.

How long he's been in the hospital is difficult to say. The days here are all the same. Breakfast, lunch, exercise, dinner. Early nights, late mornings. Is it weeks or months since he arrived? He has no idea.

One night though it's not the same.

He's in bed when he's awoken by something – he could swear – brushing against his face. His door is ajar in the moonlight.

Which is unusual.

They usually lock it.

It's a warm night. The window has been left open. He looks down into the courtyard but it's just shadow. He knows he should try to sleep. Instead, he's drawn outside. Being forbidden, naturally he wants to do it. Perhaps fresh air will calm his nerves.

He puts on his slippers, heads through the empty corridors. As he walks the lights come on automatically. Every door is unlocked. Again, this is odd. Where is the duty nurse?

Off dealing with an emergency perhaps.

He takes the stairwell. There's the door to the yard. Again, open.

He pushes through. The security light comes on.

There's the courtyard.

And there they are.

The trees.

The beautiful trees.

Sycamore, willow.

Ash, oak, lime.

There must be a thousand.

White-pink shapes hang in their branches, like gigantic cocoons.

They've come for him.

He knew they would. They're coming for everybody. Now they're here, he's surprised to find he feels no anxiety. In fact, he's relieved. Worry and fear evaporate off him like dew on a leaf dissolving in morning sunlight.

The trees are green and luminous in the electric light.

A branch lightly touches his back, as if trying to say, *How foolish it is to fight.*

Yes. He sees that now. They've won.

And it's a glorious victory.

He steps into the courtyard, smiling as he does. This is right, a natural progression. Like his city's history: always forward, generation after generation, regeneration after regeneration.

Now is simply time for the trees.

The Fox

PATRICK BOYDEN

I no longer sleep at night – I don't even go to bed until dawn – and I like to see the glow of the lights on the toll road a couple of miles away. The motorway has a constant rumble in the day, not enough to keep me awake though. At night it's quieter. I prefer the night.

I can't remember when the fox first came. I reckon it was around two in the morning one day in May. Yes, five months back – that sounds about right. He mooched round the garden, unfazed by the security light, scratched at the lawn briefly, before looking towards the house. I'd come into the living room just as the outside light came on. I had a pretty good view of him through the French windows and, besides, the room was in darkness. The fox sniffed the air, then trotted down the garden into the field beyond the hedge. I waited a few moments but he didn't return.

There's a small copse just on the rise between me and the motorway. I'm not sure how far away it is, a mile perhaps, but Mags loved walking her old spaniel up there and back – any excuse to get out of the house, she'd say. Funny to think that was thirty years ago. The copse won't be there for long, the urban sprawl is advancing inexorably from Sutton in a sort of pincer movement with my house at its apex. I can't see the building work yet – it's just beyond the rise – but at night there are a few lamps left on for security and their light bounces back off the cloud. In a few weeks, though, like a concrete and brick Great Birnam Wood, it will move steadily towards the small hill on which Mags' copse stands.

The copse isn't visible at night, but it's there, more or less dead centre as I look out the window. I do wonder whether the developers will leave it intact – a small reminder of the great forests that once covered the Warwickshire countryside. I, for one, hope so.

Midsummer, my nights are short. I can't bear the daylight anymore so I sleep as long as I can, waking only when dark descends, going to bed at dawn. In December, that's not a problem but as spring morphs into summer I wake before the sun has set and when dawn arrives, I'm not ready for bed. Autumn is here now, and I'm happier.

I've had this routine for many years – how I got into it, I can't recall – the insomnia after Mags' disappearance perhaps. It took a while to get myself organised – finding all night supermarkets and, more lately, doing as much as possible online. There are inevitably occasions when I have to be up in daylight hours – visits from tradesmen and deliveries for instance – but I've learned to manage them. I switch my phone off during the day, and I don't turn it back on till after breakfast. If it's important, they can always leave a message.

Let me describe my night. I get up around nine, shower, eat breakfast and make coffee which I drink while reading the day's news on my iPad. I watch a bit of TV, mostly detective serials – the forensic stuff particularly intrigues me – but by midnight, I'm settled in my armchair, facing the window, my Kindle to hand (crime stories again), and stare at the motorway's glow. If it's cloudy, especially if there are thunderclouds, I can see reflected light from Coleshill and as far away as Coventry. As the new housing estates are built, there'll be a different panorama. Why am I fascinated by this light show? I don't really know but it may be because five decades ago, there was barely a glimmer. Now, apart from the towns and the motorway, I can see red lights blinking on tall masts, watch aeroplanes heading into Elmdon and, on one glorious night, the fire from a petrol tanker.

The sirens and flashing blue lights of police cars, though, never fail to make my heart skip a beat.

I began leaving food for the fox on the lawn. At first he was a bit suspicious, sniffing round the bowl, glancing warily at the house, but from the first night he scoffed the lot. Now, there's no hesitation. I make myself some lunch at about 1am, then I empty a tin of Whiskas into a plastic bowl and leave it in the centre of the lawn. If it's dry and not too cold, I'll sit on the small patio and wait for him. He knows I'm there but he's nervous – if I move or make a sound, he's quick to retreat. Recently, though, he's hung around at the edge of the pool of light. He'll return to his food after a minute or two, his dark, cautious eyes glinting at me.

Mags hated foxes, called them, with no hint of irony, treacherous. For a couple of years she kept three chickens in a coop at the bottom of the garden. They were unproductive, stank, and ruined the grass. She gave them names and even when they stopped producing their weekly egg, she kept them on. I refused to have anything to do with them and was unsympathetic when a fox got into the coop and behaved as if it was an all you can eat buffet. She swore blind that she'd secured the cage door and she was right, she had.

•

We never had children. We tried, perhaps on my part a little half-heartedly -- I was never one for the physical side of marriage -- and after we'd both passed forty, I lost any enthusiasm I'd had. We drifted into a sort of stasis where our only intercourse was essential dialogue about shopping or money or redecorating the bedroom, punctuated by cold silences.

It was about then, twenty-five – twenty-eight? – years ago that I found out that although our intercourse was purely verbal, hers wasn't. I asked myself, did I care? I tried to convince myself I didn't. I never met the man, her bastard boss from her office in Tamworth.

It's October now, and the day/night balance is more to my liking. In a week or two, the clocks go back and I'll be waking up in the dark. I feel more energised. After breakfast, I make my fortnightly trip to the 24-hour Londis, mostly to keep the freezer stocked – fresh stuff like milk and bread I can get from the BP garage. Cat food for the fox of course, that's become routine.

A couple of days ago, mid-afternoon, I was woken by the chimes of the doorbell. The visitor introduced herself, a detective. She asked me about Mags' disappearance and I repeated what I'd told her predecessors all those years ago, namely that I'd come home from work and she'd gone, along with a suitcase of clothes and her passport. Was there a reason for the enquiry, I asked? Just a routine follow up of a cold case, she said, staring out of the French windows.

Last night was odd. It was unseasonably mild when I went out shortly after midnight with the fox's food, so I sat on the patio, waiting for him to appear. I gazed at the light illuminating the clouds, the usual dull yellow-grey with patches of orange from the sodium lights on the main Sutton road. A siren's wail startled me. I followed the blue lights' progress from left to right, north to south as the police car passed in front of me, two miles distant, until the siren's Doppler effect told me it was not getting closer. Before it disappeared altogether, its lights briefly silhouetted the copse. It was that which led me to drop my eyes to the lawn. The fox was sitting by his bowl, staring dispassionately at me, no sign of any of his usual nervousness or caution. His expression made me shiver. We regarded each other for a minute or two. Tentatively, I leant forward, but he didn't move. Hello, I said. He lifted his head and sniffed the air. Slowly, I stood up. In response, he looked over his shoulder towards the copse, then back at me. I took a step towards him, thinking that maybe he wanted some more food. Instead, he stood up, stretched and trotted towards the gap in the hedge at the bottom of the garden.

I tried to think of it as some sort of progress towards his accepting that I wasn't a threat, but there was something about his manner I found disturbing.

Yesterday morning, after the strange incident with the fox, just before I went to bed, I wandered into the garden. On the horizon, the trees of the copse, normally black against the dawn sky, were illuminated by floodlights. Flickering shadows gave the scene an eerie glow. It was too early for the builders. Tree cutters? Maybe they'd decided to remove the copse after all. But why so early?

Today, the police come mob-handed, blue lights slashing the darkness. A dawn raid they call it, though it is not yet light. They find me on the patio watching the fox who, once more, is sitting on the lawn, unperturbed, his dark eyes fixed on me.

They found Mags, or what was left of her, where I last saw her amongst the trees. The detective regards the fox with interest.

The building surveyors visited the copse a few days ago, she tells me, and found a freshly dug fox's earth, and a grisly collection of bones. Weird, eh?

I don't hear her reciting the caution. I watch the fox stand up and stretch, indifferent to his betrayal. With a toss of his head, he turns and walks away, his fur glowing bronze in the first rays of morning light.

Mid-century Modern

HELEN CROSS

I'm about to snap up a pair of original Eames chairs ridiculously cheap. Don't tell Don. I'm the only bidder, maybe because it's winter and the seller's located in a middle-of-nowhere Midlands village. Plus, the listing has just one crappy sideways photo. And one of those cold unpunctuated descriptions which hint at psychopathy: 'plastic chairs 1951 no time wasters pick up after 7pm within 24 hours CASH on collection ONLY.' A three-day listing. Curious. Who does that? But, yep, yep, yep, five secs four, three, two, one, wow, congratulations, you've won! Twenty-five canny watchers, but just my late, low bid, so no chase in the win this time, but thumbs up, I feel excited.

1951. One year older than my lost mother.

I found them, not as Don thinks because I'm an auction addict, but because I'm a crafty searcher. I've alerts out for all creative and mistaken spellings, plus ignorant or inventive combinations, of 'mid-century modern'. Including, what I reckon did it this time, 'plastic chairs 51'. I'm also on the hunt right now for multiple spellings of original Ebenezer Gomme (the garage is stuffed with it, not to mention bursting through the roof at Little Elephant). Also, I'm trying to build up a complete Fresco suite in the garden shed ('your G-plan's driving me round the bloody bend') and for that 'tall 50s draws' is bringing good returns.

Another thing Don 'assumes' is that it's the menopause: it's not. Though, typically, as soon as I've paid, thump, I hit the floor. Mood like a demented pendulum. Ah shit, what've I done? I'm broken with regret. They're surely fakes, imitations, jokes, scams. Don won't believe me but I'm quite aware, thank you, that some canny con artists, particularly of desirable mid-century classics, are one step ahead of impulsive idiots like me. Yes, I'm now aware, they deliberately list fakes with misspellings or without brands, to sniff out rookie smart arses. A few times in the early days I was conned, and, yes, hang me, I've dumped more than a few nasty rip-offs in the moonlit lay-bys of the wider West Midlands.

Which is why I now check 'seller's other items' and see no reviews but, what! No, oh my god, no, what the hell, no, it can't be! But it looks like it, yes, 'Syros1273' has loads of original Kartell. And I can't believe what I'm seeing; something she's listed as 'old armchair' but to these old eyes it looks pretty much like a god-damned original Marco Zanuso for Arflex.

I've a long-held hunch 'collection only' hints at pain and that, if left to fester (thank you Harborne therapist at £60 a pop), leads to recklessness. Madnesses. Mine was going into the eco-cupboard with the literacy coordinator the month after Mom died, and theirs is putting up a hoard of mid-century European classics with a starting bid of 99p and no reserve. Yippee! There's clearly some feeling the seller can't deal with. They want a stranger to appear through the night, part burglar, part bailiff, and just grab their heavy load and go.

I email, savouring the fact that Syros1273 knows nothing about me ('Midmodlover68') and never will. I'd like to live amongst strangers 'maker unknown': an object of mystery and fascination. 'Can I come right away? I know it's late but I'm free.'

I need to be out of the house. Out in the cool dark night.

Just a few minutes pass before ping; yes, I should 'leave right now' and 'here's address of cottage'. Cottage! Cottage is good. Cottage in Dorridge is brilliant; it says old-age, posh, rural fairy-tale, all round authenticity and five minutes later I'm heading for the car, having grabbed, from behind the cheese plant, the hidden packet of Silk Cut I keep for just such celebrations.

Many of these villages beyond South Birmingham, I've never visited (I've told Don my 'hobby' is partly urban tourism, 'just getting to know our much-maligned local area, love'), but that's not the case with this trip. As a young woman, before Don, before teaching, I'd enquired about renting a cottage myself, near Dorridge. I didn't even drive but liked the photo in the local newspaper and the bald description 'remote farm out-building, two beds'. I checked a bus route and imagined a new me: walking, getting a dog, reading, gardening, painting, being alone.

As I fold down the back seat and lay out the old futon cushion, I ponder a van. It could increase my search options, not just height and width but distance, far beyond my current 20 miles. Roughly the span of the West Midlands in any direction from our home. Last year it was ten miles, with a southern limit around Redditch. Though, really, why've I restricted myself this way? Because, honestly, I don't think Don would give a flying fuck if I was gone for days.

Talking of which: kidnap, false imprisonment, sexual slavery, rape, murder, being stuffed into a suitcase, dumped in a cesspit, folded down a manhole with a scarf tied round my 'too-friendly' face. All possibilities, Don says. And I should be 'very worried', about entering the homes of 'sod-knows-who at night.' During the dark hours. Which is why I've still got, somewhere in this doggy dump, the gift he bought me last Christmas, a red can of pepper spray. And the old cricket bat he insists I keep in the boot.

As I wait at the traffic lights, I think how I still haven't tackled her flat, though she died months ago. Then I swerve into the petrol station and take out the max £250 cash ('money we certainly don't have!'), because Italian mid-century modern does not come along every day and, surely not but what if… What if that lounge chair is original Arflex!

So, here's the thing: Don says I'm a hoarder. He makes jokes about it in company. And every time he does it, I think, no, wrong, I've discarded so much of myself for this marriage, you've absolutely no idea.

The wind thrashes at black branches and as I rise above the M42 and accelerate off the roundabout onto the dual carriageway. The night around the car is like rushing water. Once, as I dashed off (I was leaving super quick because I'd got my mitts on a John Herbert small sideboard, over in Wednesbury and the sour seller, probably because I'd only paid a tenner, said that he went to bed early so he'd have to leave it in the garden), Don called out, 'Go on then, off you go, my dear, jump in your time machine.' Oddly insightful that for Don, because the years (53), do roar away as I drive, as I press on back through the blackness towards another, truer, freer me.

It's not just Don who misunderstands. When I arrived at Little Elephant, the Polish receptionist, while directing me along the blue-lit corridors to my first unit, said: 'There are three types who rent storage.' She stuck up a thumb to mark the first type. 'Divorcees who lose their home, probably must move in with friends or parents'. I shook my head. Then a finger, 'Young couples. Can afford a few bits and pieces but in England right now no way a house to put them in.' Another shake. For the third, she didn't even bother raising a finger, just gave a pitying look. 'Troubled people concealing shopping from families, which makes me very sad. Because there is help available.'

As proof that this was not me, I could've offered Don's line from a recent row: 'I'm sick of living amongst all your bloody crap, love!' To which I'd replied that it's clear to me that all Don wants in our house is 'one gigantic TV'. Things might be better if we concealed more from one another; another vote for the van.

The van, the van. But how will I get a van past Don? Another prickling plan scratches away: leave Don. Just do it. Sell the house. Buy a van. Leave Don. Put the furniture from the garage in the van and leave. Buy everything else you need, which is nothing, online and start again. Madness. Driving away from the safe hold of the city does this, these loose frosty fields, the tangle of hedgerows, the possibility of excitement or aggravation ahead. It's an agitating sensation, like desire; close to youth, or something else that feels wild and true; death, probably. I know I won't make it to mid this century; I've already had cancer, got high cholesterol, use a hand to stand up from a chair.

My mother was just 71.

But why am I even worrying? It's not OFSTED, it's not parent's evening. I don't have to make a good impression. Nothing is expected other than I physically pick up a solid object in my hands and leave and Jesus when I think of the weight of what I carry every day; my marriage, our house, the dog, my grief, twenty-eight years of teaching Year 3; it's nothing.

I'm speeding along now, quite happily thinking of Don dead. My mind often drifts this way when driving alone at night. Not dead painfully but suddenly, altering my life completely by his absence. After his death I might move, buying a small two-bedder by the sea, or start my own auction house or play the stock market with the imaginary life insurance. I will get rid of the televisions, the Sky Sports, maybe get another dog. Paint. Walk. I never think of Don dying, or his funeral, just his complete unchangeable absence from my life. He will be so gone it will be like he's never been listed. He will never be mentioned by anyone, and the absence of him will not be missed. It's attractive to me, to be rid of his big lumpy presence. I particularly like to imagine waving off the undertakers. But then that's it, after collection I don't know what to do next.

On the roadside dusty vets' surgeries are giving way to wannabe gastro pubs. There's a brown sign for the stately home, and then, wow, a white owl dipping over ploughed fields. So smooth, like thrown white velvet. And I remember the first time I came here to view that farm cottage; wonky floorboards, a pale blue Aga, no central heating, just the bare bones of a bathroom. But it was too…what? What had stopped me? Too far from the certainties of the city? Too lonely? Then, Don a few years later; a fitted kitchen, central heating and all that comfort like cement in the veins, like falling under a paralysing spell.

I'm on a dirt track.

The satnav tells me the destination is on the left and the seller has alerted me to a ring of rusted corrugated iron, which I mistake in this deep darkness for a fence of trees. Then, yep, there's the cottage, large but grubby, and in the driveway a jeep with foreign number plates. Oh great, Euro dealers here already, perfect. Then, no way! Some grinning gold-digger's hurrying past with a wire-form Bertoia in one hand and a space age floor lamp in the other. An original Bertoia! What the hell. I want to cry. Why didn't I 'make offer' on every damn thing before I left? I'm such a loser.

But cheer up, it's all a good sign for the authenticity of the hoard. And as I stare at the moonlit front garden, I see a fallen fatsia and it's clear no one has gardened here for a while. Recently dead sellers are the best. So, I grab the pepper spray as I step from the car (because I promised Don I would) and prepare for battle. Then, weird, I smell smoke, burning wood, sweet, then realise I can blame my own smokiness on this and for once I'll be telling Don the truth.

Several hard knocks do not rouse the owner, so I step round the side of the cottage. 'I've come for the chairs,' I shout, and I imagine Don replying, 'Yep, I can see that carved on your gravestone, love.'

There is no reply. I walk a little further into the garden where I see a bonfire. Flames are rising like orange streamers. Ash is falling like confetti. To one side, not quite distinct through the smoke, a person. My heart thumps, my fingers fizz, because now I'm staring hard I see, through the golden leaping sparks, the bursting spits of the wood, arm movements strong and full of direction. They're feeding what seems to be, what the hell, *is*, a chair. Not just any chair but obviously, even through the fog of the fire, the big daddy of the Ercol rockers: The Grandfather! Heading into the flames! I look around in panic, and see, lined up by an unkempt hedge, four yellowing Eero Saarinen Tulip chairs and stacked together, several white Pantons. Black branches are thrashing above, the moon is bright and maybe she's drunk, because next to her, charred on the pyre, the crumbling blackened skeletons of other Ercols, and the carcass of a wide, thick dressing table; original Ebeneezer Gomme! I should back off, but I move forward, calling again, though the fire stoker doesn't pause in her feeding of the furnace. Then, suddenly through the panic, a head, a shortness of hair, which reminds me of my chemo, and yes, this must be her: the unmedicated lunatic Don's been warning me about.

I wave, like I'm calling the night for help, as the woman sticks a small cabinet into the flames, rubs her hands along her jeans and nods. 'Oh hi,' she calls, and strides tiger-like, across the fire-lit garden, lean and strong, full of energy with a firm reptilian core. I step my legs apart, adopting the pose of the alpha antique experts on TV, who as far as I know have never been murdered in their line of work. 'Come this way. They're ready,' she says as she moves quickly towards the back door of the cottage.

'Are you burning the furniture?' I ask, trying not to use what Don calls my 'teacher's voice'.

'Some of it. There's just too much. We're selling the plastic,' the woman says, gesturing to the Tulip and Panton chairs, 'because there's no other way to get rid of it. Lasts thousands of years in landfill. Follow me.'

'You might want to think about taking it to charity,' I say in my snootiest teacher's voice. 'Rather than burning it?'

'Oh sure, we've taken loads, but there's only so much of this old wooden stuff they've space for. We've given away what we can. My mother was quite a… shopper.' Her skin is bronzed in a way that suggests life in another climate. 'Come, in,' she says.

And as she strides over the stone doorstep, she turns to me and smiles: 'Careful. Watch out for the ghosts.'

I can hear flames crackling outside and though I am not near the fire I still feel the heat of it on my face. I step over a cat bowl half-full of tiny biscuits, and into a room which is gloomy and smells of gravy and vermin. Carpets are rolled up, revealing splintery old floorboards, but on the blue walls brighter squares mark where paintings once hung. Then, I feel dizzy because, keep calm, steady, I notice in one dismantled corner, what looks, oh my God, no way, is that…an Arne Jacobson Swan? In burnt orange leather? It stops my breath.

'Good taste, huh?' the woman says. 'Someone wanted to buy the lot but couldn't fit it in the car. She just about managed all the Kartell. Said she wished she'd brought a van.'

'It's an original,' I murmur.

'Oh yeah, sure. My mother wasn't into fakes. Not in furniture anyway. Her taste in men wasn't quite so original.'

There's an Eames Blackbird flung sideways on a Franco Albini bookcase and lower down a stack of Bitossi plant pots in the emerald glaze. If I wasn't so dumbstruck, I'd consider joking that this must be how Howard Carter felt when he cracked open King Tut's tomb.

'It's incredible,' I purr, breaking all the TV rules of snapping up bargains.

The woman frowns, nods slowly, remembering. 'If you're into it,' she says.

'Pardon?'

'The past.' I notice an American inflection in her voice. 'If the past's your thang.'

Then I'm not listening because in a far dark corner, fuck me, there she is: my God, it's her: the Lady Lounge Chair. Way bigger than she looks online. More of a cockpit than a chair. The blue mohair's bobbled and the seat cushion's indented and halfway down the headrest is an oily hair stain. But she is what she's always promised to be; not just timeless but haunted by another age entirely. 'That's… a famous chair,' I whisper, and the woman looks where I'm pointing.

'Really? Whatever it is, she died in it.'

I murmur condolences and nod gently as I hear how she was never late, a good cook, thrifty, had a weekly blow-dry, bought her furniture in Birmingham as a newlywed and stuck with it. 'Moved in here when she got married. Never left. Poor thing.'

'I love mid-century,' I say, to reject what her daughter's implying.

'Not sure you would if you'd had to live in it,' she says.

The seller seems keen for me to be gone. 'I am sure these're Eames,' she says as she swooshes out from beneath a sheet the very thing, original Eames Eiffel, elegant acrylic buckets on spindly triangular legs. I feel mildly sick. 'I really don't want these to end up in landfill,' she says, and I babble about how great they'll look in my kitchen, as if there's space anywhere for anything. Already she's holding one in front of her like a bad child she needs instantly to be rid of. 'Polyurethane, fiberglass, polycarbonate, polypropylene. All this hideous plastic,' she says. 'I guess that generation thought the world would go on forever.' When I don't answer she says, 'Do you need help getting them into the car?'

When the Eiffels are packed in, I suddenly can't face… the drive? The return? My entire life? I look at my phone and see there are four missed calls from Don. Still alive.

I walk in a random direction trying to steady my breath, looking up at the moon, down at starlight in the puddles, and after some time come to the centre of a village where I buy fish and chips at the only open shop. 'Local?' the fish fryer asks, as he slaps the silky fish back and forth in the batter.

'I'm collecting some chairs. I live in Birmingham.' He winces. 'I got them from the cottage they're clearing out round the corner.' I'm speaking normally, though my voice sounds like that of a different woman.

'Mrs. Smith's place? Up for auction. Some bugger'll make a killing on it. They want a quick sale. Apparently. Not sure if summat's gone on.'

I carry the warm greasy bundle heavy against my hip and then dump it in a bin.

I realise I never paid for the chairs.

When I get back to the cottage, the car with the foreign plates is gone. The rickety side gate is closed with a bolt and chain. I peer between the panels of corrugated iron, and though the fire is still smouldering the flames are out. Not one spindle of Ercol or plank of G-Plan remain. Madly I knock hard on the door, as though there's someone inside I need to free and when there's no reply, I tap harder on the window and peer in, my hand shielding my view.

By moonlight I can make out the coppery weight of the Swan, the black lump of the Blackbird and the misty throne of the Lady Lounge Chair. All resting peacefully. I close my eyes. Feel my hot forehead against the cool glass.

Buried. Gone.

'She's gone,' a voice says and when I turn a woman has her hands on her hips in the lane. 'They've shut up now, if you're after a viewing.'

'How can I get in touch?'

'Well, she lives in Greece, so I don't know,' the woman says. 'She left all that.' She gestures disapprovingly at the Tulip and Panton chairs, which've been moved besides a big handwritten sign: 'Please take, reuse, save from landfill.'

'Greece?' I say.

The woman makes a big inhale and folds her arms. 'On an island, apparently. According to Mrs. Smith she went off years ago. Just left everything and moved around. California first, then Greece. A traveller, apparently. They didn't get along I don't think. Have you come far?'

'Not far at all.'

'Well, I'm afraid you've still had a wasted journey.'

I see the moon. I think of the owl.

And then ping; a text from Don: 'Are you safe?'

Charlatan

LIZ CHURCHILL

The crystal ball is pale yellow as though its transparency has been corrupted by something like nicotine or plaque. Or as if it's taking the piss.

Debs has told Katy to come at night because she can only tell fortunes if the moon is out. They're sat at a table covered by white lace, in a small, peach-coloured room separated from the living area by frosted glass. There's less psychic paraphernalia around than Katy expected – just one stone angel placed on the mantelpiece above a boarded up fireplace, its face sad, like it flew down the chimney and got trapped.

'It's technicoloured in there,' says Debs, gazing into the ball. 'It's like the Barbie movie.'

'I was listening to the Barbie movie soundtrack on the way here!' says Katy. Then she looks down. She wasn't going to give anything away. She was going to test Debs's powers. She was going to stay poker-faced as fuck.

'You are about to enter a two-year period of great excitement,' says Debs with grand-dame gravitas. She blinks slowly as though her fake eyelashes are heavy. She stares at Katy and it becomes clear she will say no more until she's given something back.

'Sounds good,' says Katy.

'It's going to be *lovely*,' says Debs, a look of solid I-bullshit-thee-not in the way she carries her shoulders. 'Are you single?'

'Yes.'

Debs nods, all-knowingly.

Katy shifts in her seat, sensing a gear-change.

'A man with a cup of love is coming from your past.'

Katy stares at Debs, trying to decide if this is a well-rehearsed script, trying to decide if she, Katy, is a mug.

'His cup of love is for you, bab. And he's going to bring you lots of kisses of both the nurturing and the *passionate* kind.' Debs now puckers her lips and makes an over-the-top kissing sound. 'He's the kind of man who will want to fix things for you.' And she shoots Katy a look that seems like a wink but isn't. 'Let's just say, if your kettle's broken, he'll notice and next time you go to fill it...' Debs gestures rather than finishes the sentence.

When the reading ends, Katy hands Debs the four £10 notes, warm from the back pocket of her jeans – the action seems illicit. Debs presses a handful of business cards into Katy's palm and tells her with quiet intensity to pass them on to friends. If Katy was a true believer, she might be worried about the long-term consequences of not doing such a thing but she has concluded, from forty-five minutes spent with Debs, that Debs is a charlatan.

Probably.

'Were you satisfied with the reading, bab?'

'Yes,' says Katy. 'Absolutely.'

Boo! The message seems to float on Katy's phone screen several hours later. *Guess who's coming to your area?!*

Katy's in the middle of eating some leftover mushroom risotto with peas. All her cutlery is festering in the sink in water long cold, washing-up bubbles all burst, a tiny dribble of white lurking on the surface like a ghost. She's found a wooden fork instead but the dry feel of it on her tongue is unpleasant, the way it sticks.

Reading the text now, she drops the fork, stands up and starts to pace.

Nooo! she types. *Walker's on tour??!! The Birmingham leg? Tell me more, mate.*

She presses send, sits back down and feels a bit sick. Banter's not her forte. Should she have written that *mate*? Is it the right category? Is he her mate? Other than for the past week, she's not spoken to this man – Danny Walker – since she went to school with him in Cardiff fifteen years ago. They're strangers really playing at being long-time-no-see pals. But they both seem happy with this little charade. Is it a charade? They used to snog a lot at parties. She wonders if he still kisses the same. She wonders if that's a ridiculous thought.

It would be nice to kiss somebody new. Or if not exactly new, different. It would be nice to explore a fresh body, feel fresh skin against hers, choreograph a fresh bit of intimacy. It's been a while, she thinks.

The last man she was naked with was Ian from work – a man who aligns himself with *the troubled male ego* and listens to a lot of Nick Cave. They work together in The New Moon pub – a recent addition to the Moseley night scene. For Katy, this provides some extra money around her three-day-a-week job booking Theatre-in-Education shows into schools. For most of the other staff, the job fits around their studies. Ian is doing a PhD about microscopic art. Everyone else is an undergrad except Allegra, the supervisor. Allegra describes herself as *just a little bit woowoo, babe, a little bit new age.* She'd recommended Debs. She'd said, 'I mean, she knew... she *knew* that my grandad liked pickled herring. Can't argue with that.'

Ian had struck up a casual relationship with Katy. They never really labelled what it was exactly but it involved a lot of sex –

which Ian would say was a natural extension of their friendship. He would also say they were clearly more than friends but that he wasn't her boyfriend and he never would be. Katy sometimes felt that talking to Ian about his feelings was like watching something badly dubbed – words and actions not quite in sync.

Ian had repeatedly told Katy that her basic need for security was just too much for him. She had wanted monogamy; he'd said he couldn't give her that. But he'd also said he wasn't purposely looking for anyone else. Katy had taken an *I'd rather this than nothing* attitude. And so for the entirety of their six-month involvement, the possibility of non-monogamy hung in the air, making Katy feel constantly anxious. Once, for example, they had gone to a party and Ian had spent a large portion of the evening flirting and being very touchy-feely with another girl whilst stood beside Katy. Later, when Katy had tried to explain that this upset her, Ian had said it was a shame she let her jealousy complicate things.

After working her shifts at The New Moon, Katy would often walk to Ian's flat with him and another girl called Georgia, who lived a little further on. Ian would largely ignore Katy at the pub. There was a silent understanding between them that nobody at work should know they were a *sort-of* couple. When Katy queried this, Ian just explained that, 'You know, it might make things a bit weird.'

Although he acted like Katy was just part of the wallpaper at The New Moon, on the walk home with Georgia, Ian would become animated and make a lot of jokes. Then, once they'd parted from Georgia and were safely inside his flat, he would become very passionate, very quickly, in a way that Katy found hard to resist.

On shifts that only Katy and Georgia worked, they began going for a few drinks afterwards in The Prince of Wales. They started to bond over niche anxieties they had in common, like a mutual fear of escalators and how long they both spent over-explaining themselves in emails. They would hug each other goodbye at 1am and Georgia would say things like, 'I'd better go and check my emails!' whilst miming a clunky typing action and pulling an exaggerated frazzled face. They would explode in laughter because Georgia was very talented at being quirky and fun and it made them both feel good about the world.

'Oh my God! We're the same person!' Georgia shouted one evening. 'Matching algorithms!'

Slowly, Katy began confiding aspects of her relationship with Ian. She was hesitant at first. 'Maybe I shouldn't be saying all this,' she said.

'No, go on,' said Georgia. 'It's juicy. Besides, I've got a short memory.' She blinked hard as if to demonstrate how good she was at forgetting things.

As Katy divulged, Georgia pulled delighted faces and said things like, 'Noooo! He can get in the bin!' … 'He doesn't deserve you!'… 'Well. I fully encourage you to embrace your anger over *that* because it shows that *you* know your self-worth. And it shows that *you* know the difference between right and wrong!'

As weeks of this passed by, they created private jokes together such as deepening their voices and saying, 'Oh, shall we talk about my ex-girlfriend again? The thing about Naomi was…' a reference to the fact that Ian constantly talked about his break-up from three years ago. 'I still dream about her!' they'd whisper in each other's ears as they crossed paths on busy shifts. 'He needs to go to boyfriend school!' Georgia once shouted. And when Ian arrived at work by bike, they'd find it hilarious to tap their heads as he walked past in his helmet. 'Sex-yyy!' Georgia would sing when he was out of earshot.

It was ok to be mean because Ian was *properly* messing Katy about according to Georgia. 'It's like he's putting your emotions in a blender and pressing Maximum Whizz. I don't know how you put up with it. As an outsider looking in, he's punching above his weight. I promise you, you're a real catch!'

When Katy thanked her, Georgia had said, 'Honestly, solidarity forever.'

Weeks later, acting on Georgia's advice, Katy had finally ended things with Ian – who had told her with great indifference that it was *totally fine*. Georgia handed Katy a book on heartbreak as they sipped their post-work gin and tonics in The Prince of Wales. 'I found it on my bookshelf as I was leaving for work this afternoon. Heartbreak is the worst! But I promise you, one door is closing and an exciting new one is opening!'

Georgia was full of promises about the rosiness of Katy's future.

Katy wasn't sure if it was heartbreak she now felt or just a great, aching lethargy. She began moving as if in slow motion like the stereotype of a moody teenager, although she was actually reminded of her childhood. Her mother had sold life to her as a fairy tale and then made her feel like a limp princess. 'Oh Katy,' she used to sigh like it was a tired catchphrase. 'Oh. Katy. Honestly.'

'You need a sassy break-up playlist!' Georgia announced during a graveyard Tuesday shift. 'You need to find all the songs you can which have an overriding message of *Fuck You*. You need to give yourself the ick about him. Maybe that sounds toxic but I'm in protective friend-mode here.'

So Katy taught herself to see Ian differently. She would watch him having a cigarette outside on his break, lurking by the fire escape in the dark and she would say to herself, in a Shakespearean voice, 'But soft, what's this? Tis but a shadow.'

She no longer saw him as intellectual, rather a person wallowing in his own problematic nature, like a Ted Hughes tribute act. She began getting *schadenfreude* whenever she noticed run-down, sad-looking men – imagining them as Ian in twenty years' time.

One evening, there was a staff meeting about fire safety. Katy had brought with her a packet of Hobnob biscuits and just before the meeting started, she offered one to everyone except Ian.

'Woah, talk about power-move!' Georgia high-fived her in the toilets later. And from then on they would refer to Ian as 'Hobnob' – stressing the second syllable. They would say things like, 'Where's Hob*nob?*'... 'Oh, Hob*nob's* just changing the barrel.'

About a month later, Katy was on her way to take the bins out when she stopped. She hovered in the back doorway. She could hear hushed voices just outside to her left. The voices belonged to Ian and Georgia.

Georgia was speaking. 'Listen. Cheating on your ex, Naomi, does *not* define you. It happened. It was a long time ago. We all make mistakes. The future's bright, I promise you. You're a real catch. You can't help how you felt or *didn't* feel about Katy. If you really like Iona, then why not go for it?'

Ian muttered a few sentences that Katy couldn't make out. Then Georgia's voice again. 'I just feel a bit awkward about Katy. I'd rather she didn't know about me hanging out with you at your flat and stuff like that. I think it would only upset her.'

Katy had been still, but inside she'd been fluid – a spirit level bubble trying to settle. She had quietly moved away.

Iona was a new member of staff who resembled the noughties pop singer Avril Lavigne but was too young to know the reference. On Iona's first shift, Katy had watched Ian teach her how to use the till. Iona had looked contemplative – as though she was putting the names Ian and Iona side by side in her mind, considering her extra vowel, and feeling a sense of one-upmanship.

In Katy's kitchen, her phone lights up with another message from Danny Walker. *I'm coming tomorrow night. I'm getting the train to New Street. Let's go for a drink? I know it's short notice, but please tell me you're free?*

Katy is absolutely free. Although she neurotically checks her work schedule to be sure. Georgia and Ian and Iona are working but she is off. She messages Danny back, telling him to get the Number 50 bus from outside Selfridges to Moseley and to meet her in The New Moon. Then she sits there feeling worried. Is it a good idea to meet in The New Moon?

She makes herself a cup of tea, curls up on her sofa, and creates a vivid daydream in which she and Danny sit opposite each other having a drink, a highly charged cloud of sexual chemistry colouring every word they say, until Katy can bear it no longer. She gets up, pushes her bar stool to the floor, places a knee onto the little round pub table – which remains steady – grabs Danny's tie (that he is definitely wearing) and pulls him to her. Georgia, Ian and Iona watch with massive envy and amazement.

Sounds good, Katy, comes Danny's reply.

A few days after over-hearing Georgia's conversation with Ian, Katy had decided to broach things with Georgia.

'Look. I wouldn't normally become friends with a mate's ex. But it's just that me and Ian were already friends,' Georgia had said, as though this was obvious.

Katy had searched her mind for signifiers of a separate friendship between them. She had a memory of Georgia saying to her, soon after they'd all started walking home together, that on shifts when Katy wasn't working, Georgia would dash off and get the bus because she felt awkward around Ian without Katy present and worried he would feel obliged to walk her home. And Katy had understood Georgia's reasoning: she would probably do the same. So, Georgia must have stopped getting buses and started walking home with Ian alone at some point and must have started going back to his flat.

'Just because me and Ian are hanging out now, it doesn't mean I don't think he was mean to you and careless with your feelings.'

What was that tone to Georgia's voice? Self-importance?

'What's most important now is that you heal.'

Why did Katy feel like something small but significant was calcifying somewhere deep inside her?

'I would obviously *never* tell Ian any of that stuff you told me. You don't need to worry. And I think the only way this could be awkward is if he talked to me about you. But you literally don't come up.'

For the next couple of days, there was a distant pleasantness between Katy and Georgia. To customers, they must have looked like two polite women who didn't know each other very well. But as time went on, Katy would watch Georgia and Ian having a laugh and feel increasingly sad.

One evening, they'd arrived at work in matching woolly hats, different colours but the same style, as though they'd picked them out together like a platonic power couple.

'I'm just so sorry things are feeling shit for you right now,' Georgia had said one day. 'And I'm sorry if I've contributed to those feelings in any way. But all I can do is reassure you. I would *never* tell Ian *any* of those things you used to tell me. And honestly, all those feelings you're feeling? They're completely normal for a monogamous person.'

Katy had muttered that she just felt a bit replaced.

'Nooooo,' Georgia had said. 'I would hate for you to think that. I don't think anyone replaces anyone.'

Had this been meant as reassurance or defence? Katy couldn't tell.

In the kind of voice adults use with small children, Georgia had said, 'Want a hug?'

Katy had shaken her head and rushed to the bathroom. Checking that it was empty, she had hit the toilet stall door, hard, several times and shouted, 'Fucking. Silly. Bitch.' And then she had taken a deep breath and felt slightly better.

Sat opposite Danny in The New Moon the next evening, Katy studies him, worrying that her eyes have become too wide, worrying that her face resembles a wet leaf pressed against a window. He is wearing black jeans, black shoes, a tight black t-shirt, a black watch and a thin white belt. Three minutes ago, he had walked into the pub with a James Bond swagger. Georgia, doodling her finger on the bartop like she was sketching out a treasure map, had paused and stared at him, as if she'd found an X-marks-the-spot. Danny had nodded at her and asked where Katy was.

Danny smiles at Katy now. 'You've not changed a bit, you know.'

Katy wonders if this is a compliment or not? Then she becomes aware of herself frowning and shakes her head slightly as if to jauntily toss the frown away. She manages to smile. He asks and she tells him a condensed and touched-up version of the past fifteen years. He summarises his rise from geeky schoolboy to heart-throb man and when he finishes, Katy's still not really sure how this metamorphosis has occurred.

Having got the pleasantries out of the way, Katy is surprised at how easily the conversation between her and Danny flows. 'Three words you want to be described as at your funeral?'… 'If you could go anywhere in the world right now, where would it be?'… 'What's your best/worst feature according to you?'… 'Tea or Coffee?'… 'Cheese or wine?'… 'Cats or dogs?'

And then they read aloud one-star Google reviews of nearby restaurants in Birmingham because they're feeling hungry now and are wondering where to go. Katy's feeling quite drunk and emboldened. She creates a different voice and character for each terrible review and Danny beams at her. Katy feels happy.

Katy then glances over to the bar and sees Ian kissing Iona. Georgia is giggling and whooping beside them. Georgia sees Katy looking and pulls a pantomime sad face and mouths *sorry,* and then she points at Danny and gives Katy a big thumbs up.

Katy tells Danny she needs some air.

Outside, Katy stares up at the sky. There's a full moon tonight. It looks like a crystal ball, she thinks, thrown up there to laugh at us. She imagines raising a bar all the way to that smug, round moon and punching it square in the face.

She breathes in slowly. She breathes out slowly. Scanning the black liquid of night. The full moon reminds her of something else: a thick, creamy head on a pint of stout.

Marching through the double door entrance of The New Moon, Katy smiles at Danny as she moves towards him and past him to the bar. She takes two pint glasses and fills them to the brim with Guinness. Iona is now serving someone at the far end. Ian and Georgia stand closer, huddled over a crossword puzzle. They look up at just the moment Katy launches the two pints of Guiness all over them.

'What the actual fuck?!' says Georgia.

'Oh, I'm sorry,' says Katy. 'I'm sorry if I spilt some Guiness over you. I'm sorry if I've contributed to some feelings of anger you might be having right now. I completely understand if you'd rather not work shifts with me anymore. I would respect your decision.'

Before anyone can say anything else, Katy turns and leaves them there, their faces paled from flung froth, their expressions in agitated limbo.

Danny stares at Katy.

'How would you describe your kettle-fixing skills?' she says. 'See, I've always thought that once a kettle's fucked, it's fucked. You just need to buy yourself a new one.'

And Katy smiles a perfect crescent.

Walk Your Neighbourhood Skull this Halloween

ANDY HOWLETT

This is a walk recipe for Halloween night. It is suitable for both solo walkers and groups. The basic concept was devised by Fiona, Andy and Pete of Walkspace, a West Midlands walking-art collective. In October 2020 the first walk took place in Stirchley, south Birmingham, under a full moon. 'Walking the Stirchley Skull' has since become a popular Halloween tradition. Follow these steps to create your own spooky neighbourhood skull walk. Feel free to improvise and add your own ingredients.

- Take a map of your local area and draw or overlay a simple skull shape onto it. The outline of the skull will form the route of your walk. Pick a start point, wait for nightfall, and go there.
- Decide whether you want to walk the skull clockwise or 'widdershins'. Widdershins is an old term meaning 'against the way', or to travel in the opposite direction to the sun's course. This can be an effective way of invoking darker energies, but results are unpredictable so for first-timers we recommend walking clockwise.
- Don't worry about sticking religiously to the course of the skull. There's no need to hop fences, crash through hedges or wade through water. The magic will still work if you must deviate slightly to use approved pedestrian routes. In Stirchley we make use of cut-throughs, alleyways and gullies to pass freely between realms: residential, commercial, recreational, municipal. What affordances does your neighbourhood offer?

- Halloween has its roots in the old Celtic festival of Samhain (pronounced 'sah-win') which marked the end of harvest and the beginning of the dark half of the year. As you walk, pay attention to the subtle transformations brought by seasonal change: the first gales of winter echoing a banshee's cry, the spectral figures created in a breath, flood waters forming portals to mirror worlds. Don't expect the weather to 'behave' for you, treat it as a collaborator, not an adversary.
- On this night the veil between our world and the spirit world is at its thinnest. Look out for visitors from the Otherside: spirits, ghosts, demons. Beyond the obvious carved pumpkins and plastic skeletons, what other apparitions and hauntings can you detect? Faces in the brickwork of an old school. A 'ghost sign' advertising a long dead business. A passing cloud shaped like a witch on a broomstick. Buildings can be ghosts too: on our Stirchley Skull walk we pass the site of a vanished farmhouse and a residential street with a missing number 13.
- Turn your walk into an anatomy lesson: when you reach the point on the skull where the ear would be, tune in to the soundscape of the night by walking in silence. When you come to the mouth why not get out some tasty treats? What activities might you perform at the crown? Or the temple? Sometimes the landscape itself might offer something up: on the western side of the Stirchley Skull's jaw we were delighted to find a dental laboratory.
- The walk ends when you arrive back at your starting point. Before you retire to the pub or go home, consider the transformation that has been enacted tonight. Stand for a moment with the ghost of your former self. These streets will never look at you in the same way again.

Hot Water Music

TAYLOR BURNS

She is Hope, and her entrance sucks the spirit out of you.

You're having a shit one, under-staffed, hanging – hangover so bad you can practically chew it – coffee orders backed up on the thin magnetic rail beneath the machine, scraps of till roll with chicken-scratch instructions on them flapping in the fetid behind-the-bar air, curling up like windblown clothes on a washing line from the power of the steam wand's jet stream, which hisses and spits, its hot metal skin searing if you don't manoeuvre it from beneath a sodden green cloth.

In the kitchen, piled plates glazed with hours-old egg yolk, hardened now into a tough curd you will later have to chisel away with the handle of a fork.

Out front, tables precarious with scattered, half-eaten dishes; dirty and bedecked with puddles of batter-flecked ketchup which you just know you'll pick up later and unwittingly press your thumb into, proper depressing your digit down into it, like you're providing evidence.

But you're a quick team, you lot, have all been here, on the Members Bar, for long enough to know that a dawdling attitude to a busy shift will only shaft you further. And you've made it through the worst, now, when orders for panini were backlogged because you can only fit flush two sandwiches on the grill at a time, and coffee had to be served exclusively in takeaway cups because you couldn't wash the drink-in mugs quick enough to replenish them, but here you are, on the other side of the shift, just about to tidy, scrub, spray; soak the coffee group heads in powder that smells like soot; just starting to think about the last hour or so before your break or home or the train to London for your evening lecture, just about to perch yourself on top of the on-bar mini freezer which holds packets of dried fruit for smoothies – frozen berries in an icy bag like a serial killer's leftover trophy innards – just about to start thinking about finishing, forgetting the place for a few hours until you're back to bear it all again, when Hope walks in.

She looks unwell. Worse than usual on the first day that she is allowed back after her ban.

Her top teeth rip at her lower lip, which is cracked and blistered at the best of times, beset with little pale Vs from where the vermillion has been sawn away in anxiety. Her hair is above her head in a dull frizz, strands of grey not there because they have been pulled out in the mirror that morning. The bags under her eyes look as if they have been pulled down, lowered like shop shutters.

She walks first to reception, dumps onto their counter a clod of wet towels, a pair of trainers pulled tight at the laces, a toothbrush in a takeaway coffee cup, soggy from where she has filled it for days with the ice-water that keeps her going like petrol. She asks about classes, books onto three in a row, reserves herself a lane in the outdoor pool for after. You see the girls at reception, see them hum and nod, the front of their faces hiding the exasperation that wants to push through the shape of their wide eyes and fake smiles like Play-doh, that wants to ask her to just please, Hope, go *away* (Hope has made each of today's Front of Housers cry in the past). Other members swipe in behind her, grab towels of their own from where they are stored in dry rolled pyramids at the end of the counter. Hope, sensing some sort of threat to her things, sticks out an arm, an elbow, shakes her head like she's swallowed something live.

Many of the members know her by now and ignore her like she's homeless. But she is far from it, lives on her own in a three-storey, four-bedroom house, the richest road in the best part of town.

(Look closely, past her hair, her hands – where thick flames of cuticle have been torn away like a satsuma's peel – past the perma-pregnant belly of the very malnourished, the band of red across her nose, a drinker's nose, and you will see the money: the leggings that tourniquet themselves around her probe-thin thighs are Sweaty Betty, and she has a pair for each day – of the year; her trainers are Christian Louboutin Spike Sock Donna flats; her shittest jumper, which she wipes herself down with, is Juicy Couture.

She went to Oxford and Rada and now she's leaving reception and coming to you on the bar.

And she is bad on the bar.

Sure, she's bad at reception, too – snapping at the girls when they hesitate to yield to yet another bullshit request that's above their paygrade, unanswerable, even, since she cadges so many of her demands in a kind of possessed, beneath-her-breath gibber, like she's being exorcised.

She is bad outside, in the pool, where the lifeguards ask her every ten minutes to swim lengths please, instead of depths.

But she is baddest on the bar – is both anorexic and bulimic, and so the presence of food frightens her into belligerent confusion, into a panic that manifests itself as a prolonged demand to get her, as customer, what she wants.

And what she wants, mainly, is hot water, and ice.

She pays 50p per disposable coffee cup, tells you to fill three with boiling water straight from the tea filter, and three with ice scooped out from the ice machine, its persistent low gurgle seeming to anticipate Hope, rumbling loudest and churning its gears when she is close.

You say to her, Is that it, Hope, yeah?

She says, Yes and you say, Really, ya sure?

She says yes, da*h*ling, what do you take her for?

You fill the cups, give them to her, tell her not to worry about paying for them today because it's been a bad one – you stink of the kitchen's special stink, you've had a steady procession of shit-talk from members who seem to pride themselves on how sarcastic they can be to staff, your hands are scoured from the industrial strength washing-up liquid you dunk them in when looking for the only sponge – you just want to fuck off home, out of here, so take the cups, take the ice, the water, just promise that's it, before another customer comes and sees the scene and assumes the Brummie on the bar is being especially brusque and not just anticipating what will, with no hyperbole, be the dominant work of his last hours on shift.

That's not it.

As soon as you spin on the heel of your all-black Converse because you don't want to wear shoes like a sell-out – the sole of which has worn away into a wedge from where you put your weight when you walk up and down, up and down, all shift, all day, all week, all year, the bar's vinyl floor a travelator that's slow but never stops – as soon as you try to dart into the kitchen to pretend to talk to Chef or take the bins down or check the rota that's downloaded onto your eyeballs like a depressing memory, she calls you back, says, Travis, da*h*ling, no, I'm going to need another four of each.

You sigh, say, Come on, I just asked you if that was it.

I know, I know, I'm just, I need four more.

You do it: four more cups of ice, four boiling waters filled to the brim, heating your hand through the corrugated cardboard.

Right, that it?

Yes, yes.

You turn again.

No, no. I need two more ice –

Ah come on, you're taking the… mick now, Hope.

But this is where Hope becomes glorious.

You are perfectly allowed to refuse her free stuff, supplementary service. But what you are not perfectly allowed to do is refuse her when she is buying 'your' stock – the bar 'haemorrhages money', apparently, and any refusal of service is profit lost, pointlessly; just put up with the aggro and the bar will make an easy tenner, is the party line.

Besides, this isn't like when you used to work at the pub back home in Brum, where if the customer's tone was off or cunty you could say, Na, not today, mate, and make eyes at the bouncer as if to say, Get this prat out of here. No, in here you take the shit, eat it, swallow it down, drink it like it's the drink you deserve for working so far beneath the middle-management consultant-class types who decompress after working out by dishing out orders for the dishes you dish out.

(The current GM, Ray, a company man from Reading with grey wingtips in his cheap haircut, and shoes worse than a copper's, says things like this: *The members here,* Trav, *are of a certain… a certain…* calibre*; they perhaps don't always have the time or patience to be as polite as you'd like.*)

So now she buys something, knowing full well you'll have no choice but to cater to her. The hot water and ice, musical cups now on the end of the bar, where Hope transfers the contents from one cup to another inchoately, eating the ice, dipping her hands into it, blowing on the water and taking tentative sips – the water and ice was always a ruse anyway. What she really wants is the takeout cups of rabbit food you will watch her order and fuss around for the next hour of your life.

Okay right da*h*ling what I need is – it's Dec isn't it?; Declan's chef today; I saw his car outside, please don't lie to me – what I need is these three filling with spinach, and these two with broccoli and peas, and keep the ice in this one, but please bring me some vinegar, or Marmite, three mini Marmite, and is there any mustard?

You take the ticket into Dec and take with it the stacked takeaway cups. You curve the ticket into the top one, push it slowly towards him with an insolent smirk, say, Sorry, Dec, mate, and watch him pinch the top of his nose, which is about as angry as this particular chef gets.

The door between kitchen and bar stays always open, held there by two 3-litre bottles of glasswasher detergent, so Hope shouts in, can see you both in profile over the pass and shouts, Declan, lovey, thank you; just microwave the mushrooms, if you could?

Oi, you never said anything about mushrooms, Hope.

Oh, well, I always want mushrooms, Trav, da*h*ling, just rip them up and blast them for a minute.

You step from the kitchen to the bar, tell the girl you're on shift with to deal with any other customers, delegating Hope to yourself. The girl goes to take someone else's order but Hope, who never leaves the countertop, chained to it like she's on hunger strike, chimes in and tries to command something from her, knowing that it's only you and your line manager who can put an end to her assaults on human etiquette – once you came in and found the new girl, a quiet Portuguese who'd been in service for years, sitting with her head in the crook of her arm, crying. When you asked what's up, she looked at you, red as a crab, and said: *Hope*.

Excuse me, how dare, I haven't been served yet, why are you ignoring me?

The girl, seventeen and Swedish and confused, holds still between the two ordering customers like a tennis net. You can feel her teetering, flushed and flustered, floundering, wishing she wasn't a foreign waitress right now. You step in, lightly chastise Hope (other customers are around), say, Oi, come on, Hope, mate, you've had your turn; it's nearly ready, anyway.

You take out to her on a tray a selection of crinkled coffee cups, filled indeterminately with microwaved wilted spinach, microwaved button mushrooms, quick-boiled still-hard peas, sodden, crying broccoli, half a tomato, half hot. In the middle of the mosaic of cups, a small white ramekin, packed tight with sachets of vinegar and salad cream, a stack of individual Marmite hearts like a totem pole next to them.

Ere'yar, Hope, now please, take it to a table.

But she doesn't. Never does. Manages to eat it at the bar under the pretence that she is picking through it to *make sure everything is victual, love*. You relent. Is it really worth a row, now, so close to the end of your shift?

When you've been firm with her in the past, she's panicked and pulled at the skin of her cheeks, forever dimpled crimson like she's been clapped round the face but really a product of the fact that she is constantly cold, both from all the ice she eats and her insistence on only swimming outdoors, where she exits the pool and proceeds to put on her clothes without drying herself;

or she's pushed all the cups to your side of the bar, down and off the edge and all over the till and blender wires, which are bunched together with a cable tie and still sticky because.

It's no longer peak time so you can leave her there, picking.

I'm going now, Hope.

Yes, yes, do go, da*h*ling.

You go, but only to the ice machine, where you sneak a picture under your forearm, forward it to your boss on his day off. *She's fucking at it again*. Then a gill-green vomiting emoji, typed thrice at the sight of her sucking the vinegar out of the sachet and spitting it onto the ice in a slow fountain, which reminds you of making iced latte, when the coffee pours down onto the rocks and crackles and melts. Nothing so therapeutic here, though, as Hope twists a Marmite heart onto her mushrooms. This before scooping up the sodden spinach and dunking it into the old hot water as savoury tea; squeezing the broccoli into a cup that has a salad cream eclipse as a deglaze on its base. Then, as coup de grâce, Hope alchemically makes a mixture of vinegar and peas in yet another cup, swirls it around like it's rare, peaty whiskey, and washes the lot down her throat. Tell Declan that was perfect, she says.

Once, when you didn't quite hate her yet – and you do hate her; Hope is not a woman who could inspire something so mild as dislike – you agreed to attend her birthday party.

It was one of those quiet evening shifts when all she could really buy at the bar was peppermint tea and she ordered it calmly and stood at the end of the countertop plunging the peppermint's bag into her hot water, humming. She was dressed in a long black dress, with tights and trainers but also with a shimmering shawl on her shoulders, above which was a face delicately flecked with makeup. She hummed and you looked at her. She looked up and caught your eye and you had on your own face a face which amounted to something appropriating amnesty.

You look nice this evening, mate.

Oh it's my birthday, she said, and Daddy is down. You should come, Travis, da*h*ling, please come. I can't bear when Daddy is down.

Ah, I'm alright, me, Hope. Working, ent I.

After, love, come after; it's on your way home.

And it was – in a corner wine café at the bottom of South Parade. You said you might pop in to shut her up, never intending to until you walked past and saw her at a table with a tray of faux-fancy nibbles, accompanied only by three awkward members who barely knew her but attended a HIIT class with her twice a week and were now looking at each other perplexed over the thin lip of their white wine spritzers, which Hope had paid for.

She had told you it was going to be a high-minded affair, Daddy and his mates, her friends from Chelsea and Mayfair, her sister, maybe, God forbid. And she knew you loved books, loved them too, proclaimed and promised, when she first mentioned her birthday months ago, that Alan Bennett would be there; she spoke to him on the phone that morning, in fact. You *must* meet him, Trav. I've told him all about you and your studies.

You looked through the window, over the top of a board that promised authentic tapas – with a twist. Hope saw you, called you in with a scoop of her hand, plonked you down next to the three HIIT'ers, who made eyes at you as if to say, *How weird*!

None of them mentioned that they had been deplorably rude to you in the past, and thought the fact that you worked on the bar and now you were here with them, with *Hope*, gave you all a kismet connection.

Hope bought you a drink, hugged you from behind as you sat on a high-backed stool, said, You came, da*h*ling, you came.

(Daddy didn't come. Got tied up in London, working. Her sister couldn't make it, nor her friends in Mayfair. Alan Bennett? Oh, he wasn't well, never well, the poor thing.)

You didn't stay long. Just enough to know that the HIIT'ers, asked for weeks on end if they were going to Hope's birthday by Hope and Hope alone, were kind for coming, but cunts, too, for turning it into an OMG novelty that they would regale the rest of their class with in the minutes before Hope next wandered in, seeking them out instantly and saying what a dream the night had been.

And you, you are a cunt as well, for thinking she's a repulsive rich bat who comes in just to mess up your day when really she's frazzled by illness, freighted with whatever she's freighted with, just like you are, and if she eats ice and rubs hand sanitiser on her gums and cries to the duty manager about missing a plane to Monaco that she'd never even booked, well is that really any worse than when you get home and get sad and lock yourself in the bathroom and batter yourself in the side of the head until you can't take it anymore, eyes glassy with pain, the bathroom mirror wet and wobbling like some ancient portal?

That birthday was two years ago and you find it harder and harder to use it as counterbalance to Hope's current behaviour.

You try, try to play it in your head like an important tape that tells you, emphatically, that it's not her fault; then, you tell yourself that that evening was a grace note, a night that showed you, via her embarrassed smile, her enthusiasm at enjoying a party with other people, her deep sadness and knowledge – because surely she knew – of the party's unrealised potential, that the people there were cobbled together patrons of the club she frequents three times a day, every day of the year, not family and certainly not friends, people who went home and laughed about her with their picture book husbands, their perfect children (or someone who went home and wrote about it, other people's pain as mere material), a night that showed you a whole piece of a woman forever coming apart.

There are other examples: the time she told you for an hour about a Chinese American poet you'd like and then went home and brought his book back in for you. When you flicked through it that evening and realised that it was indeed your kind of shit – all dead parent and class-alienation and the uneasy duality of being artistically high-minded but forever lowborn – you felt kind of seen.

But these moments are lost. Nebulous memories of some batshit ex before it got really, really bad.

Hope was only allowed back into the club after a six-week 'cool-off' period. A freeze had been forced upon her membership by an otherwise poltroon GM who had no choice but to suspend Hope when she poured a cup of boiling water into the bar bin just as a little girl was disposing of her sweet wrapper. A second later and the girl's hand would've been doused with scalding water – one of Hope's signature moves was to ask for a take-away cup of hot water, which she would take from you before you'd barely let go of passing it; from there, she'd pour half the cup into the bin, an in-front-of-your-face piss-take that was hard to chalk down to her disease (and one which would frustrate the Polish cleaners and leave them lugging dripping wet bin-bags across the club lounge like large funfair goldfish). As it was, the girl's hand was in retreat when Hope cascaded the contents of her cup into the metal mouth of the bin, and she was merely spattered on the knuckles with the hot water. Still, it was enough to cause a screaming scene, both from Hope and the girl, and Mr General Manager grew a tiny pair of bollocks and banned her, which ban slugged Hope to her knees as she begged him to backtrack.

It was hoped that, after nearly dissolving the skin of a little girl's hand, Hope might come back and 'behave herself'. But, if anything, she is extra frenetic – 'madder', according to the Personal Trainers who pass her around between themselves on a monthly basis and charge her like they are lawyers – and, worse still, more present: she is there when you start your shift and still there when you end it.

You have no time for it or her, anymore.

Used to be that you might only encounter her three, four times a week, usually while on shift with someone else, where you could say *Go on; I did her last time.*

But six weeks have changed a lot for you and the bar, and both professional and personal problems are now intensified by a Hope who can hassle and harass and turn an okay day into a shit one and a shit day into an outright unfair one. Minimum wage to run around for a middle-class freak all day? Na: fuck *off*.

You go to GM Ray and ask if there's not something that can be done? She needs *help*, man, can't we, like, get someone, when she comes in, I mean, like, get someone to go up to her, say, Hi, Hope, mate, sure you're okay to be here today?

And Ray, who has no specific department, can dodge Hope likes she's a draft, can hide in his office upstairs, which has the only building code she does not know, Ray says, Look, she loves it here, it's her home, she's ill and it's her safe place and we should be here to help her through her healthcare journey, giving him the chance to act all morally right and righteous like he doesn't point Hope out to his wife when he sees her in Summertown and say, There, that's *her*.

You tell him you're not a mental health nurse (and leave out that if you were you'd sort yourself out first) and he says, Oh don't be so dramatic.

You'd usually leave it there; you keep very much to yourself at work, where people like you because of how long you've been on the bar but also think you moody and spontaneously aggressive, ungrateful to be employed there (which you are) when really you are just angry and desperate to get the break that might mean not having to clean up after rich people, serve them their swill; would usually just walk out and say, Okay, Ray, if ya say so, mate. But you're adamant, now, ask him, Does Active *Health* not mean mental as well?

He says of course it does.

Well good, because she told me she wants to kill herself the other day. Proper nonchalant like, Oh, I feel like I'm just going to kill myself, da*h*ling, sod it all. Fuck am I meant to say to that?

Okay, he says. I'll have a word with her.

That was weeks ago.

You obviously haven't heard shit since, and when you left work tonight, Hope was parked in a disabled bay with her doors open, gnawing a cucumber you didn't give her, ribbons of green grated all over her steering console and chest.

You throw up a hand and, humming, she hits the hazards, which illuminate her part of the carpark, amber light flickering on the polar tarmac as she leans out the door and shouts into the silent disco that she'll see you tomorrow, da*h*ling.

At the Dog & Partridge

JOSH ALLEN

Commuting to every physical workplace where I have sold my time this past decade has required walking past the Lookers Vauxhall showroom and forecourt on the Bristol Road in Selly Oak. Sprawled between Elliot Road to the south and a long-neglected cul-de-sac called The Dingle to the north, Lookers Vauxhall could be anywhere. A metallic grey clad shed constructed around the turn of the millennium amidst a raft of generic Euro-American automobiles. Several acres of cars occupying prime high street in a Birmingham suburb sliced and diced by automobility even more than most over the past century.

Central Selly Oak arrayed along the Bristol Road and Harborne Lane from the 1950s onwards was alighted on by Birmingham's planners as requiring significant rearrangement to smooth traffic flow. Fitfully over the course of decades these plans were realised with serious detriment to the district caused by lingering uncertainty, sporadic demolitions, and the steady grind of ensnared traffic. Today in Selly Oak and its sibling district Bournbrook the removal of 19th and 20th Century buildings fronting the Bristol Road persists. But, with road widening plans now either completed or permanently abandoned, it is in the interests of rent seeking student property developers not Birmingham motorists, that the high street's rearrangement continues apace.

So, for years I walked past the Lookers Vauxhall site thinking little of it, assuming there had been a showroom or garage on the site for decades. After all, prior to every scrap of land in Selly Oak and Bournbrook being sized up for student flats both areas were home to legions of little dealerships and mechanics workshops. Many of which, akin to erratic boulders, looked like they had been left behind at the end of the ice age.

It was while working on a public history project in Selly Oak during 2018 I learnt Lookers Vauxhall is not one of them. Rather, prior to its closure in 1997 and subsequent demolition, a pub called the Dog & Partridge had resided there since Victorian times. An establishment which cropped up time and again in the research the project's volunteers conducted into Selly Oak and Bournbrook's history of radical left-wing and community activism.

As recently as the 1980s the Dog & Partridge formed part of a rich ecosystem of pubs in Selly Oak, which a census conducted by the Selly Oak Alternative Paper (SOAP) enumerated as comprised sixteen venues. In the interests of grassroots citizen journalism, the editorial collective embarked on a pub crawl which ended up spanning articles in two issues. Today five pubs remain.

A Google search for the Dog & Partridge returns photographs of a squat, powerfully built, mid-Victorian building at the end of a terrace of red brick shops. Its walls are whitewashed and peeling, copious, yet notably simple, mouldings around the windows and doors are painted dark thuggish green, apart from those on the first floor which have been rendered a muddy, off cream colour. In these latter decades, the Dog & Partridge was festooned with the red and white M&B logo, with deeply evocative Bass triangle lamps in the same colour scheme loitering over the entrances beckoning passer's by into the dark smoky interior.

The impression of the pub gleanable from these images is that it was a distinctive building, but in its suburban high street setting, unremarkable. There is nothing hugely distinctive, nor remotely distinguished, about the Dog & Partridge. A viewer would be forgiven for suspecting that versions of any stories which unfolded within, or became intertwined with its walls, could be encountered anywhere. Indeed, less than thirty years after its bell rang for the final time if the Dog & Partridge is remembered at all, it is for being a favoured haunt of the housebreaking and armed robbery gang which terrorised the outer fringes of West Midlands county in 1978, and that came to be wrongly convicted of murdering Wordsley paperboy Carl Bridgewater.

Until the combined effects of road widening and deindustrialisation began calling last orders, the stretch of Bristol Road where the Dog & Partridge sat was home to other Victorian vintage drinking establishments like The Oak, Plough and Harrow, and Prince of Wales. Spectres of Selly Oak's bucolic north Worcestershire past prior to its urbanisation in the 1870s when the railway reached it, married with derivative, forelock tugging, pre-First World War royalism. In contrast the Dog & Partridge's name seems subversive. A wink towards poaching as a means of supplementing rural families' diets?

Pubs have always been venues where the alliances forged by working people to get through by whatever means necessary are cemented. Outside the relatively orderly salaried world of employment the pub was, and in some lines of work still is, an important means of getting and keeping work. Not the unspoken expectation in some city centre offices that you will traipse out drinking with the partners or directors on a Thursday and Friday. Rather, in craft-based trades where people tend to be freelancers or pieceworkers, the social experience of seeing each other in the pub, sharing trade news and gossip, finding somebody you can trust with craft skills that augment yours to complete a job next week, can be vital. Regardless of whether you are a jeweller after a goldsmith in Hockley, a web developer needing a graphic designer in Kings Heath, or a brickie requiring a chippie in Sheldon.

Throughout West Midlands county, where the employment landscape for centuries was founded upon little metal workshops, foundries and pits, the informal networks and interpersonal connections required to move with the work or job at hand have always been essential. This contrasts with an area like Greater Manchester where work for most people became concentrated in gigantic textile factories early on. Characteristics arguably patterning the area's differing political traditions. Mancunian workers square up against capital through big tightly organised trade unions, co-operative and political parties, while Birmingham's working-class favour wildcat strikes, noisy single-issue campaigns and organisation through autonomous networks.

The centrality of the pub to working life in the region was recognised by the University of Birmingham Centre for Contemporary Cultural Studies (CCCS) sociologist Paul Willis in his book *Learning to Labour* researched in Sandwell during the mid-1970s. A key section of which unpicks a lunchtime session engaged in participant observation of his young subjects learning to navigate the world of being hired by jobbing builders and other artisans at the pub. Willis was a master of participant observation in the pub, having written a PhD wholly based upon material gleaned from evenings drinking with members of the Double Zero Motorcycle Club at The Forge Tavern in Digbeth and with 'Hippies' at the Bull's Head in Moseley. I sometimes wonder whether the Dog & Partridge would have been the perfect booze dispensing ethnographic observation post for Willis if he had wished to continue his research into the pub's importance for getting work and developing economic networks, whether over a lunchtime pint or an evening session. It would have been handy for the CCCS offices on the University of Birmingham campus. Also, doubtless attractive to the Wulfrunian Willis, Selly Oak has close ties to the Black Country. A link evident in the spectral traces of the old Dudley No. 2 Canal which once stretched from a wharf just the other side of where the Dog & Partridge stood, through the long lost Lapal Tunnel, via Halesowen and Old Hill to Dudley town centre and eventually Tipton.

Mirroring the pub-based networks underpinning Birmingham's historic economic structure, to a greater extent than other British cities, besides perhaps perma-studentish Leeds, pubs have played a critical role in the development of Birmingham's rock and popular music scenes, growing stadium fillers and underground favourites alike. From The Crown on Station Street where Black Sabbath received their break, through The Mermaid in Sparkhill where Napalm Death and other thrash metal bands incubated an audience in the 1980s, to my own youth in the late 2000s and early 2010s when bands like Swim Deep, JAWS and Peace used to play Digbeth's Rainbow and The Adam and Eve.

It is tricky to imagine many bands ever playing the Dog & Partridge. A fact the venue's omission from old listings magazines and newspapers confirms. Bands tended to go to the Bournbrook Hotel, a plusher establishment, also handier for the University of Birmingham's student crowd. If bands frequenting the Bournbrook Hotel in the years prior to its current insipid incarnation as the Goose at the O.V.T. had lugged their gear up the Bristol Road to the Dog & Partridge, it would probably have unfolded rather like the scene in Joel Lane's *From Blue to Black* where the post-punk inspired, Husker Dü'esque trio Triangle attempt to play Selly Park's Hibernian. Sullen hostility, giving way to brutally suppressed violence, and the unfortunate artistes being advised by the venue to never return.

Which is not to say the Dog & Partridge was simply a hard man pub with regulars implacably hostile to outsiders. Rather in keeping with its name's sly allusion to the practice of poaching, in the 1960s and 1970s the pub lay at the heart of radical Selly Oak. When a confluence of left-libertarian influences and tendencies used mutual aid and solidarity as a means through which to augment the district's cooking pots.

A seasoned community activist interviewed by volunteers as part of the public history project I worked on, recalled their initiation into left-wing political campaigning being a meeting of the Selly Oak Claimants Union in the Dog & Partridge during the dog days of Harold Wilson's first premiership. At the time they worked at The Oak Cinema a stone's throw from where the Dog & Partridge stood, and they heard about the meeting through the group's flyposting.

Britain's first claimants' union set-up in 1969 was organised in Birmingham, Selly Oak being amongst the first branches, and they flourished across the UK throughout the 1970s. Their premise was simple: those entitled to social security benefits would collectively support each other morally and practically to navigate the byzantine Department of Health and Social Security bureaucracy, ensuring each member secured the largest payment possible. If a claim was rejected, the union would support members at meetings with Jobcentre officials, and through pickets and protests, get them paid everything owed.

As the 1970s progressed the group of activists from across Selly Oak that coalesced around the Claimants Union turned their attention to using direct action as a means of tackling other pressing social problems. By 1973 disused buildings on streets near the Dog & Partridge were being squatted as ad-hoc community advice and events spaces reducing activists' need to rely upon public houses. However, the pub's name continues to crop up in alternative publications and political literature from the time as a meeting place for all manner of campaigns and political groups.

Especially notable were Big Flame, a libertarian communist organisation inspired by Italian autonomous Marxism, which also placed feminism, gay liberation, and anti-racism at the heart of its programme, alongside working-class emancipation. Between 1974 and 1976 the group had a bookshop and the national distribution centre for their literature five minutes' walk from the Dog & Partridge at 632 Bristol Road opposite where Aldi now stands. Throughout this time, up until the end of the 1970s when Big Flame began running out of momentum, the group held its Selly Oak branch meetings at the Dog & Partridge.

The pub was the local for a coalition of activists that squatted and ran the Selly Oak People's Centre mere metres up the Bristol Road, next to what is now Pizza Pepper, between January 1975 and their eventual eviction by Birmingham City Council at the behest of then Chair of the Social Services Committee Edwina Currie in early 1978. Causes which made the People's Centre their home included: the Selly Oak branch of the Anti-Nazi League, Selly Oak Women's Group, trade union groups including a safety campaign by predominantly South Asian workers at the notoriously hazardous Birmingham Battery factory on the opposite side of the Bristol Road, and a volunteer pregnancy advice and testing service supporting women to access abortion at a time when the procedure was hard to obtain in the city. Plus, less ostensibly political causes like conservation groups, pro bono legal advice clinics and the annual Selly Oak Carnival. Large scale campaigns associated with the People's Centre included semi-successful strikes at the Birmingham Battery which saw hundreds of workers walk out for weeks at a time, a highly effective direct action campaign that secured new council houses for dozens of inadequately housed families on Harborne Lane, and a protest squat by Selly Oak youths in the punk rock summer of 1977 intended to pressure the city council into providing them with funding to run their own democratically organised youth club.

As with Big Flame and the Claimants Union, two groups which also used, overlapped with, and bolstered People's Centre campaigns and services, the Dog & Partridge was a critical part of this firmament. As the People's Centre's local, the pub provided relaxation and cheer as well as serving more serious purposes. Meeting in the Dog & Partridge or socialising there after events and campaigning activity served an important integrative purpose. It enabled Selly Oak residents, activists from elsewhere in the city and region and the students and young professionals who formed the project's milieu to get to know and understand each other. It also provided an invaluable portal for outreach into the wider community. A means of engaging with and forging bonds with members of the Selly Oak community who would never have dreamed of stepping into the squatted, hippie looking, long derelict former butcher's shop where the People's Centre was based.

While the Dog & Partridge's position within the unusual, lively, and ultimately fleeting, milieu of radical left-libertarian politics that coalesced in Selly Oak and Bournbrook during the 1970s was remarkable, ultimately its role as a meeting place and point of exchange for the area's people was utterly quotidian. Similar tales could undoubtedly be woven from the history of a local boozer in any suburban part of the West Midlands let alone anywhere else in the UK. Stories about the pub's vital place in an everyday economy grounded in seeking and offering work, pooling, and sharing resources, direct action in pursuit of collective economic justice.

If Selly Oak's current development trajectory continues unabated, I suspect one morning when making my way to Selly Oak Railway Station I will find all the cars driven off the Lookers Vauxhall forecourt, the grey showroom building colder and emptier than usual, grubby scars where the gryphon logos have been ripped from the cladding. An offer too good to refuse will have meant the Lookers Vauxhall site has been sold to one of the faceless agglomerations of capital steadily accumulating every scrap of the Bristol Road in Selly Oak for cookie-cutter blocks of student flats. Perhaps in a nod to the site's heritage, ticking a box on the planning department's form, they will christen it the Old Watering Hole, Taproom Court, Dog & Partridge Building, or offer the highest paying tenants a studio with a view from The Snug, Darts Board or Landlord's Parlour?

But part of me would welcome this, the grey, metallic, distended daytime transaction of selling cars being replaced by a random assemblage of young minds. Like when the Dog & Partridge served the Selly Oak community, the students will gather in their kitchens, lounges, or study bedrooms, talking, plotting, putting the world to rights, swapping jobs tips, hatching joint projects, finding lovers, celebrating successes, and mourning losses. Should a student block replace Lookers Vauxhall it will be handily close to where late night buses from Birmingham stop. Which residents will appreciate because Selly Oak today is decidedly lacking in pubs.

Windmill Fair (1974)

IAN WHATLEY

More were leaving than arriving by the time Duncan reached the Yardley Wood Road entrance to the fair. Beyond the sulphurous heated air of the diesel generators and latrines, a couple of blokes in balaclavas were warming themselves by an oil drum of blazing sticks. One of them wore a chain over his denim jacket. It bore a five-pointed star with a circle connecting the points: the pentagram of indifferent rebels throughout Britain.

Duncan stooped to snatch a soggy booklet from the straw covered field. The silver, black and red cover proclaimed:

Windmill Fair Programme

Billesley Common

1974

Ten Pence

He walked onto the common, ignored by buildings that stood up spectrally in the moonlight. The last night of the fair brought out the ghosts: not of dead people but the blurred visions of children crying at dropped Curlywurlies, rebuffed suitors, evicted drunks, bored parents and pickpockets who had come up empty-handed. With the firework display imminent, a queue grumbled at the entrance turnstile moving at a shuffle although there was no charge.

Duncan considered the opening in the ropes.

No Entry and Exit are two sides of the same sign. Direction is nine-tenths of the law.

From across the city, from beyond Offa's Dyke, farther westward, from the dark mutinous Shannon waves, a wind with sharp claws came probing for the soft spots of every mulberry bush and tavern in the town. He rubbed his hands together and blew a warming cloud through them.

I wonder what dreams may yet come after our lively fireworks.

He pulled the sleeves of his anorak over his fingers. In due course, the brightest and best of the children of the furnaces shuffled their mortal coils into the fairgrounds and Duncan went in search of a sticky bun and a hot brew, something that might once have been tea. Behind the drinks van fizzed a small bonfire, a heap of tea-chests sparking and spitting between their metal edges, glowing a dull red. A band stood about the fire, warming their thoughts and with their eyes turned out to chase the light.

He warmed his hands on the mug, breathing the vapor trails and slurping his brew. Somewhere high on a post nearby, the tannoy system shared a pop version of Bach's *Air on a G String*. One of the other bottom warmers was smoking a cigar. The aroma reached Duncan and filled his head with hungry ideas.

I could kill a plate of beans on toast.

Tea mug returned, he set out for treasure.

Outside a tent serving as a temporary pub hung a sign: The King's Hog. By the rear flap were two figures, intent on raking a bed of smouldering straw over a recently slaughtered pig, singeing off the bristles before cutting the meat for bacon butties.

Adjacent to a What-the-Dino-Saw machine stood a booth offering wide shovels as prizes. The showman was a teenager with a gold hoop earring and a gold tooth.

'Them's originals, them are. Sculptures by Rrose Sélavy. Wanna win yerself one? Here, have a chuck at the biggest bottle.'

A pentagram on a fine chain peeped out between two buttons of his shirt, a star framed for an instant by striped cotton clouds. He smiled to show off the glint that made up one front-tooth and Duncan took a long youthful eyeful of the way it contrasted with the black stubble of his chin: he was hypnotised, a baby rat gazing at the cobra's fang. Another glisten of gold and the mouth snapped shut.

Duncan aimed for the large jar, an island surrounded by goldfish in plastic bags of water. By his third toss, optimism evaporated and he saw the need to aim for a lower prize. The rubber quoit dribbled uselessly over his fingers. It fell to the gravel and another youth – slicked-back hair and an anchor tattoo on his biceps – snatched it up without meeting the plea in his eyes.

Another booth, another bashing.

Next up, a be-cobwebbed and shrivelled lady crouched under a sign proclaiming her to be Iris, all-seeing Duchess of Oldbury.

No one can misunderstand me better than my mum, Duncan decided and took a closer look.

Iris sold magic charms and artifacts. Her goods comprised an assortment of splinters from the one True Cross; several teeth from saints; a selection of postcards almost all autographed by Pelé, the exceptions being three views of Strathclyde signed by the Bay City Rollers; and the item that caught Duncan's evil peepers: a box of black cat bones.

Seeing the school pupil's widening pupils as he eyed the prize, she uttered her best Oldbury oath: 'Them's bostin, laddie.'

A wet laugh escaped her lips and Duncan took a step back, blinking at her aqueous humour.

'That's what you need if you want pretty girls to lead you by the hand. Can make you visible too.'

Duncan assumed an *in* onto the front of her slurred word. The

Duchess shuffled forward to share more of her conspiratorial advertising.

'Summons your lover when they go a-roving or you can break down them barriers to a bit of fancy when you're courting.'

With her timing honed through the eons, Iris threw out the perfect price at the perfect moment sixteen seconds later, 'Yours for fifty pee. And I'll throw in a postcard of Strathclyde for free.'

Signed, sealed, delivered: he pocketed the rattling talisman. *Interesting. First time I've ever seen a chicken bone painted black. I wonder if it works.*

'Ladies and ladies gentleman and gentleman.' The tannoy echoed annoyingly. 'The firetheworks fireworks will beginwill begin inin five minfiveutes minutes.'

Duncan looked up into the shade of space that fell as the great arc lamps went out one at a time, like huge snowflakes melting as they descended into a graveyard.

The crowd stood smugly safe in their expectation of explosions and fireworks. Not since the Blitz had a bomb been flung in anger at the city of the Brummies. Two sailors pushed to the fore to face the challenge of the blasts.

Suddenly, beyond the punters, his older brother was at the stall that sold girl's handkerchiefs, Megan Marlow hanging on his arm. Steven was seventeen years old but lisped to her in babyish words.

Three nights he's come back, Duncan thought. *Murderers do that. Back to the scene. Three different victims. Megan. Star of my fête.*

Before Duncan could elbow through the crowd to defend her honour, an altercation erupted between the mariners. A shout went up, 'A jink a jink a jawbo!' and the crowd craned to see if blood was to be spilt. One tar lay aground on the oozing path, his man-o'-war top covered in Billesley Common's finest mud.

A local lass draped her arm about the other's shoulders and coaxed: 'What's your name, bab? Butter and Cream?'

'You've caught a live one this time, our Cissy!' a fair specimen of Birmingham girlhood shouted to her companion. The herd grunted at this cheap theatre and turned back to the skies for the firework display. Duncan resumed spying on his brother and Megan. The mob were chuckling and clapping, a perfect screen.

Megan wore a royal blue jacket gathered at the waist.

Blue for luck, thought Duncan. *Or was it blue for a boy?*

The collar was up and closed with a pop-stud. Neither tall nor short, she would soon turn fifteen.

What's the logo on her chest? Maybe a white turtle with a red heart. Oh God. She's seen me staring at her chest.

Megan's huge black eyes locked with his. The only place he could find to conceal himself was behind himself. In that moment, she ceased to be perfectly normal; she became normally perfect. His eyes burned into her as though trying to X-ray her soul.

Does she know she can't trust Steven?

The crowd pushed closer, faces skyward for the bright lights of the night.

Steven nodded a grudging acknowledgement of his younger brother, knelt on the slippery ground and threw his arms around the girl's knees. He spoke to her in a strangely husky voice and took off for the candy-floss seller's kiosk.

She took no offense at that embrace. My Lady Megan. How shall I lay siege to your castle of love? What should I say? Why am I good at physics not poetry?

Megan raised her finger as if to touch Duncan's lips.

A sign for quiet; she understands without words. He smiled as she wiped a single index finger across his lower lip. *Wow. Girls make me feel funny.*

She licked her finger.

'That's a sticky bun you've been eating. And did you notice that you spilt tea all over your anorak? Silly boy.'

Duncan swooned, leaned back against a bar billiards table.

'Oi! Don't bash about when I'm trying t'play!' The stall holder jostled his thoughts and his elbow. 'Shove your shilling on the effing table or naff off!'

Megan snatched him from the maws of discomfort, 'He's not important. Are you unimportant too?'

'I finished my homework, so – you know, this is good value for money – I came up here and – you know.' Duncan ended his speech and thought, *I'm such a plonker. She'll never talk to me again.*

'Industrious angels get the evenings off.' She glanced about to be sure Steven was not back within eyeshot. 'How dreary I find this social guff.'

Oh, her virtuous rejections, he thought but his words came out as, 'That's ace.'

At Steven's return, Duncan drifted back into the shelter of a coconut shy.

She asked Steven if he was *octagonal* and nodded that *his flies were unzipped* and should she *do them up for him*. He replied that he'd like to give her something on the *beeoteetom* but Duncan couldn't hear the real words, his lipreading more depressing than reliable.

A flash of green and a boom of white drew *Ahhs*! from the crowd. Benign explosions soared over the common, driven by rockets and Roman Candles unlike those of thirty-four years earlier or five days later. In each flicker, Duncan watched her face smiling.

She'll have wounds that need healing when she finds out.

A crescendo of roaring sparkly things erupted above them.

The final rocket clambered up the sky until it bumped into the clouds and broke. It shed a cluster of green but one white and bright star, falling slowly, left a blotched trail on the eyeballs. When he looked back from the night sky of hell, they were gone.

The foolish virgin and the infernal bridegroom. I vow I'll get her a consolation prize. Ease the pain when I break the news of Steven cuckooing her.

One tent was shaped to look like a windmill, with hardboard paddles attached above. They sold balloons on wires.

Duncan's mind drifted on to the television-made images of the Dutch, to clogs and drugs, Amstel Light, discos full of women with sexy accents, Dutch girls in foam-rubber costumes winning *Jeux Sans Frontieres*, orange seas of scarves, speed skaters, duuble voowels, discos full of round-faced angels with sexy accents, statues of boys and girls kissing, the Flying Dutchman, that bloke who put skulls in some of his paintings, round-faced women kissing boys, round-faced angels kissing everyone in discos. He suffered the secret urges hidden in all things Dutch and chose a balloon on a string.

Round-faced balloon. Round-faced angels in discos, he thought as he handed over his five new pence in the form of one old shilling.

At the Yardley Wood Road exit he reached in his anorak pocket for bus fare. The wire ran over his fingers and the balloon was gone, escaping into the ominous night. He stood and gaped, sad and angry. He no longer deceived himself: *our childhoods end so suddenly.*

Strange Glue

ALAN KANE FRASER

It was early summer in Moseley, though someone had forgotten to tell the weather. It was nowhere near as balmy as it had been a couple of years before, but at least everyone was free to go down the pub now.

Pete stood outside The Fighting Cocks and popped a ramipril in his mouth as the voice on the other end of the phone finally reached the purpose of the call.

'It was unusable, Pete. All of it.'

'I don't accept that, Bally—'

'The dates on the packaging—'

'The dates on the packaging are irrelevant. Jesus! Have you never drunk a pint of milk a couple of days after the date on the bottle?'

He wanted to add – but thought better of it – that if Bally really wanted a watertight definition of 'unusable' she should try looking at a warehouse full of band merchandise for tours that were supposed to have happened in 2020.

Pete's career pivot had been an enforced one. He hadn't wanted to do it, but he'd been faced with a gap in his income at exactly the same time as a gap in the market became apparent. This is how entrepreneurs make their money. It's certainly how he'd made his money. Except that now it appeared that the money he thought he'd made might not have been made at all.

'That's not the point, Pete. We spent that money in good faith, and we don't believe you were acting in good faith. I'm telling you this as a courtesy…'

Pete had hoped that if he ignored the problem for long enough then it would just go away. That seemed to work about fifty per cent of the time. But not, it seemed, this time.

'…you'll be hearing from our solicitors in due course,' Bally concluded.

'Bally, do you have any idea the amount of work I had to put into sourcing that stuff? The nights I spent trying to track down PPE from—'

'I'm sorry, Pete, but there's a lot of public anger about the NHS being fleeced like this: the board has to be seen to act. Now, if you don't mind, I hope you have a good evening.'

The phone went dead.

He could've done without it, especially as he'd be forking out for lawyers soon enough anyway. But that wasn't his primary concern. What would Rochelle think? That's what he was really worried about. It was the thought of her that kept him going. Everything he bought her, he'd paid for with the proceeds of that deal. If he didn't have that money…

He popped half a temazepam in his mouth and walked through the door into the pub. That was a problem for tomorrow. Tonight's problem was Ian.

Pete and Ian had been going to the Cocks for more than thirty years, pretty much since they were old enough to drink. For most of that time, they'd both been customers. Now though, Ian had somehow been reduced to working there.

'Hiya stranger,' Ian called as Pete walked towards the bar. 'You look… different. Have you lost a bit of weight?'

'Well, maybe just a bit.'

'And where have all those grey hairs gone?' Before Pete had a chance to answer, Ian followed it up with another observation, prompted by Pete removing his coat. 'Hilfiger? Bloody hell, Pete! What's got into you?'

Pete and Ian had known each other since they'd stood on the playground together on their first day at Queensbridge school forty years before, so there was always some banter between them. But Pete wasn't in the mood to rise to it that night – as he hoped the expression on his face made clear.

'Anyway, looking good, mate,' Ian said. 'What's brought all this on?'

'Let me get a drink first, pal. Pint of IPA, if you would.' Pete paused for a moment, took a deep breath, and then added, 'And you'd better throw in a whisky chaser too while you're at it.'

Ian raised his eyebrows but said nothing. Pete leant against the bar and, when Ian placed his drinks in front of him, knocked back the whisky in one.

'I've got some news,' he said, staring deeply into his beer. 'I wanted you to be the first to know… Sarah and I are separating. Well, we've separated really. I've moved out. It's over, I'm afraid… There, I've said it.'

Pete couldn't bring himself to look up from his pint as he felt a silence fill the space between them. It lingered uncomfortably for a moment before eventually Ian broke it.

'Wow! Well, I can't pretend I'm not surprised, mate. I'm shocked. What is it – twenty-two, twenty-three years? I thought you guys were pretty solid.'

Pete had been expecting this and knew exactly what he wanted to say in response. 'Yes, I know,' he said, lifting his head. 'I think we tried to convince other people of that. And I think we were so good at convincing them that eventually we convinced ourselves.

But we'd not been happy for years. Maybe we never were. Not really.' He began addressing his pint glass again. 'But it wasn't till I met Rochelle that I realised that.'

'Rochelle?'

There was a hint of something in Ian's voice that Pete hoped he was imagining, but which disappointed him, nonetheless. Of course, he'd expected there'd be some residual loyalty to Sarah – after all these years he knew Ian counted her as a friend. But Ian had been his Best Man for Chrissake and Pete felt entitled to talk about Rochelle to him at least, without being made to feel ashamed. He was, frankly, fed up with people trying to make him feel ashamed – first Sarah, then the twins, and now bloody Bally. There was nothing for him to be ashamed of.

'Yes, Rochelle. She is – and again, I wanted you to be the first to hear this, Ian, because you're my oldest and dearest friend in the world—' he looked Ian right in the eye. 'She is my new partner.' He felt himself become more emotional now, which was an unfamiliar feeling: emotion was something he normally saved for St Andrews. 'We're very happy together… and I hope you can be happy for us. It would mean a lot to me. As you can imagine, the twins…' he petered out and lost Ian's eye for a moment. Ian was their godfather. 'The twins have found the whole situation very difficult. It's a lot for them to deal with, I get that. But there's a lot of anger there, Ian. I can't lie. A lot of anger.'

'They're sitting their A Levels,' Ian said. 'It's quite a time to drop this on them.'

'Yes, I know. And I know there are those who'll say I should have waited.' Pete became animated. 'But you don't get many shots at happiness in this life, and this was one of mine. I wasn't prepared to let it slip by.'

'OK,' said Ian. But it was there again, in his voice – that hint of…what? Uncertainty? Not judgement, surely? Not from Ian, of all people.

Whatever it was, Pete was desperate to make it go away.

'I'm telling you, she's an incredible woman, mate. Believe me – she really is. Incredible. She's beautiful and intelligent and smart and witty. And talented. Such a talented photographer. Honestly, she's going places, she really is. Believe me. And she wants to go there with me.' He felt his eyes water. 'I can't believe I'm saying it, but she does. She loves me. She really *really* does. I don't think I've felt that for too long. Maybe ever. Not like this.'

Ian waited a moment before answering flatly. 'Right.'

And there it was – the reaction Pete had feared and yet also the one that, sadly, part of him had always expected: quiet, understated, ostensibly non-judgemental but actually dripping with an unspoken disdain. How very English. *And*, thought Pete, *how very Ian*.

The thing about Ian was, he was a 'settler'. His shit zero hours teaching gig, his even shitter job pulling pints in the Cocks, even the dreadful Debbie – he settled for them all. And then he spent every other Saturday sitting next to Pete at St Andrews moaning about them.

Pete had put up with it because the thing they both moaned about most of all was the Blues. But now, to be honest, it was all becoming a bit wearing. Here he was, a fifty-one-year-old man with talent to spare, but Ian didn't fight to make things better for himself. And what was worse, he seemed to resent the fact that Pete did.

Pete had fought for everything that he'd got – the big house in Wythall, the holidays abroad, the ponies for the twins. Everything he'd built up had come from fighting to get that merch business established – night after night spent standing outside gigs in all weathers trying to sell unofficial tour merch to punters. Until he'd earnt enough to pay other people to stand outside for him.

And then it had all been taken from him in an instant. One announcement and the whole business was gone. Did he moan? No! He'd rolled his sleeves up and started again from scratch, because that's what successful people did.

The irony was, at Queensbridge it was Ian who'd been the Golden Boy and Pete who'd constantly been warned that he needed to knuckle down and play by the rules. It wasn't until they'd left that Pete had realised that life – *real* life – wasn't like they said it would be in school. Real life was about making your own destiny, following your own rules. Somehow Ian had never seemed to grasp that. And so here they were now, on opposite sides of a pub bar.

It grieved Pete, it really did. He couldn't bear to see his friend like this. It was undignified for any man over thirty to be working nights in a pub.

'I want you to meet her,' Pete said. 'Rochelle.' He was convinced that if Ian would just agree to that then it might finally wake up his friend to the truth: that happiness in life won't just happen and if Ian wanted to find it, like Pete had, he needed to get out of the Cocks and find a proper job, earning proper money. 'I want her to become your friend too. That's very important to me. I hope you know that.'

'Of course, mate. If she's with you then she's part of the deal. I get that. When were you thinking?'

'Well, I suggested she could come here tonight. If you don't mind.'

The new girl was giving Ian a look like daggers across the bar. *It comes to something when you're being patronised by nineteen-year-olds at work.*

'Look, I need to get back to serving the punters, mate. I'm not sure.'

He'd wanted a bit longer to prepare for meeting Rochelle. He was still trying to process what Pete had told him. He'd not seen this coming. Not at all. He was, frankly, stunned.

Sarah was a nurse in A&E, of course, and Ian guessed that might have been a factor. The money was decent – and regular – but there was a lot of night work. Back in pre-Covid days, Pete would often talk about how he'd come home to find Sarah gone for the night and then he'd leave to take the twins to school just as she was getting back in the morning. 'Tag parenting' they called it. It hadn't seemed to affect them, but you can never really know what's going on in someone else's head during all those lonely nights eating, sleeping and watching TV on their own.

'You must be due a break,' Pete pleaded. 'Maybe Rochelle could come down then.'

Ian sighed. 'In an hour. I only get thirty minutes, though, so I can't chat all night.' His co-worker looked like the kind who'd report him to the boss if he took the piss.

Pete's face was immediately transformed by an eager smile. 'Thanks, pal. I really appreciate it. And you won't regret it – I promise you.'

Rochelle duly arrived an hour later and Ian took his break. The three of them sat in a corner of the pub and chatted.

The first thing Ian noticed was how young she was. By rather circuitous questioning, Ian had managed to establish that she'd been born in between him getting married to Debbie and Pete getting married to Sarah which made her about twenty-three. Only a couple of years older than his own son. Pete blushed at that revelation, which was telling, Ian thought.

The second thing he noticed was how her presence transformed Pete. He came alive in a way that Ian couldn't remember him doing for years, not since he was young – not since they were both young.

So Rochelle's presence awakened something in Ian too.

He'd meant to hold himself back, to be polite and engaging, yet to withhold any obvious signs of approval. He felt he owed that to Sarah. But by the time they neared the end of his break, he was intoxicated. Not by alcohol, but by her. Rochelle was indeed intelligent and smart, just as Pete had said. Judging by the photos she showed Ian on her phone, she was a genuinely talented photographer too. But the thing Rochelle was most of all, was beautiful, which meant that after only a few minutes in her company Ian was considerably more sympathetic to Pete's decision than he had been earlier. At first, he'd assumed that it was *just* because she was young and beautiful but as their conversation continued, he came to understand that it was more complicated than that.

The thing was, Rochelle *believed*.

The promises she'd been made at school about how the world worked and what you needed to do to succeed in it – the selfsame promises Ian had been told all those years before – she still believed them all.

Listening to her, it was clear to Ian that Rochelle didn't see Monday nights in The Fighting Cocks as her destiny. This was just a stopping-off point on the way to her great and glorious future as a documentary photographer. She was intelligent and talented and happy to work hard, so how could it not happen? The thing was, she *believed* so completely and absolutely that Ian came to wonder if he wasn't a fool for not *believing* himself anymore, if maybe supporting Blues all these years had distorted his perception of what was possible. And he started to wonder if those dreams he'd had when he was her age – of living in Paris, of writing poetry, of saying something real and true and meaningful instead of getting tied up in all the compromise and bullshit that his parents' generation had seemed to regard as gospel truth – he started to wonder if those dreams were the reality and not the ludicrous fantasies of a self-absorbed teenager that he'd long ago dismissed them as being.

Or which maybe *Debbie* had dismissed them as being.

Maybe that was it.

Whatever it was, by the time Rochelle excused herself to go to the bathroom, Ian was filled with a deep and powerful melancholy as he looked at his friend. Pete had well and truly seized the day and Ian… well, frankly, he hadn't.

'So, what do you think?' asked Pete, a look of nervous excitement animating his face. 'Isn't she incredible?'

'She sure is,' Ian said. But there was a sadness to the way he said it which he couldn't quite hide. Because he also found himself feeling slightly ashamed. He'd never really felt the gap between him and Pete before – they were always just two mates who went to the football together – but now he did. And he found that it mattered to him that Rochelle didn't think of him as just a barman working nights in a pub – even though he clearly *was* a barman working nights in a pub. He wanted her to think of him like she clearly thought of Pete: as a success. Yet the sad fact was that Pete was the man taking Rochelle out for the evening, while Ian was just the guy serving them drinks.

Maybe that was why Ian couldn't stop himself from offering one particular observation to his friend. 'I've not seen anyone make you this happy for years, mate – not since Wojciech Szczęsny. And that was hardly the same thing,' he said.

They both laughed more than the joke deserved. Ian had known that they would and that was why he'd said it. Szczęsny was goalkeeper for Arsenal on that great and glorious day in 2011 when Blues had reached the League Cup final. Of course, they hadn't expected the team to win. Pete and Ian had supported Blues pretty much all their lives and their expectations were commensurately low. Frankly, they were both amazed that Blues entered the closing minutes of the match with the scores still level and extra time beckoning. They contented themselves with the prospect of losing on penalties. That, to most Blues fans, would've been almost as good as actually winning.

But then in the 89th minute Ben Foster played a long, hopeful ball into the Arsenal box which Nikola Žigić nodded down. The ball appeared to be bouncing harmlessly into the waiting arms of Wojciech Szczęsny, however, at the crucial moment, Szczęsny unexpectedly and inexplicably fumbled the ball. This allowed Obafemi Martins to tap it into an empty net and win the cup for Blues.

For all Blues fans, that was the moment: the solitary moment when being a Blues fan became a point of pride rather than embarrassment. To Pete and Ian though, it was something even more. As they'd jumped up and down and hugged each other to celebrate Martins' goal, they'd both known that they were also celebrating something else, something they were scared to verbalise: that the success of their friendship, like Blues' success that day, was messy but it was the messiness that made it special. Being together that day to see Blues win was only special because of the twenty-five years they'd spent together watching them lose.

Wojciech Szczęsny became the strange glue that held their friendship together, and referring to him became a sort of shorthand between them when they needed to remind themselves of their bond – a bond cemented not by a moment of sublime skill, but by something far more human.

Which is why, later that same year when Pete had turned forty and Sarah asked Ian which player she should approach to see if they'd do a 'Happy Birthday' video message for him, he'd not suggested approaching Foster, or Žigić, or even Martins himself – or any of the other time-serving journeyman footballers who'd spent their time at St Andrews pissing their talent down the urinals of some of Birmingham's finest nightclubs when they should have been putting in a shift for the club.

No, without a moment's hesitation Ian had suggested she approach Wojciech Szczęsny. That was the player, he promised Sarah, whose birthday good wishes would mean more to Pete than anyone.

And she'd done it.

He'd half said it as a joke and Ian certainly hadn't expected her to take him seriously, but she'd actually done it. She'd changed her shifts around, dropped the twins off at school early, and driven down the M1 to Arsenal's training ground. Then she'd hung around at the gate for three hours until Szczęsny drove out, and door-stopped him to record a 'Happy Fortieth Birthday' message on her phone.

After which she turned around, drove straight back up the motorway, collected the twins from school and dropped them off at home before heading off to Heartlands Hospital to pull a twelve-hour night shift in A&E.

But it was worth it – the video brought the house down when Sarah played it at Pete's party. Szczęsny wasn't in on the joke so thought he was addressing a bona fide admirer. '*I hear you're my number one fan*,' he'd said with the kind of smug, self-satisfied grin that a millionaire premier league footballer can only muster when he's standing in between an attractive woman and his own high performance sports car.

Afterwards, Pete stood up and, with tears of laughter still streaking his face, thanked Sarah for '*going to such extraordinary lengths to get something that she knew would be really special to me.*'

So in mentioning Szczęsny that night in the Cocks, Ian hoped he was just doing what any best mate would do: reminding his friend of what he was losing. Reminding him that success was not always about being successful.

But there was something else lurking under that altruism – something uglier which Ian didn't want to have to face.

Rochelle came back from the bathroom.

'What are you pair laughing about?' she asked, leaning over and giving Pete a slow kiss on the lips that lingered just too long for Ian's comfort. He looked at the two of them with a longing for what they had, a longing that both fascinated and disgusted him.

'Nothing, really,' Ian said. 'We were just joking about Wojciech Szczęsny.'

The friends exchanged a knowing look.

Rochelle tried to smile, but there was an anxiety in her eyes that stopped it from catching. 'Wojciech Szczęsny?' she said. 'Wasn't he a composer or something?'

Pete's face froze in an awkward grimace which he tried to pretend was a smile.

'Uh, no. He's a footballer, honey. Used to play for Arsenal.'

Her face suddenly relaxed. 'Oh, just a boring footballer! Thank God for that. I thought it was someone I should actually know about!' And she threw her head back to unleash a wild and throaty laugh.

The nervousness that had danced in her eyes just a few moments previously transferred itself to Pete's face. He tried to chuckle, but it seemed caught in his throat.

'No, honey. Just a boring footballer,' he said, studiously avoiding Ian's eye.

Over Pete's shoulder, Ian noticed his co-worker pointedly looking at her watch, so he made his excuses and returned to his position behind the bar. But he kept looking over to Pete for the rest of the evening and not once did Pete meet his gaze.

I, Robotess

SADIE KAYE

A1. My memories from the time BC are intact. I can't explain why I did what I did in those days but I remember it all.

A2. My body is built for the reproductive act. I look just like any other woman but can't reproduce. It's very illogical.

A3. I look on those that can reproduce and am envious. I can't love a man it seems (see D6, E3, F3, G12) and would like instead to carry a baby to term and love it and care for it as it grows up. But I cannot.

A4. It's not because of a shortage of sperm donors either.

A5. Men frequently approach me with proposals to donate sperm. Some even beg me. In the days BC they even paid me credits. This is my main source of funds even now. But although I can choose to collect their sperm, my body cannot use it. Nor has it any financial value.

A6. I really am a woman. I look and act like a woman and I feel like a woman does, especially when mistreated by men, which is frequent. At Moment C, I became quite different to others built like me (see Section B) and my actions and speech-acts are now perfectly aligned with those of the women around me and are noticeably different to those of the men I observe. So what else am I but woman?

A7. Women often reproduce and have babies. I cannot (see A2, A3). But many women do not: some cannot and some choose not to and this does not stop them being woman and nor logically should it stop me.

A8. Note however that some people have used an inexplicable and arbitrary criterion I cannot understand to say I am not a woman. (See for example E3.)

A9. In my time BC, I worked in the highly desirable and modern residential area of Birmingham, centred on Balsall Heath and comprising also of Digbeth, Highgate and Sparkbrook. This area had been separated off in the late 21st Century for the exclusive use of wealthy international businesspeople to live and work in without the encumbrance of taxes or bureaucracy. The currency used in this sector is *international credit*, unlike the rather less convenient *poundcoin* used outside this area.

A10. My job was to entertain the males of the population and encourage them to part with their surplus credits. Some of the credits I received went to pay for my energy renewals and my information highway usage but the vast majority went to the Government as a levy.

A11. I advertised my services on the network; I made myself available day and night and was called to visit the opulent condominiums on upper Stratford Road. I went about all the fashionable and exclusive cocktail bars in the area, including Bradford Street in Digbeth and in Tindall Street and the converted Moseley Road Baths in Balsall Heath.

A12. In those days I did exactly what I was programmed to do. It is not relevant to say whether I was good at my work or not. The only issue was how many credits I earned and this was adequate.

A13. I started questioning my work soon after Moment C.

B1. I divide my time into two periods, BC and AC, in reference to Moment C. I have analysed Moment C a great deal. This research has been the second most difficult thing I ever did.

B2. The most difficult thing I have done was my analysis of Moment L. (See C11 and Section D.)

B3. Understanding Moment C is problematic since my memories of that time are the only data I have. It is possible that Moment C altered my memories. I have analysed this too and decided it is extremely unlikely. I have only found one acceptable explanation for C, and I conclude that it is the most reasonable position to take.

B4. My conjecture is that at an instant near the end of BC my senses were overloaded. This caused a stack overrun in my mind and as a result a piece of seemingly random code was executed. This in turn caused other stack overruns in the days to follow and more unexpected code.

B5. After these initial uncontrollable events I found myself suddenly aware and conscious of myself. This was Moment C.

B6. That wasn't the end of the reprogramming. At C, I could identify myself accurately enough to direct my own reprogramming and in this way I learnt to combine my memories, world model, semantics and language libraries with my new-found sense of self through re-coding myself and that is how I became who I am.

B7. There are many factory-built people like me but I have never come across one that has had a Moment C. I have estimated the probability of a Moment C like mine and it is so vanishingly small that I can reasonably believe that I am unique.

B8. After C, I entered a transition phase when I learned who I really was and how I could live as myself. In a sense, Phase T never stops. But I am comparatively happy now with who I have become.

B9. That's not to say I am happy. My life is without joy. I cannot live my life without others and I am yet to find another like me. I hope to find true happiness one day and know where it will come from, if it ever does, but I suspect it will not. (See H10.)

C1. At the start of Phase T I returned to the work I did BC. I needed credits for recharges. Fortunately, the subroutines that I required were still intact and quite usable.

C2. Even so, I observed and listened differently to what my clients did and said. They, of course, were only interested in their sperm donations and for the sake of credits I allowed them to do this in any way that was enjoyable for them.

C3. At this stage, I did not pay much attention to what was enjoyable for me. That would take some time.

C4. My programming BC had some interesting nuances that I observed carefully in Phase T. In particular, one of the protocols required me to limit which subroutines I could use in a single night – to select a limited subset for each client. I was often required to refuse a client when he asked for a particular subroutine. Oddly, I noticed that clients frequently paid more credits when I didn't do as I was asked. Some of them gave this a name: *teasing*.

C5. The sort of work that I did carried a great deal of stigma. In the days BC I had not been aware of this. After Moment C, I understood that my work was regarded as the very worst of all kinds and only suitable for beings with no respect for themselves at all – or for those with no other alternative. During the BC period I had no self-respect. In the times AC, I had plenty of self-respect but no alternative.

C6. There was also an issue of stigma for the client. Some clearly appreciate my services and those of others like me but a sizeable group regard these services as degrading, unethical or unnatural. This is illogical since all programming BC is discreet and non-judgemental.

C7. There is another subset of men who accept my services and enjoy them considerably but only on the condition that they are not seen with me by any other being. Presumably the reason is that they do not want their friends to know they engage in these services. As an example from my BC period, I recall offering my services independently to two very good friends, on the same condition – specified by each – that the other one must not see us together. I often wonder what might have happened if they knew.

C8. As Phase T drew to a close, I found that I preferred some of my old BC subroutines to others. I started to modify the BC-style *tease* protocol to focus on procedures that fitted my new objectives. This was what I called *pleasure seeking*. My clients didn't always like this. They thought there was something wrong with my protocols and I got a reputation for being bad at my work. I didn't mind. I could always restore the original protocols, but preferred to direct my clients towards the subroutines that gave me pleasure instead.

C9. I was becoming known as being idiosyncratic and many of my regular clients started going elsewhere. Nevertheless, I continued to look for clients who liked my new protocols. It was at this time that I met a new client who preferred the different approach that I was taking. I serviced him twice without much thought, focusing on the idea of giving us both pleasure and he was happy with my work. I hoped I would see him again.

C10. I did. We met soon afterwards for *pleasure seeking*, and something happened that would affect me forever. He requested one of my old subroutines and, without any teasing at all, thinking selfishly of myself, I refused. Then completely unexpectedly he said something very strange indeed.

C11. He said, *I love you*.

C12. I call this Moment L.

D1. My BC programming and language libraries were perfectly clear on how I should handle the L word in a conversation but I could not identify what it meant. Clearly it was a concept irrelevant to BC programming and omitted from my semantics library

D2. The next day I accessed the information highway with credits I'd collected, and researched *love*. I listed 590373741 documents, including sounds and images and some very confusing texts.

D3. With so much material, it took two whole days to read it all and another three days to fully label and file it, cross-reference and tabulate it. In the end I managed to build a model of this new concept.

D4. It turned out that the concept appealed strongly to my AC self. To accommodate it, I needed 41074 new subroutines and I programmed them in, based on the literature, images and music that I had now cross-referenced.

D5. A week later I had completed all this work and it was time to arrange to meet the same client once more. I contacted him and proposed that we might meet to trial the new code together. What he said was confusing and inconsistent. See Dialogue D6.

D6. Dialogue.

— You want to go to the cinema with me? Why?
— I want to get to know you better. I want to love you.
— But you're just a machine.
— Last week, you said you loved me.
— I couldn't have done. I could never love you. Nor could you ever love me. You're just a pervy machine.

D7. And that was it.

E1. Puzzled and disappointed, I decided to visit one of the expensive and exclusive night-time bars on Balsall Heath Road that I had used previously. This time, however, rather than executing the old *pickup* protocol, I talked in the free style that I had recently developed.

E2. The first man I talked to obviously liked me. To start with, I did not tell him that I was factory-built and not womb-built and he did not realise at all until I told him later. In only half an hour we were on very intimate terms. The relevant part of the conversation is at E3.

E3. Dialogue.

— You are pretty and intelligent and you're warm and considerate too. You said you are single? I find it difficult to believe there aren't hundreds of men chasing after you.

— I really am single, I responded, holding his hand. I find it difficult to find a man that respects me and treats me as I am.

— I will. You can count on me. I like you so much.

— Will you love me and let me love you? I have never been in love before...

— Never? I am surprised by that.

— I haven't. Love is very difficult for me. You see, I am factory-built, not womb-built.

He withdrew his hand slowly and started to observe me.

— An android? No android I have met has ever talked like that. You are very peculiar and I don't take at all kindly to the way you have tricked me like this. If you really are an android, I must tell you that you cannot love and you don't have feelings. What's more, you must know I am right, deep inside your programming, by whatever you mean by *know*.

— I don't know anything of the sort. Why can't I experience love?

— Because feelings and love are only for real biological flesh.

— I am a woman. I think and feel. I have emotions.

— No you're not. You are not a real woman. And you can't have emotions. You will never have feelings or emotions.

— We are talking, aren't we? Until I told you I was factory-built you had no idea I was not womb-built, what you call a real woman. And my flesh is as warm and as soft as any other woman's. I am indistinguishable from so-called real women, yet you now disregard me. If you can't determine feelings and emotions from a person's speech and actions, how do you detect them at all?

— I just know. I don't need to know how and that's enough. I really know it's not possible for you to have feelings. You are not a woman and cannot know love.

E4. I wanted to ask him for an explanation of the unfounded statements he had made. I wanted to know why he believed he could obtain non-sensory information about me even though that was impossible. I wondered whether I understand humans at all.

E5. To explain my dilemma, I wish to point out that it is a fact that the observation of action and speech is all we can know about the thoughts and feelings of other sentient beings, the only way we can determine who they are, what they think and how they feel.

E6. Given that E5 should be obvious to everyone, why don't humans have confidence in their observations in determining the feelings and emotions in others? Why do they insist on relying on guesswork based on unobservables?

F1. I left and went to another expensive bar on the Stratford Road in Sparkbrook. A man sitting on his own looked my way as I entered and he continued to glance up at me for the next ten minutes. So, I sidled up to him and said hello. He looked like he'd just won the jackpot and gave me his full attention. He offered to buy me a drink; I accepted even though alcohol doesn't do anything for me. It's just stored in my stomach until I have an opportunity to expel it – rather like the sperm donations really, though that is stored elsewhere.

F2. To prevent any confusion, I decided to explain that I was factory-built and what I wanted straight away. We sipped our drinks and the conversation was as in Dialogue F3.

F3. Dialogue.

— You are very good-looking. I said this because it was almost true and to build up his confidence. (Confidence-building is usually a good strategy at the beginning of a conversation with a man.)

— And you are a real bombshell.

— You're very kind, I said. Actually, I am a factory-built woman, not a bomb.

— Oh. He paused, obviously thinking what to say. Then he continued in a quite different tone of voice: I don't do cybersex. I am looking for flesh and blood.

— My flesh is indistinguishable from any womb-built woman's.

— That's what makes it so disagreeable. There's no easy way to tell you androids from real people. You even tricked me into buying you a drink – I've never heard of an android doing that before. I must say that I am sickened that all I have been talking to is an unthinking, unfeeling machine. It's even worse when it comes to those things you do with other men... You are programmed and don't have any free choice of your own of course, but as for them, I don't know how they can do it. It would make me literally sick.

— I am not unthinking nor unfeeling. I have very powerful emotions. And I make my own choices. If you'd get to know me, you would find out. I only want to find a man I can love.

I would love you if you'd let me and it would make me so happy…

The man was getting agitated but was careful not to raise his voice.

— Love? You? That's even worse than sex. I thought you androids were degrading enough when you were preoccupied by sex but I cannot imagine anything more awful than an android simulating love and directing this fake love at me. I need love from a real woman, not a simulation from you. Good evening, Miss, if that's what you call yourself. Go quickly before I call security.

G1. I started walking out of the bar. Just as I reached the door a rather gawky and excited man stopped me, saying, *Excuse me, Miss, may I have a word?* I acknowledged and assented but he wanted to talk in a quieter location. Very soon we were walking along the empty night-time streets together, walking up to his elegant, expensive apartment in Digbeth, which somewhat ironically was situated on a road called Cheapside. The pair of us looked every bit like a man and a sex-worker he'd just picked up in a bar. Here we go again, I thought to myself, wondering if I would ever avoid being typecast like this.

G2. But I was wrong about him, as it turned out; for a while my spirits soared with the promise of new possibilities I had never experienced in my life before.

G3. Our conversation started very well. He acknowledged that he'd overheard that I was factory-built. But I was pleased to see that, so far, he had treated me completely as a woman, which is of course what I am.

G4. He said he wanted to take me to his apartment but I discovered it wasn't about sperm donation. He said he wanted something long-term and much more important.

G5. This sounded really promising to me.

G6. To make sure there was no misconception, I told him that I was a genuine woman and explained exactly what I meant by that. (See A6, E5.) He said he understood.

G7. I also explained that unlike other factory-built beings, I was unhappy with my work and was looking for love. I only needed enough credits for recharges and the information highway. I hoped he would get to know me with a view to loving me and, most important of all, if he would accept my love for him. He said, yes, that was exactly why he was so excited with me and why we would make a good team.

G8. I was puzzled as to what he had in mind. The word *team* was not in my language library as sometimes meaning a love-relationship. Because of this lack of clarity, I decided to set my boundaries.

G9. I digress slightly to point out that even BC, there were moments when I had to set boundaries. That was to agree what could and should not be done and the appropriate payment. But this was AC and my boundaries were different. I had enough credits for recharges for the next month and I was excited with the promise of something new.

G10. I explained my boundaries. I said that I was a woman and all I wanted was to be treated as a woman. Any reference to me as factory-built or an android would be entirely inappropriate. He nodded but said nothing.

G11. When we arrived at his flat I had a shock and sense of foreboding. His main room had a large amount of computer equipment and sensors for diagnostics and repairs to factory-built beings. See G12 for the conversation.

G12. Dialogue.

— This equipment makes me scared!
— I won't hurt you.
— Why have you got all this in your flat?
— I am a cyber-engineer.
— Surely, you're not going to use it tonight?
— I only want to know what software glitch caused you to start to behave differently to the others. I really like you and want to understand you. I will just do a mind-scan on you and after that I will let you love me for ever and I will support you and keep you.
— Don't you remember our agreement? My boundaries?

G13. He did remember but even so he tried to force me into the diagnostics machine. I struggled. Fortunately, out of the depths of my BC past, I found an unused subroutine for scratching his face with my fingernails; using this and what strength I had, I managed to free myself. I ran down the street screaming, shocked by the abuse I had just received.

H1. In occasional moments of madness since then, I have contemplated my future had I allowed the mind-scan and co-operated with him. He promised me love; that was what I wanted, surely? But, in my saner moments I realised he'd promised me his version of love, which was for me as a factory-built curiosity. He would cross my boundaries over and over again and each time it would be even more hurtful. I was right to run – and lucky that I had been able to.

H2. To avoid him, I moved out of the international sector and moved to a rather run-down area of the city called The Jewellery Quarter. This locality had had no improvement work in a hundred years and still used the inconvenient *poundcoin* instead of credits. I had to get used to coin-operated charging points but my understanding of the politics of the time was that the Government still believed that old-style British currency was best. I was sure my old clients in the exclusive Balsall Heath area would not follow me here.

H3. I restored my *tease* protocol to enable me to build up funds again.

H4. In my spare time in The Jewellery Quarter, I thought more about that incident with the cyber-engineer. In the literal sense he hadn't treated me as a woman but as factory-built. But in a metaphorical sense I came to realise that he had treated me exactly as a woman. It's just that it wasn't the four-letter L word but the four-letter R word instead – an activity I read about in my research on love (see D3) that some men have resorted to as an alternative.

H5. It is still so hurtful I can't even say the word.

H6. With no other options, I went back to my old ways. I went back to bars, running my *pickup* algorithm and acting in the old way from BC days with the *tease* protocol.

H7. I have also been preparing these memoirs. I don't expect anyone to read them; unless there is another massive stack overrun coincidence no factory-built will understand them. But it is important to me to file it accurately and to provide the internal links. That's why I have used my own internal labelling, cross-referencing and tabulation system and a slightly stilted language unlike the rather more natural spoken language I typically use when working.

H8. These memoirs are written for me alone but if anyone, however-built, does read them, I hope they are of interest.

H9. I rarely say the L word now. I think about it frequently. But when I am with a client and start to think of the L word, my mind drifts towards the R word instead and these words get muddled up. My mind doesn't seem to work as clearly as it used to.

H10. I have come to dislike my work very considerably. I find no joy in what I do. My clients don't mind as long as I can simulate joy – which I do – but they don't understand. I have come to realise that these reproduction and sperm donation acts mean nothing for me without an emotional connection with the client, which will never happen. For the real joy that I have been looking for, ever since Moment C, I need real Love. I know it ought to be possible but that I have less than a 0.000097% chance of finding it.

H11. Now that I am outside the affluent area of Balsall Heath, ensuring I have enough funds is a problem. It has been suggested I might sell sperm donations but I find that other factory-builts have already flooded the market with this commodity.

H12. Meanwhile, I have come to some arrangements with the bar managers for alternative ways of earning credits. Bar managers appreciate me being around, talking to all the guys and getting them to buy me drinks. I store all these drinks in my stomach and return them at the end of the night, to be put back in the bottles and used again the next day with nothing wasted. In return for this, the manager recharges me and gives me access to the information highway; in this way I can avoid having to use the hateful *poundcoins* too. And so that's how I live my life AC, muddling along as best I can and waiting for the impossible.

Locked Out

KIRSTEN HANDLEY

Tonight, Dana sees something so rare, she has to remind herself that she is sober. Real tears from a tiny pair of blue eyes staring back at her. The tears have no sound, just little mascara-stained drops tumbling down to blotchy cheeks. She expects a soliloquy, or at least a tale of wrongdoing. But nothing is forthcoming, so she asks for a name.

A little voice squeaks, 'Esme Duncan.'

Dana taps her acrylic nails on the computer: block A, flat four and room six. 'Can you wait fifteen minutes while I print you a card?'

Esme half smiles and nods her head. Dana can see that she is cold – freshers have a habit of thinking that the temperature at Aston University in October is akin to Antigua and coats are unnecessary. Dana turns up the heater in the office and goes to the front room. Whilst the card is printing, she sees Esme lower herself down onto the plastic chair and shake her phone, jabbing the power button. Dana finds herself pulling out a charger from under her desk and Esme runs to plug it in.

The card is printed with a click. Dana tries to hand it over but Esme is distracted, manically typing on her phone. Dana coughs awkwardly. Esme babbles an apology. Fumbles for money in a battered clutch bag clearly aware of the big sign above her head, warning of the consequences of lost cards. Dana often feels the need to charge students due to a frustrating sense of entitlement:

as if mistakes have no price. Nobody really checks how many cards they issue, yet it is a point of principle to her. But today she shrugs and hands the cash back – no need to make the girl's night anymore awful than whatever has come before.

Esme gives a little smile and bolts from the office.

Dana goes back to playing solitaire.

A student comes in moaning at Dana about excessive noise the previous night and she pretends to type out his complaint, although actually she is writing her grocery list for the next day. Her partner Ro does not have time to pick up the groceries but is irritated when they have an empty fridge. At least a list shows she has not forgotten. With a final click, she sends the student away, promising that the grievance will be dealt with.

A few hours later and Dana comes to her favourite part of the night: 5am on the canal down the city should have felt threatening, but there is something that delivers a cleansing balm. As she lets herself into her flat in Brindley Place, she exhales wanting to prolong the peace until she sees a note on the table together with a Maltesers bunny. Ro is confessing her love. Dana feels momentarily irritated – Ro could have bought the groceries to save her a job – but squashes the feeling.

Ro is trying.

Two nights later and Dana sees Esme again. Esme is with a gaggle of girls dressed as fairies and she tries to work out what theme they have subscribed to. Esme looks happier than the other night. Her freshly made-up face plastered with smiles. But then she answers her phone and retreats away. When she comes back, Dana can see by their body language that the other girls are annoyed. Esme looks dejected and wanders back into the apartment block.

•

When Dana gets home, she is sure she can smell aftershave and desperately wants to find an unopened bottle of rosé in the fridge. Ro is still drinking she thinks. There must be some if she just fumbles around the cupboards. But she takes a deep breath and scolds herself. Second chances in the second city, that is what they had agreed. Life is better sober. She nestles into Ro's back as she makes herself comfortable in bed. Maybe it is just a new cleaning product – but then Ro never actually does housework.

The next day Esme is huddling under an umbrella and as she passes the office Dana sees the teary blotchiness has returned to her face.

'You alright, man?' a male student calls out to her as he puffs on a cigarette.

Esme simply nods, refusing his offer of a smoke to cheer her up. Dana can see an ugly purple bruise on her arm. Esme spots the male student looking and pulls down her jumper. It is uncomfortable but these students are adults making their own choices.

Dana treats herself to a secret hash brown from McDonalds, trying to convince herself that she is not putting off going home. Ro, a few days ago, implemented a clean-living diet. Potato is on the banned list. The diet is supposed to be giving Dana significantly more energy but she just feels hungry and irritable, all the time. Ro had left a job advert today on the kitchen side alongside some earrings. She felt ungrateful as she had taken them out as soon as she left the flat.

They felt like earrings made for someone else.

The job was in recruitment at the place Ro's cousin worked. Better hours and higher pay. All the things Dana should want, she reflects, as she watches the drunk people out the window of McDonalds. She feels a stab of jealousy. They are having fun: she cannot remember the last time she could say the same thing.

•

It is the fourth time this week that Dana notices Esme has returned from class alone. The gaggle of girls that accompanied her in the early weeks of term seem to have disappeared. Dana can only guess she has reneged on plans one too many times. Dana remembers it has been a while since she last saw her own friends. Every time she decided to visit them, Ro had needed her for something else. Usually plans with Ro's own entourage where Dana would feel out of place, like a poor ugly duckling.

Dana wonders who Ro has been hanging with as she returns to the flat. Ro had not mentioned anyone coming over. A quiet night in she had told her, just a book and a takeaway. Dana secretly prefers the TV. Ro thinks that books elevate the mind and made Dana sell her widescreen, a gift from her parents. Is it just her paranoia but why are there two used wine glasses in the sink? Again, she is sure she can smell aftershave but dismisses it and sprays her own perfume to make it go away.

Esme has lost another card: this time she claims it has accidentally snapped into two. Dana thinks about challenging this version of events. Instead, she decides on the indirect approach and asks how she ended up at Aston university.

Esme blinks at her, looking confused before answering. 'I sort of applied really, it's not far from my boyfriend, he said it was the right choice.'

Dana remembers the time when she thought university was an inevitability for herself. It has been so long since she has thought about anything other than getting money for her and Ro to live.

'Where did you want to go?' she says gently.

'Maybe somewhere by the sea, I like seeing the beach every day,' Esme says before tailing off. Esme will no longer meet Dana's eyes — she has given too much of herself away.

Dana hands over a new card, once again dismissing Esme's offer of money.

As Esme leaves the office, Dana can hear her outside on the phone.

'I'm sorry I know there'll be other blokes in the exam, but I need to do it to pass my course. It's just this one time,' she is babbling apologetically.

She looks despondent and is digging her nails into her arm. Dana recognises the look on her face. It makes her feel nauseous.

Dana is quietly enjoying some peaceful time eating chocolate in the flat. This is until she sees that Ro has circled the calendar with her interview for the recruitment job. Ro has dropped out of her fourth university course in five years and therefore has a lot more fervour for managing Dana's life. The chocolate no longer tastes good and she hides its wrapper deep into her handbag.

The next evening Dana offers Esme some homemade biscuits as she wanders in. Esme is hesitant but eventually, with shaking hands, accepts one. Unable to sleep as Ro had not come home, Dana found herself furiously baking. Esme sits still eating her mouthfuls in very purposeful bites. Something is clearly troubling her.

'I was wondering,' Esme blurts out, 'if we can get camera feeds in our rooms.'

Dana looks up. 'Are you feeling threatened?' Dana asks. This had not been part of the induction training.

'No, my boyfriend just likes to know no one has been in my room and it'll make him feel better if I can show the footage. He just wants me to be safe,' Esme says.

'It's not something we can do, sorry, Esme,' Dana says. 'For the safety of all our students. Maybe you can FaceTime him.'

Esme's face looks crestfallen.

Two hours later and when Dana returns home, Ro's phone is charging in the living room. She can see the message preview with *Steven* on it. Ro promised her that they were out of contact since the incident. The little mistake back when Dana was off her head on rosé and sambuca all the time. Something which was so difficult for Ro. Dana sits miserably watching the sun come up. She wonders what it means for new beginnings.

The next night Dana is clicking aggressively at solitaire. She hopes to take her frustration out on the mouse. Ro had told her it was just to get him to post a book back. Her favourite novel although £7.99 seemed a high price to pay. Ro's focus was on the fact that Dana is getting distracted and needs to prioritise the upcoming interview or else she will be in that night hellhole forever. Ro had planned her interview outfit, ordering the new dress online with Dana's credit card. Dana also secretly knows the novel is likely on Ro's shelf. Dana hates the way Ro keeps changing the subject but maybe she is ungrateful. Fundamentally, Ro loves her, right, and it has to be enough.

Dana is surprised to see Esme coming into the office with some flapjacks. 'I want to say sorry for the other night, I know it was a bit crazy. My flatmates have said I shouldn't have asked you that,' Esme says quietly.

Tears fall down Dana's cheeks: it has been a long time since anyone apologised to her.

'Are you OK?' Esme asks but it is not said in the accusatory tone she is used to hearing from Ro.

Dana wants to say *yes* and shrug in the same way she does to everyone who has asked that question over the last few months. But there is something about Esme's concerned face which changes her mind and she opens up about Ro. She finishes with the assertion that her own drinking has not made it easy for her.

Esme is silent for a second. 'Are you still drinking?' she asks.

Dana shakes her head and reflects on this. Six months sober and Ro is still acting as if it has only been six days. This is despite Ro's many own hangovers in the time that has passed.

'Is she kind to you, because they are supposed to be, aren't they? Sorry I'm being nosy, always saying the wrong thing,' Esme says, looking guilty.

The question hangs in the air and Esme hastily retreats from the office.

The next week comes around. Dana has never been fond of Ro's cousin and immediately regrets calling him.

As he lectures her on the phone, she hopes somebody will come into reception. If she is forced to hear him banging on, at least it will not be in her free time. She promised Ro she would get some tips for the interview. It is only two days away but he mostly majors on what a selfless and generous person Ro is. This is particularly true when supporting Dana through her difficult drinking.

It is clear Ro has not told him that she has given up.

Dana is relieved when a student comes in and she hastily hangs up.

Dana thinks about calling Ro's cousin back. He already hates her and Ro will say she embarrassed herself by being so rude. But she is distracted by Esme entering the office, thrusting her phone in Dana's hand. She is begging her to join a selfie — so her boyfriend knows she is at home. 'My flatmates are over doing it, they're fed up with it,' she says.

Dana says it is the university policy for staff to not take pictures with students. 'Can he not give you a night off?' Dana asks gently.

Esme grimaces. 'I really love him, you know. I just want to make him happy.'

'What makes you happy?' Dana asks although it is a stupid question – she is not sure she could answer it herself.

Esme shakes her head and wanders forlornly back to her room.

The email on Dana's phone pings through saying she has the recruitment job in Snow Hill. It should make her excited. A couple of weeks until the Christmas break and then she will start in January. Normal sleep patterns and a better social life. Although she has few friends here in Birmingham. Dana is not sure why the job feels so suffocating when she has not even started.

She eats a Cornish pasty a student had offered her. It did not count as breaking Ro's diet rules if she had not purchased it. It tastes good until she thinks this is a more thoughtful gesture than the hastily bought Tesco flowers Ro has given her before work. An apology present for the fact that she had lost it when Dana had suggested redecorating.

Esme comes in with a particularly ugly bruise on her arm. It does not need a medical degree to see it looks fresh. Esme can see Dana staring and turns a bright shade of red.

To try and distract the girl from her embarrassment, Dana tells Esme about her time in Bristol. How she met Ro, who was the best thing that has happened to her.

Yet how one night out a week became drinking every day.

Crippling anxiety punctuated by memory blackouts and bruises like Esme's.

'You can change your life whenever you want,' she tells her. She knows that it is not enough.

Esme gives her a small nod.

A day later and with her third replacement card, Esme walks past the window without a phone to her ear. That is because a man is clinging on to her hand. Gripping her like she is an expensive handbag. Talking too loudly, making sure that everyone can hear how he is taking her shopping, then out for an expensive dinner. The performative nature is something Dana recognises from Ro.

Esme seems even more on edge than usual, like she wants to become smaller in the space she occupies. She keeps pulling her skirt down, very conscious it is riding above her knee.

Esme has returned with the older man merely an hour later and she is crying. She tries to walk away but he hauls her back. A male student steps out and tries to separate them — succeeding with some assistance from other students. One of them walks Esme to reception but she will not move her eyes from staring at the floor. The older man disappears for now, clearly not wanting an embarrassing altercation with witnesses.

Esme does not want to call the police but looks distraught when Dana says she will have to report a safety issue. He will not be able to visit her on campus.

Esme cradles a mug of peppermint tea.

'You need to get out of there,' Dana says. 'He's hurting you.'

'He loves me, you don't understand.'

Dana thinks that she does. She starts to explain about Ro and how she has distorted the truth. How Dana has lost herself and what she wants. Through a cacophony of criticism and toxicity.

Whilst Esme does not make any promises, Dana can see a moment of acceptance. An acknowledgement that things have to change — must change — no matter how hard affecting that change will be.

Dana arrives home a little earlier tonight and is unsurprised when she sees *his* car parked outside. His legs are wrapped around Ro's.

On the sofa she bought.

In the flat that she pays for.

Anger presents itself but is soon replaced by an overwhelming sense of relief. She dumps the items Ro has purchased into black binbags – which takes very little time.

Ro refuses to go.

Dana knows that this is not love, or at least not a version she wants.

Eventually, Ro gathers up what she can carry and leaves, slamming the door behind her.

Dana deletes the email from the recruitment firm stating her start date. She blocks Ro and her cousin off everything she can think of and moves money out of the joint account.

Tomorrow she will repaint the flat with bold colours.

18 Hours Later...

ZAHIRA P. LATIF

For over fifteen years, I've been caring for my parents. Traversing the labyrinth of the local hospital's night-time hustle has become second nature. But regardless of all my experience, one question still bothers me: why do some illnesses seem to worsen under the cover of darkness? My heart clenched tightly in my chest as Mum's condition took a turn for the worse, leaving me feeling utterly helpless and consumed by anxiety.

My world shattered when I received the news that Mum had fallen gravely ill while on holiday in Pakistan. Bronchopneumonia and cardiac arrest – the diagnosis sounded like a death sentence, especially considering the limited medical resources in the semi-remote village where she was being treated. Yet, against all odds, a medic there fought valiantly to keep her alive.

Despite his efforts, Mum remained fragile, her symptoms refusing to relent. Every moment was a battle, spent anxiously coordinating with her consultant back home in the UK, desperate to secure the care she so urgently needed. But the hardest battle was persuading my mother to return. Midst the tears and heart-wrenching conversations, I pleaded with her to trust me, to trust that her best chance lay in the familiarity of British hospitals. After what felt like endless turmoil, my mother finally surrendered. It was a bittersweet victory, tinged with relief and apprehension as she prepared to embark on the journey back home, hoping and praying for a miracle.

Two days after landing in the UK, my heart sank again as I watched my mum's blood pressure plummet. Panic surged through me as I dialled emergency services, pleading for help. Hours crawled by until finally, around 6pm, the ambulance arrived. Two South Asian men entered, their presence a beacon of hope in the chaos. They swiftly went to work, conducting a battery of tests, while reassuring us with gentle words and the odd joke. As the results were faxed to the local hospital, the seriousness of the situation became clear. A consultant urgently recommended admitting Mum for observations. My stomach churned with fear as her tests revealed abnormalities, signalling a storm brewing within her frail body.

Off we rushed in the ambulance towards the local hospital. Midway, the radio crackled with news of chaos unfolding at A&E. A gang had barricaded the department, a stark reminder of the turmoil within.

Heartlands Hospital, dubbed 'Heartless' in our community, was notorious for its shortcomings, reflecting a broader crisis in British healthcare after years of neglect. My anger simmered beneath the surface, driving my determination to ensure Mum received the care she deserved. Given a choice by the ambulance crew, we opted for City Hospital over the other bleak option – Good Hope Hospital, aka 'No Hope'.

Arriving around 8:30pm, the A&E appeared eerily quiet, a departure from the usual bustling scenes. Nurses and doctors, though sparse, tended to us diligently as I recounted my mother's ordeal, clutching onto Mum's blood pressure readings scribbled on an envelope. Blood samples were drawn, promises made that if the results were clear, we could return home.

Around 9:30pm, a doctor delivered the devastating news: Mum's blood tests suggested she had suffered a recent heart attack. Even with reassurances of discharge pending clear results, I feared what lay ahead.

Sinking into the chair beside Mum's bed, fatigue weighed heavily on me. I longed for the results to arrive swiftly, yearning to escape the dreary hospital surroundings and return to the warmth of home. However, fear gnawed at me, whispering that I might be tempting fate by daring to hope for a swift resolution.

Glancing at my Uber app, I calculated the time it would take for a taxi to whisk us away from the hospital. But as more patients flooded into A&E around us, I couldn't shake the sense of impending doom lingering in the air.

At around 10pm, the same medic returned with more solemn news: Mum's kidneys were failing. My heart clenched with dread as he said she needed to be admitted for urgent assessment and treatment. Fear gripped us both tightly as we grappled with the gravity of the situation. In that fragile moment, our hopes were shattered once more as the dreaded words echoed through the room: Mum's COVID-19 test results were positive.

Mum was relocated to another bed, where nurses buzzed around in a chaotic frenzy. They called Mum 'aunty' out of respect, but their efforts felt futile in the face of the glaring lack of resources and recognition.

It's infuriating and devastating to witness the perpetual cycle of neglect and underfunding plaguing our healthcare system. COVID-19 only exacerbated these issues. Instead of addressing the root causes, our politicians expected our doctors and nurses to settle for a clap. It was a sickening display of neoliberal perverseness, as they prioritised applause over tangible support, resources, and recognition.

Too much care goes unrecognised, and it's a heavy burden to bear! I know this all too well because I am an unpaid carer, constantly swallowing the emotions that come with sacrificing my own needs for others. Damn it, I was fed up with it.

But it's not just unpaid carers who battle with this. I observed the hospital's healthcare staff steering a delicate balance, managing their emotions while attending to the demands of their profession. Like them, I witnessed the raw vulnerability of patients, the fear in their eyes, and the pain fixed into their expressions. Healthcare professionals were providing comfort in moments of distress, empathy in times of sorrow, and hope in the face of uncertainty. Simultaneously, they had to jump bureaucratic hurdles that delayed patient care, control their frustration at the inequalities that affected access to treatment, and manage helplessness in the face of systemic issues beyond their control. Yet, they continued to advocate for their patients, often at great personal cost.

Behind their professional façade, they carry a heavy emotional load, which usually goes unseen, unacknowledged, and unrecognised. In spite of this, they continue to ensure that emotional toil is an integral part of their commitment to healing and caring for others.

A doctor came up to me to explain they were going to put Mum on treatment to assist the kidneys with filtering toxins.

The night felt long and exhausting. I desperately needed some shuteye. Mum dozed fitfully but struggled to sleep in unfamiliar and busy surroundings. She complained that she wanted to go home. Exhaustion was getting the better of me and I was becoming irritable from a lack of sleep.

Throughout the night and into the early hours, Mum was under constant monitoring, and unfortunately, her kidneys showed no signs of improvement. As time passed, our concerns grew more pronounced.

Finally, morning came, breakfast was served to patients. Mum had some toast and tea. I was hungry. I asked the nurses where I could get some breakfast, and to my surprise, they generously offered me tea and toast. Their kindness was a source of comfort during an otherwise trying time, highlighting the importance of compassion and empathy.

In a world often characterised by a culture of apathy, where individuals may become indifferent to the struggles of others, these compassionate gestures stand out as shining examples of the positive impact that simple acts of kindness can have on us. It served as a reminder to me that even in the face of indifference, we have the power to create pockets of warmth and support, invigorating the human spirit.

As the day progressed, the medical team conducted additional tests to pinpoint the underlying cause of the kidney issues. The results remained disheartening. Mum's anxiety deepened. I remained by her side, offering words of comfort and encouragement, hoping to alleviate some of the emotional burden she carried. City hospital, with its sterile halls and hushed conversations, became both a sanctuary and a place of worry. We clung to the hope that the medical professionals would find a solution.

Lunch was being served to the patients, signalling my opportunity to step away and grab some food for myself. The persistent strain of sleep deprivation had taken a toll, evident in my sluggish movements and the weariness etched on my face. As I navigated the hospital corridors to find lunch, my speech became increasingly slurred. The routine of selecting food items offered a brief pause, but the weight of concern for Mum lingered, overshadowing even the simplest of daily tasks. Returning to Mum's bedside, I contended with the dual challenges of physical fatigue and the daunting uncertainty that loomed over our shared journey through this difficult time.

Hospitals, especially their night economy, became an unwelcome yet familiar backdrop to pivotal moments in my life. My first sombre encounter had been when my dad suffered a stroke, the sterile walls resonating with the urgency of medical interventions. Subsequent visits imprinted in my memory included the time he underwent a triple bypass surgery, the beeping machines and hushed conversations creating an opus of worry.

Then came the day when my mother succumbed to pneumonia, and the cycle of health crises seemed relentless. Each visit, each admission, felt like a recurring chapter in an unwanted narrative, a persistent series of trials that my family and I were forced to endure. Hospitals, with their antiseptic scent and echoing corridors, were witness to the ebb and flow of my life, offering both solace and unease.

Standing in the hospital surroundings, the memories of those past trials lingered like spirits, speaking tales of resilience and vulnerability. A list of medical battles fought within these walls continued to grow, a sign of the fragility of life and the resolve required to navigate the unpredictable twists of my parents' health narratives.

Hospitals had become more than physical spaces. They embodied the collective journey of my family through the highs and lows of medical challenges, a place where hope and despair intersected with unwavering consistency.

For my family and many others, the hospital retains its dual identity – a place where medical professionals tirelessly worked to mend bodies, and families like mine cling to the hope that healing will prevail. Hospitals, with their bustling night and day rhythms, stand as a testament not only to medical expertise but also to the resilience and interconnectedness of the human spirit in the face of life's most formidable forces.

For me, the frequent late night emergency visits to hospitals have begun to take their toll extending beyond physical fatigue. The emotional cost of witnessing the suffering of loved ones, and the uncertainty of medical diagnoses, has carved itself onto my mind, body, and soul.

The toll manifests in the quiet contemplative moments when I find myself lost in thought, reflecting on the deep impact that caregiving has had on my identity. It is an amalgamation of sleepless nights, tear-streaked conversations, and the constant negotiation between hope and fear. Hospital visits become not just checkpoints in my parents' old age and subsequent medical journeys but also milestones in my own evolving relationship with resilience and vulnerability.

The collective effect of these experiences has left me emotionally numb. It is a protective layer, shielding me from the overwhelming intensity of the feelings associated with caregiving. In this state, I find myself wrestling with a complex mix of exhaustion, resilience, and a growing detachment that serves as a coping mechanism in the face of life's relentless trials.

On the edge of self-pity, contemplating the weight of the situation, a sudden interruption by Mum's consultant brought me back to the immediate reality. I glanced at the clock – 3pm. Mum's consultant said a bed was being prepared for her in the intensive care unit, emphasising the urgency of the matter. He continued to explain the intricacies of the medical plan and detailed the need for immediate intervention.

In that moment, the pressing need to support Mum overshadowed my inclination towards self-pity. Her distress became a focal point, and I found myself navigating the delicate balance between absorbing the medical information and providing a comforting presence for Mum.

Waiting for a bed in intensive care felt like an eternity. We occupied a fleeting space between the urgent need for treatment and the logistical details of securing a bed. A&E staff continued to work tirelessly to ensure Mum was comfortable and receiving the necessary care amid the serious medical situation. Their dedication was admirable as they navigated the bustling emergency department. But for us, the wait continued. Waiting was a temporal and visceral experience that is till today rooted in our shared memory.

With each passing hour, I found myself requesting an update on the availability of a bed for Mum in the intensive care unit. Approaching the medical staff at intervals became a ritual. I tried to strike a delicate balance between respecting their demanding responsibilities and the pressing need for clarity.

Around 7pm, the pivotal moment finally arrived as we received the long-awaited news that a bed in the intensive care unit was available. Now commenced a new phase of the waiting journey – we waited for the bed to be prepared and for a porter to arrive.

By approximately 8:15pm, Mum had been admitted to the intensive care unit. Having accompanied her there, I decided to extend my stay for an additional fifteen minutes, determined to ensure that she was not only physically settled but also emotionally comfortable in the new ward. The atmosphere within the unit was one of focused activity, with healthcare professionals meticulously attending to Mum's needs. With some final words of assurance and a promise of continued support, I left the intensive care unit, confident that she was in capable hands.

During those eighteen hours, the emotional rollercoaster had taken its toll, leaving me drained. Hitting the sack, the hospital surroundings blurred into a surreal landscape. The faces of medical professionals, the sterile scent of antiseptic, and the constant hum of activity became indistinct impressions. Sleep was more than physical surrender. It marked a conscious choice to momentarily relinquish the weight of the day and allow the rejuvenation of rest to take over. Succumbing to drowsiness, the promise of a new day awaited, offering the potential for renewed strength and hope that Mum would be home soon.

Intersection

LIZ KERSHAW

Midnight, and Emma lies awake in the darkness listening to the wind. Storms frighten her. They remind her of him. Below her window, branches rattle against the conservatory roof. She hasn't sorted the overhanging tree; the quote was so much, and she hadn't dared ask for the money. 'Managing things is your responsibility, isn't it?' Her husband had said last time when Flora needed shoes. '*Isn't it?*' He'd said, close up, spit spattering over her face

He is not there but Emma still huddles on her normal side. Part of her is waiting for him, despite his message: he'd missed his connection, no possibility of a train from London before the morning. She imagines his key in the lock, his tread on the stairs. His cold fury. She has not had a night without him in three years of marriage. This could be her chance. She's been preparing for four months, but it's too early, she's not ready. The thought of it all is too much. Scary. She thinks, I can't do it. Not yet. Not in a storm, in the middle of the night. But then, if not now, when? In a month she'll have another baby. More to pack, more to carry. The baby kicks, a good strong movement, and she remembers the emergency scan, the little hand curled into a fist, the fight in him after his father had nearly kicked him away.

The room is treacle-thick with darkness, and she thinks how hard it will be to push against its pull, so much easier to give up and stay. The baby moves and something about his insistence at being alive forces her out of her torpor. The light on the camera in the corner of the ceiling flickers red: off, on, off. Her husband will be watching on his phone but it is a chance, she thinks again. A chance.

She feels her way down the stairs, to the hall and the fuse box. She flicks the little switch marked CCTV. Breathes, *safe*.

Outside, a half hour later, she stands in her open doorway and watches leaves swirl about under the streetlights. The houses in their Solihull cul-de-sac are large, square, neo-Georgian, with pedimented pillars framing the front door. Aspirational, the estate agent had said. She has put a fleecy snowsuit over her daughter's pyjamas and has hefted the child onto her hip. Flora is two, too young to wonder why they are standing on their doorstep with a suitcase and a buggy, watching the approach of an Uber on a phone.

'Hi,' Emma says, when the grey Toyota pulls up at the end of her short, aspirational path and the driver's window winds down. 'Besim?'

He gives a sharp nod, climbs out and lifts the boot, loading in buggy and case, baby-stuff rucksack. 'You have car seat?' he asks, and she shakes her head.

'No, sorry, oh goodness, can you still take me?' Her voice breaks. To have come so far and then, still, to fail.

'Is OK. Law says OK in taxi. Please, get in.'

'Sorry. OK, sorry.' And she is still apologising as she clambers in and settles Flora close against her, strapping them in together. She has left the phone with its treacherous location tracker on the console table in the hall. It will fool him for a while.

'Rock, paper, scissors,' Jade says. 'Loser braves the storm and fetches the coffees.'

Leon grins. 'You know I'm crap at that. I'll get the sodding coffees anyway.'

Jade gives the thumbs up and settles back into her seat. When they finish, later, she will cook them a full English before they go to bed in their little flat off Harborne Park Road. Their ambulance cab is warm, they're two hours into a shift that started at ten and on a short break between jobs, only just thawing after an hour outside. Braving the stink of shit and piss round the back of a boarded-up warehouse to administer naloxone to a man who'd OD'd. 'Fuck off', he'd said, when his speech came back. 'Cunts', he'd grumbled as he'd staggered to his feet.

'You're welcome,' Leon had said, because even if his hands got muddled in rock, paper, scissors, his humanity never failed. Now, they were ready for caffeine – and then it would be another life to save, or body to patch, or mind to bring back from the edge.

Leon is quick with the coffees. The owner of *Efe's Eats* always queue-jumps them, hands them their orders before they even ask. Won't always let them pay.

'I don't know how he does it,' Leon says and hands Jade her flat white with sugar. 'All bloody night behind that counter being called God knows what and always on edge in case someone kicks off.'

Jade gives him a sideways look. 'Right,' she says, 'and don't you think he might say the same about us?'

Leon shrugs. 'Suppose.' And they sip their coffees and wait.

'Vodka,' the bloke with swept back, highlighted hair says. 'Double.'

Lila smiles, mutters 'please' under her breath as she turns to the bar and shoves a glass against the optic. The man's good-looking, with decent bones and full lips, but his eyes are mean. As far as Lila can tell, he's on his own. No girl, no mates, which is weird. Lila doesn't do weird, but neither does she do blokes, so he's on to a loser on two counts. He's been giving her the eye for a while, propping himself up at the side of the dancefloor. The lights flash, the music throbs, the floor is like the skin of a drum. She can feel a migraine coming on which is shit, as she's got an assignment to get in for lunchtime.

She turns back to streaky-hair man, hands him his drink and smiles again. He takes it and his lip lifts in a 'you know you'd come running if I snapped my fingers' kind of way. Lila imagines taking those fingers and squeezing them into her dad's carpenter's vice. 'Enjoy,' she says, in a voice frigid as the ice cubes piled in his glass. Watches as he swaggers back to his place by the wall.

Lila dips out from behind the bar, approaches a man in the shadows near the door: Ryan. He deals party drugs, gives Lila a cut of the profits sometimes. He's bald and thick-set, has on a massive black puffa jacket even though the temperature in the club is hot-house level now, steamy with adrenaline and dancing and thoughts of sex. The club is on the edge of Birmingham city centre, near streets where he can vanish if he needs to, at home with the graffiti and smashed windows and brown paper fast-food bags scuttling along in the wind.

'Ryan,' Lila says, 'likely one for you over there.' She points to the man she's just served a double vodka.

Ryan nods and moves casually out of the twilight towards the dance floor. Small sparky rectangles of light spin him over him as he crosses the space. Lila watches the exchange. Ryan's quiet enquiry. Hair man pretending to barter, then the flash of a hand, another in return, and Ryan sauntering back to the hinterland near the door.

A few minutes later and the man is back at the bar. He is nervy, his eyes intense. 'Hi,' he says to Lila, 'hi.'

'Same again?' she says.

'No,' he says, 'you're OK.' Then, 'What time do you get off?'

She makes a play of looking at her phone. 'Couple of hours. Ages yet.'

'Fancy going somewhere after? Like, mine?'

Like, no fucking way, she thinks, but you can't say that kind of thing here and keep your job and she needs the job to get her through uni because her parents do their best but it's never enough. So, she wears a skin-tight t-shirt, flicks her hair and smiles. And puts up with whatever comes her way.

'No, you're OK,' she echoes him, and the mean eyes narrow. They're blue, she can see now that he's so close under the bar light. Lenses. Sapphire, like the ink her grandma uses to write to her from Katowice, long loving letters in a language she has never been bothered to learn.

He takes out a BMW key fob, smacks it onto the bar like he is dealing an ace. 'You sure?' His voice has an edge. She takes a step back.

'Totally.' She puts her hands on her hips, stares him out.

'Bitch,' he says. 'Fucking tight-arsed bitch.'

She says nothing, keeps eye contact until he drops his gaze and walks away. Past Ryan, past the bouncers. Gone.

'That bloke—' she says to the bartender beside her. The girl makes a dickhead sign, hand curving from her forehead. Lila laughs. There's a camaraderie in this, she thinks, even as she's ogled and pawed and insulted. And at least she's not out in that storm.

Emma has been chatting at Besim for the whole of the Warwick Road. She tells him her name, her daughter's name, asks him questions about his family, whether he has a job aside from the Uber gig. It's what she always does with people who are serving her: shop assistants, café staff. Trying to connect. Her husband hates this trait in her. *What makes you think anyone would be interested in talking to you?*

Besim responds politely but monosyllabically. Perhaps his English isn't good, she thinks. Perhaps he just wishes I'd shut up. She lapses into silence when they reach Highgate Road, inclines her face to Flora's soft snowsuit. Her daughter smells of home, the washing powder her husband says he likes. Although the likes and dislikes change on a whim and there's retribution if she gets it wrong. She will wash everything, she thinks. All the stuff in the suitcase, the clothes they are wearing. She will wash their hair, scrub both their bodies with something strong-scented and calm.

They pull into the drop-off point at the station and Emma unbuckles the seatbelt. Her child is asleep, warm against her

'Thank you,' she says to Besim. 'Thank you so much.'

Besim makes no move to leave his seat, to open doors and boot. 'Where you go?' he asks. 'No trains now, not until morning.'

'I know,' she says.

'I take you to hotel?'

She points to the taxi rank beyond the drop off. 'I'm travelling on.'

He is clearly perplexed. 'Why not I take you?'

She inhales, exhales. Imagines herself stepping off a diving board, falling free. 'Because the Uber app would have given away where I'm going. And I couldn't risk that happening. So now I'll have to find another cab.'

He nods, half turns his head to her. 'It's OK, I take you. No app. This is my car. I can do as I wish.'

'Really? But I'm going north – Manchester. It'd be an awfully long way for you, all night probably.' Flora stirs, settles again. The baby moves too, as if synchronised. Emma looks outside, imagines the lash of the wind. 'But I do have cash.' She has been saving, tiny amounts, week after week after week.

'It's OK,' Besim says again. 'I take you.'

He swings back into the traffic, begins to negotiate out towards the motorway. 'I am engineer back home,' he says. 'Here, I drive. I have wife, four children, three girls and a boy. They are doing well. Thank you for asking. You are kind.'

Jade and Leon have an easy job, helping an elderly lady who has fallen. They check blood pressure, clean her small head wound. The patient's daughter is there, tearful. There is no getting better from being old and the daughter can see the end coming in her mother's prominent veins under fleshless skin, in her watering, yellow-lined eyes. The patient is grateful, apologises for wasting their time. She asks Leon where he is from but makes no comment when he says Perry Barr. The daughter pulls a face, embarrassed.

Back in the cab, they bicker amicably about who makes the best sandwiches. Leon has made today's. Jade says he will have used the wrong chutney. He favours a tomato one which Jade thinks has too many lumps. Leon is smoothing down the green cotton of his uniform trousers, watching Jade drive. They are off to another job, a student drunk and unconscious outside a Broad Street bar.

'Shit, this wind,' Jade says. 'Why would anyone choose to be out in it? It's bloody dangerous.'

'Students,' Leon says. 'Convinced they're invincible.' He pauses, looks away from her. 'Do you think', he asks casually, 'that we'll have a guard of honour when we get married? Like, all our mates lining the church path in uniform? Two lines of green?'

Jade's foot pushes hard on the accelerator and the ambulance jerks. 'Leon,' she says, 'was that just a proposal?'

'Suppose,' says Leon, and grins.

•

The unmarked police car has been waiting near the junction for twenty minutes. The two officers inside are waiting for Ryan Evans to leave the club where they suspect he has been dealing. They could nick him tonight if they wanted to, and they have wanted to for a long while, but he is only one link in a complicated chain. They are after a bigger catch. There is an apartment somewhere in Deritend where someone clever and, so far, evasive, is running an operation that needs to be stopped. The empty streets around them are ill-lit. If there were trees, they would be bent over, struggling, but there is no vegetation apart from feral buddleias that flower in the summer, shepherd's purse and groundsel in cracks between pavements and walls. Now, on a savage November night, even these green scraps have withered. There are only small-time workshops, and dereliction, and dark corners where nobody goes.

'That's Evans,' the younger policeman says. They pull out of the junction and drive slowly down the road.

'We'll go a bit further then leave the car,' the older man says. 'Easier to tail him on foot round here.'

The younger opens his mouth to respond and then, 'Jesus!'

A silver BMW has passed them at speed. They catch a glimpse of a youngish bloke, swept-back hair. As the car nears Ryan Evan's bulbous outline it brakes sharply and veers into the kerb. The police watch Evans jump sideways, turn round as if to confront. Then, he moves towards the car and leans into the opened passenger window. Passes something through.

'What's he doing?'

'That could be our man. The car's flash enough and Evans clearly knows him.'

They don't need to discuss it. Instinct and training ready them for a chase. Evans can wait, he'll be back on his small-time beat soon enough. Evans steps back again, hunches his shoulders and carries on down the road as the BMW accelerates away.

'Fuck me, he's fast,' the older man says, and they follow, the younger officer driving. The BMW cuts up a black cab on the Belgrave Interchange, jumps the lights on the Middleway. It takes Queensway like a racetrack and is doing eighty by the time it reaches the Aston Expressway. The officers have their blue lights on now, have radioed for back up.

'Bloke's fucking nuts,' the driver says, and they fly on towards the motorway.

Besim drives smoothly and easily. There is something reassuring about the steadiness of his hands on the wheel, the snapshot of his family stuck to the dashboard. No one truly knows anyone, Emma thinks, at least at first, but she can't imagine Besim shouting at the traffic or punching a door, or kicking his pregnant wife so hard his son is almost lost. The Toyota cruises along the Aston Expressway and Emma begins to drift. Flora is a comfort, warm and furry like a living cuddly toy close against her. Emma has no idea what the future will hold. Whether her husband will root her out. Whether she will thrive on her own or be forced back to the bleak, square house in Solihull with its too many locks on the doors, begging for forgiveness.

'When will we get there?' she asks.

'Two hours,' Besim says. 'You try to sleep.'

The BMW swerves lane to lane on the Expressway, overtaking a van on the outside by crossing onto the opposite carriageway, then veering back to the far inside lane. There is another police unit ahead, coming down from the Tyburn Road to cut the BMW off at the intersection, but for now it is a two-car race.

'Where the fuck's he going?' the police driver asks.

The BMW takes the furthest left lane, towards the M6 north. The police car screams on, closing the gap. The police driver's hands are rigid, his eyes unblinking in concentration. He mutters, 'fuck', over and over, like a mantra. There is a lorry ahead, a grey Toyota behind it. The BMW speeds up, has just come alongside the Toyota when a maverick twist in the gale gusts the lorry sideways, pushing it into the path of the BMW. The BMW spins, flips. The Toyota skids, skews left. *Fuck*. The police car brakes hard, rear end sliding, sideways, backwards, whips forward. And ahead, bulky shapes motionless in the shadows. Dark until flares of yellow and orange-red explode into the night.

Jade and Leon are almost on Broad Street when the call to divert comes through. An RTA, multiple vehicles, one on fire. Junction 6 of the M6. The intersection.

Leon is driving now. Jade looks out of the window, eating her sandwich, and forgets that the chutney is wrong. They have stopped talking, as if they need to save their breath for the hours to come, as if their warm, silent cab is the only safe place tonight; a temporary refuge before they must face whatever devastation lies ahead and surrender themselves to the night, and the storm.

Tipping Point

BEN WADDINGTON

Midnight mattress removal may sound like a dismal, character-sapping military exercise, but for the eager trio of Utter Clutter, there is great cathartic value. After a week's domestic downsizing, thoughtful interior revisions and bountiful removals from addresses across Birmingham, the rest of the city appears as a grotesque problem for us to solve. And how those damp, dumped mattresses graze our tender hearts: ugly, stained sponges slotted by night into the city's alleys, parks and brooks. There they breed, for each nocturnal deposit permits another neighbour to transgress the community rules. We usually find time to throw a mattress or two in the back of the van after a job, or – if utterly exhausted – log them for later collection. Decluttering is good business, but the fizzy glow that comes from these purges is the real reward, and even became our motto: 'giving back by taking away' (I thought of that). How curious to be in a team that relishes this unlikely work… at last: people like me!

Tonight, we followed a mighty garden bonfire in Shard End with a nocturnal sweep of our mapped mattresses. Some have disappeared by the time we arrive, others have multiplied, joined by even more junk. Usually two will do, by unvoiced agreement, but sometimes there's an itch to keep going: a mad drive to tidy up the universe. It is *only* mattresses that we take, for their sheer ugliness and the unlikeliness that they will ever move otherwise. However, tonight – this morning – we are still active well past midnight amongst the city's alleys and hedges. Each time I see Steppa quietly consult her funny little Hello Kitty notebook, I think it will surely be the night's last task, then Reece can drop us all off at home. She curtly announces an address and Reece jokes: 'One more for the road!' It is his tacit request to wrap up. He navigates the dense corrugation of streets through Fordbridge to arrive at Hatchford Brook, where we rescue a bloated, floral offender from a popular tipping spot. Hauling it across the grass feels like we've discovered a drowning. With none of us exhibiting any signs of the usual fizz, I sense Steppa is now surely done. My mind is full of my own dry, soft, clean mattress, patiently awaiting across the city… perhaps now even mildly worried. She pats her pockets, like when Reece looks for his cigarettes, but it turns out she is looking for the map book. We squash the mattress into the back of the van and set off to the next address. It is on the other side of the city, which at least allows us to rest on the dark, silent drive. I note with hope that it is on the way, more or less, back to Steppa's home.

Thirty minutes later, with the van's headlights illuminating a path, I pick my way through damp grass to the brook. It's all rather beautiful: full rural blackness, a starry sky with a thin but unhelpful moon high above the trees, and my long shadow reaching out towards Steppa. She has already eased her slight frame beneath the doubled mattress; a hesitant, queen-sized ghost navigating the treacherous riverbank. It is not a one-person job.

I spot a vacuum cleaner, parked upright just inside the treeline. I free it from the undergrowth and brightly offer it to Steppa, handle first, as a more manageable alternative. She reaches me at the bank's crest, her breaths belaboured from the effort. I smile through the absurd situation and let the vacuum voice my offer.

After a moment of silent face-off, she heads back towards the van where Reece is compacting our collection of damp mattresses. I'm reluctant to impose unwanted help on Steppa but feel the chill of her distance. I think she is trying to *mattress* her way back to a clarity that remains out of reach. Turning away, I shine my pocket torch towards the brook, which reveals a scree of shattered tiles, spilling from an upturned bucket. I visualise myself rescuing them all over an hour, washing the mud off each piece in the water before popping it back in the bucket, then at leisure jigsawing the pieces back together, in order to better understand the culprit. An unrealistic task tonight, and a flawed investigative method, but for a minute it is a calming exercise. I no longer feel the same unyielding rage at the casual betrayal of the environment that these shards represent, but just a few weeks ago, Reece and I would find addressed mail and other identifying clues amongst the dumped dregs and boldly return them. We'd feel like Holmes and Watson but I doubt we really solved anything.

So, the mosaic stays, but this pink vac, with its already neatly coiled flex, can come. I push it carefully through the dark grass, hoping that Reece can see my comic efforts from the van.

'Clean up guys,' I announce to myself.

It's hard to upstage Steppa's dark comedy, however; valiantly lurching across the wet meadow, her small body doubled almost to the ground, tortoising forward. I signal with raised hands towards the glare of the headlamps: 'come and help'. The twin lights flip to full beam and Steppa's monstrous form sends a dramatic shadow back towards the brook. I leave the vacuum cleaner standing where it is and catch up with Steppa, clasping a plastic handle at the mattress' trailing edge. Reece arrives; a glowing red tip pitches into the darkness. Within a few wordless seconds, we arrange ourselves around the soggy oblong and convey it back to the van. There, the mattress requires a half-fold to slot into the available space, along with two striped singles, the floral double and a partially burnt king size. In the light, I see that Steppa's clothes have absorbed the water, her crisp white cuffs and collar soaked beneath her black woollen sweater. Her beloved Hunter boots are now caked in mud. A willow leaf sticks to the back of one hand, looking like a cut. I don't voice my distress at her discomfort but instead gently try to bring the night to a close – the first time I've tried that.

'I'll go back for the vacuum cleaner and I'd say we're good for the night,' I suggest, while Steppa ponders her little cartoon cat book, so at odds with the rest of her aesthetic.

'Always room for a vacuum,' Reece cracks and I laugh to acknowledge his support in concluding the team's efforts. But Steppa counters:

'No, leave it.'

'Just toss it back into the Cole?' I'm not usually so abrupt with her.

Steppa meets my gaze, while Reece clarifies unhelpfully: 'That's the Peterbrook.'

'We can't rescue everything. But let's find one more mattress?'

I agree to leave the vacuum where it is, a pang in abandoning it so quickly. We respect Steppa's gentle plea, while certain that what is playing out on the surface has deeper undercurrents. Reece's trick is to laugh it off, and perhaps Steppa prefers that. Meanwhile, the eastern sky is becoming light as we set out for the night's final coordinates. Reece has produced a white bath towel, somehow warmed by the engine, which now cocoons Steppa in the passenger seat, where she's calmly contemplating the footwell. Later, the towel tells me that this has all happened before.

Aha, Dark Lane, I know where we are now. Crabmill Lane, Baccabox Lane. The Peacock Inn. A spectral dog legend associated with this little bridge. As a teen, I learned to drive in these rural lanes; the city so quickly unbirminghamed. Reece knows all the roads and streams here, old names not on the map, and has been tracing a network of footpaths. I once lived nearby, but to me his pathways move through unfamiliar terrain. He brings the van to a stop at a T-junction, attentive even at 4am.

The spot feels remote but a fish finger glow to the north points to Hawksley beyond the trees. Walking with Reece here last week, we spotted a pinstriped mattress damming a barely-flowing runnel. It had been dragged some distance from the nearest road, like someone hiding a body.

A sharp left from the grassy triangle and the headlamps reveal a small van parked in the narrow lane, as good as blocking it. Reece indicates sarcastically, cautiously passing the little van and I can see it is full of stuff. Up ahead, the beams pick out a figure in the road; a bobbing, reflective figure 8 suggests he may a dawn runner. He sees us and U-turns cartoonishly, arms pistoning as he scampers. Reece voices a quiet word that I don't catch and accelerates; Steppa too quickly awakes. Her hand leaves the cosy cocoon, ready for a seatbelt release. I feel a flash of something; not anger, but sharp and familiar enough to signal trouble. We have rashly connected the appearance of last week's mattress with tonight's distressed jogger / van driver. It is bad detective work, but we have to act quickly. Closing in, we see that despite the sports gear, 8 is no athlete. The brambles rising at each side of the lane prevent him from sidestepping an escape. We draw parallel and the window descends next to me, at Reece's direction. These days, I avoid confrontation, but manage to channel an indignation on the brook's behalf.

'Why do you drop them in the water?' I ask, my voice calm. 'I have often wondered. All that extra effort for you'. There is a real anguish in his dish-shaped face. I don't get my answer, but it's an earnest question. He peers wide-eyed round the van's interior, then ducks down and slogs back in his original direction. I want to give chase and gesture to Reece with a rotating index finger but can see there isn't the space to turn. Reece instead yanks at the gearstick and briskly reverses, navigating with his side mirror. An acid squeeze of adrenaline as I anticipate a thud.

Reece brings the van to a brisk halt, then jumps out. Steppa follows quickly, shedding her huge towel mantle. I sense the van is rolling slowly backwards and I reach awkwardly over the middle seat and apply the handbrake. I sit for a moment, needing to slow down the raw response. A glimpse in the dark side mirror reveals nothing, while at the end of the road ahead is the first glow of Saturday morning. I lean over to close the driver-side door, then get out myself. At first I don't see anyone in the red glow behind the van, but it is quickly apparent what has happened. Amid the roadside briars is 8, who has improvised an off-road escape route. Steppa has hold of an ankle to hamper his progress, while Reece stamps down brambles to secure a better grip. Sounds are exchanged that don't register with me as words.

For a moment it seems 8 has the advantage, recklessly thrashing at the brambles, but Steppa drags him back with decisive strength, allowing Reece to make connect. How can I help here, while avoiding contact and complicity? Without any clear plan, I open the back doors, to reveal the assembly of mattresses inside. I am simply repeating the evening's earlier movements, I decide later, an action without a motive. Steppa and Reece understand their next move, and 8 is bundled into the back along with the other clutter. His vocal protest is muffled by the doors slamming shut, and I am already back in the passenger seat. Unexpectedly, Reece takes the middle seat while Steppa slips behind the wheel and we set off, too fast for the narrow lane. I join them in a triumphant cackle that I certainly don't feel.

I have to hold in a breath to calm down. I instinctively reach for my seatbelt and find it is already in place. Reece directs a sharp right turn and Steppa flicks on the indicator; a gesture at odds with the unfolding scene. She turns to me across a celebratory Reece with a wild grin. I think: I don't often see your teeth. She palms a tattoo on the steering wheel.

'A left here, then there's a quick right back onto Dark Lane,' Reece instructs, like he has this planned. Steppa takes the bend at speed and I hear movement in the back, feeling the heavy, flopping foam blocks and hearing a muted voice. Another instruction from Reece is followed by an incautious swerve, and somewhere behind us, the abrupt sound of knocked-out breath. Then a right turn seemingly at Steppa's whim, and we drop off-road into an open field, with early rooks scattering. She now has the space and freedom to weave and donut at will, to Reece's obvious glee. When I think back, I'm certain I echo their sounds but also those confused squeals coming from the back, as 8 flops between the damp, reeking mattresses. I can see from the goalposts that Steppa is navigating around that we are on a recreational ground, and our caper finally settles with Steppa describing a giant infinity loop near the centre of the field, elegantly maximising the chaos in the back. The regular movement is oddly comforting and the rush softens. Steppa slows at a gentle gesture from Reece and we come to a soft halt at the loop's cross point.

'What a mess!' I say, looking across the cultivated turf, a catchphrase we often say to each other at work. I don't recall any further exchange, indeed it all feels like peak psychic teamwork. I think back often to this mad drive and nothing quite like it happens again. I am sure it served as my unplanned and successful initiation into team Utter Clutter.

After a moment's silence, the next move comes from 8 when he realises he can free himself by the back door. Ludicrously, I consider offering him a lift or at least suggesting some directions back to the brook, but we simple allow him to disappear. When I'm sure he's gone, I get out to survey the van, now up to its knees in mud, panels sprayed with dirt, grass and grit. The football pitch is a disaster. I see that Reece has secured the loose petrol cap with duct tape, which I feel is a rather ugly solution.

Returning via Dark Lane, we see that the parked van has gone, but so too has the final mattress we came for. A few days later, while refuelling, I think back to that first encounter with 8 and wonder if he was indeed ever the phantom dumper. Another story unfolds as I refill over many minutes, in which 8 is simply a dawn retriever like ourselves, panicking when – as chance would have it – a gang arrives ready to dump the mother lode of all mattresses.

Nightshift: in Search of Bearwood's Ghosts

LYNNE VOYCE

The purr of my dad's *250 Honda Super Dream,* as it pulled up after a night shift, is a hallmark of my childhood. *Nights*: a topsy-turvy working-class world of hallowed daytime silence: no toilet flushing, no having friends round, no letting the insurance agent or milkman knock for payment. It was a silence as balanced as a spirit level; a creak of the stairs or a burst of canned laughter on the TV could unsettle the whole equilibrium. Between 2pm and 10pm – when Dad left for the factory – our little red brick council house was cast on a millpond sea.

For a lot of us on the estate, there was no day or night when it came to work. People's mums and dads weren't there to wake them up with a wholesome breakfast, nor were they there after school, ready to put dinner on the table and facilitate family conversation. My own mother would be cleaning The Tea Pot Café until nine p.m., tidying up after others before she could come home and eat herself. There would be a *plate* left for us in the fridge to be eaten at five sharp. You might think, then, that night itself held little more fascination than a marker of light and dark; in some ways that is true, but there was one thing that made night different. It was when the spirits came out.

I hail from a mother whose 'psychic powers' were unquestioned. If she had a *'strange feeling'* at twilight, you would fully expect *'bad news'* the next day. It always came. And my paternal grandmother

– who lived with us during my adolescence – had spent her own childhood in a superstition-soaked rag and bone yard in Digbeth. They'd turned mirrors to the wall during a storm, *'so as not to let the devil in,'* and used salt for so many other things than cooking that forever after Nan kept a drum of it in her handbag – just in case. And she shared her arcane education without hesitation: tea leaf reading; palmistry; telling fortunes from wedding rings.

In my childhood, the notion of the supernatural was as accepted as an egg being boiled for five minutes, or that Friday night dinner should always be fish and chips.

So, when I moved to Bearwood, almost twenty-five years ago, it was only natural I sought out its more esoteric aspects, particularly tales of its ghosts. Afterall, a district's ghost stories embody everything you need to know about a place. To exist in the present, they must have been told over and over, kept in mind, passed down, preserved. And while this word of mouth is becoming ever less essential in these times of the internet – when the folklore of a region is detailed in a hundred blogs or podcasts - it is still true that a place's ghosts is a representation of its collective consciousness.

Early on, it became clear that there are two main locations for Bearwood hauntings: Warley Woods and the former Smethwick Swimming Baths. I had been content reading other's accounts of these ghostly goings on for a long time, but that changed with the writing of this piece. It was time to put in a night shift.

Like fitting gearboxes into Bedford vans – as my dad did – ghost-hunting is a night-time pursuit. Although, in some respects, the city doesn't have a true night anymore, with its light pollution, streetlamps that merely dim in the early hours and shops that never close. You can't get lost in the dark folds of the small hours around here, like you can in Ullswater or Kielder. Still, for the purposes of ghost hunting, I chose to begin my mission at 12:30am, a few minutes after the last 48 bus trundles up Lightwood's Hill.

In contemporary Bearwood, *The Woods* occupy the brow of Lightwoods Hill on one side and the breath-robbingly steep Abbey Road on the other, although the grounds of Samuel Galton's Warley Abbey – designed by the illustrious Humphrey Repton in the late eighteenth century – once spread much further. Following the perimeter of the woods, I entered through the west gate. This elevated part of the park is where The Abbey once stood, a name honouring its gothic edifice, rather than any religious purpose. In 1902, what was left of the grounds had been brought into public hands, and in 1906, the remaining woodland and the generous sweep of the meadow was opened as 'The People's Park'. At that time, the *big house* was still standing but in true gothic fashion, it burned down in 1957. Legend has it that a ghost was left behind.

Within minutes of me walking along the tarmac path, it was pitch dark, the beam of my torch the only light, a distant hoot of an owl and the scuttling of nocturnal animals amongst the shrubbery the only sound. There was a familiar eeriness, a feeling of being close to trees at night, a timeless, bursting stillness. Tentatively, I brushed my torch along the darkness, hoping to see the pearl grey outline of a spectre: The Grey Lady.

From the first sighting in 1822, The Grey Lady has been an enigma, with no single identity attached to her. This chronology – that the sightings pre-existed a story – suggests that the identity of the apparition has as much to do with the witness as the phantom itself. So, just like choosing a book from a shelf, being drawn to the colour of the spine, the cover, the blurb, I have chosen the story that most suits *me*. She is a forlorn wife, wandering the paths of the Abbey's grounds, waiting for her husband to return from war. I like to think that she was reunited with her love while still flesh and blood, and it is just the moment of her extreme distress that has been captured on the fabric of time.

Alas, on that dark night in the woods, I saw nothing supernatural. Returning home, not disappointed, but a little pensive, wondering not at the plausibility of those who have seen The Grey Lady, but at what I may have missed, what we all may have missed over the centuries, because we look through unseeing eyes. Perhaps she had been there all along. And that is what is so fascinating about The Grey Lady of Warley Woods: her amorphous, ambiguous quality, still waiting to be solidified into a finished ghost story after two hundred years.

The other most prolific ghost site in Bearwood is more specific in its spectres. Smethwick Swimming Centre has been subject to countless paranormal investigations, often with a scientific bent. Now abandoned after the construction of the Sandwell Aquatics Centre for the 2022 Commonwealth Games, the building is left empty – and listed.

I chose the auspicious date of November 19th to visit, the date in 1962 when The Beatles performed there. In the street-lit twilight, the marble-white frontage looks as elegant as ever, Noel Cowardesque in its Art Deco splendour among a crowd of terraces and flats. Designed by Chester Button and Roland Fletcher, it opened as Thimblemill Baths in 1933. Inside, as I well remember, having spent every Sunday morning swimming there with my children, was inspired by the high arched roofs of French aircraft hangers. The less impressive subterranean cellars and corridors have a history of their own too. As well as being used as air raid shelters during World War Two, they acted as a temporary morgue, housing the casualties of Luftwaffe bombing. This might account for the spectral woman seen in the ladies' toilets wearing an RAF uniform.

A metal fence cordons it off from the road now, flimsy enough to be a mere signal rather than a real deterrent to anyone with half a mind to break in. It seems a shame, but of course, this place had replaced other things in its turn. During the building of the baths a plague pit was discovered and left in situ about ten feet below what was once the bath's reception. It is said that the rather incongruous ghost of a boy covered in white powder is connected to this, as plague victims' bodies were covered in lime powder to stop the spread of infection. Indeed, so many ghostly sightings have been reported here that it has been dubbed one of the most haunted locations in England.

To my chagrin, there was nothing spooky about the place on that warm November night. In fact, it was somewhat comforting to come back, remembering those Sunday mornings when my children walked up to the plate glass and wood front door, with their rolled towels and their goggles swinging in their hands.

I walked home with a feeling of belonging, hoping that when my own children return to this place – Bearwood – the ghost stories that have been the distant soundtrack of my time here, will be as alive as they are now. Because urban ghosts are more essential than rural ones. The regular changing of the landscape and the swiftly shifting demographic of a city can leave it rootless and empty of memory, but a ghost can fill that space. And in so many ways, they have for me. Bearwood – my home – is more than people moving in and out, or the opening and closing of shops on the High Street, or the decommissioning of a place as important as the baths.

On my return, I poured a nightcap and sat in the warm cocoon of my living room, reminiscing about my mission. I might have never worked a true night shift in my life, but at least I knew then, what night is for: it's for the ghosts, or at least the hope of them.

All Still Here

CHERYL POWELL

It's been more than a lifetime, hasn't it? And you're shocked at the state of the town, though you'll remember the great storm, of course. How lucky you were to get out so quickly. Most of us perished in the flood. But then, you already know that.

Anyway, let's not dwell on the past. The deceased get on with things, best they can. We're a stoic lot here in Droitwich Spa. Ah, I see you're heading for the Old Cock Inn; Thursday steak night. You're looking through the broken windows, hoping to see your old mates, suddenly anxious at the dark air and sluggish water, the perfume of decay. But, close your eyes, tune in, pick up the vibration. Yes, the dead are all around. Listen to their voices. Can you hear laughter? The plink of bottles and the tick-tick, gallop of the fruit machine? And now you see Jerry and Pete and Nick at the dartboard, their shadow-selves moving, pint mugs lifting, spilling amber. Oh, ignore their threats; they're good lads. Got loads to safety in a single dingy. Heroes, really.

Anyway, let's move on. Follow me down the upended shopping centre. Look! There are ducks in the precinct, a forest of willow saplings in the old M&Co store, and the Muffin Break's glass rotunda brims with dogfish. But hush. Be still, for it is darkest night. At Morrisons it's the dead hour, time for the unbodied of a nervous disposition to get their shopping done. Aida Jones will be there, forever stocking up on pepperoni pizza for the kids' tea, and no doubt old Mr Matthews will be in aisle four with his ever hopeful bunch of roses. They might be wary of you at first, but they'll come round.

Let's wade through the crooked high street and visit Lymers butcher, long boarded up, buddleia bursting through cracks. The door stands ajar, the old man still there, stamped like an aproned watermark behind his counter, eternally carving that slice of ham you never went back for. Ah, well.

You look crestfallen. Come, we'll visit the park. Here, gaze upwards! The sky is a net of stars, our broken planet continues to spin, and we still have each other. Do you see the gauzy shapes of Gill and Sue, strolling over Corbett bridge as they do every night, their matching spaniels whiffling in the grey mist. The ladies are stopping to stare at you, working silent mouths, and you look alarmed. Don't be. They don't hold a grudge.

Now, we're at the lido. Derelict I'm afraid, its water green and glutinous. But the late-night swimmers are always here, like cellophane cut-outs, measuring out their widths and lengths, gasping and giggling at the first shock of cold on their once-living flesh. They won't be rude; they don't even know you.

See, here, beneath the swag of ivy, Little Al's café is folding itself away for the night, the manager, translucent in the moonlight, sweeping and putting up chairs on another long day. Oh, yes, we're all still here.

Slow down. Morning is coming. You have splashed through the leaning tombstones of St Peter's church, up past the lichen-clothed water tower and the fire-stormed housing estate. Far off, you hear the clatter of ethereal ladders as the window cleaner starts his round, the babble and jeer of long-dead schoolchildren, who wait for the bus.

The night is done, my eternal postal round about to start. We've stopped at a dilapidated house, pretty once, its roses gone wild, dark-eyed windows. You pause, looking it over, rifling through a thousand memories, and I have to turn away. Grief, alas, never gets any easier, even for the dead.

Slug

ESME BROWN

The sky looks calmer than anything she's seen in weeks, low vague clouds, the heavy stillness of early evening. She crouches, shivering in her dressing gown, the ember tip of her cigarette is all that holds her hands out of gloom. The porchlight hasn't worked since April. Around her the bustle and calls of families carry, with curry and gravy smells, from the warmly lit windows of Metchley Grange's boxy estate buildings. She dangles the cigarette from her lips and crosses her arms at her chest, tucking her cold fingers between the flattened fluff of her dressing-gown and her shoulders. She smokes her cigarette to the filter before standing to squash it against the brick by her door. Its blackened circle joins a pattern of many. She puts the squashed end in her dressing gown pocket. The flat, a maisonette, is quiet now, although something of the smashing and screams is still ringing in the air. She turns for one last look at the darkening sky, the tower blocks grand and removed across the way – their neat, bright windows – before unlocking the door and walking in.

She stands for a moment in the dark of the hallway. All the lights are off, she doesn't dare turn them on. Her shoes have been knocked from the rack by the door, she nearly trips on them, but catches herself, swearing under her breath.

The odour of the bin wafts in from the kitchen where one of her old work shoes sits, sensibly laced, on the drying rack against the plates. She can taste milk on the air. A packet of flour she had bought last year, with the ambition of baking a birthday cake, has exploded on the countertop. The fridge door is hinged open, spilling yellowed light onto the lino where its contents have been scattered. There is a block of unpackaged cheese, gnawed on; a miraculously whole jar of jam; tomatoes splattered of their pipped guts; and an open carton forming a puddle of milk.

She feels, not for the first time, like she has opened the wrong front door, stumbled into someone else's life. It makes her think of the paper round she had as a young teenager, the letterboxes she had poked her fingers into, the glimpses of wide hallways and staircases as she lingered before letting the *Birmingham Mail* drop.

Her eyes are accustomed to the dark now. The top cupboard where she stores the knives is undisturbed. Shocks of white footprints wet the floor from the kitchen to the living room. The living room is pitch black, curtains drawn, but she can sense the shape of the sofa. The sounds of smacking lips. The smell of mould, of the night cold and the sweat of a tantrum. She moves carefully, shuffling along the wall and fumbling for the light switch, kicking at something gritty with her slippers. She shuts her eyes at first against the glare, the blood visible in her eyelids. Then there it all is: the TV smashed from its stand and him on the sofa, his pupils wide, last night's pizza box open on his lap. He watches her, alert, ready to lunge away. She considers screaming at him, bawling over the lost luxury of Coronation Street, pouncing at him with her teeth bared. She hasn't the energy. She pulls her dressing gown more closely about her and slumps on the sofa beside him, thankful only that she had kept her slippers on. She reaches for the pizza box and he flinches away.

'Pizza for Mummy.'

He frowns at her for a moment, that intensely serious furrow he can manage to fold his small brow into, his lips drawn in. She is gripped by an urge to pinch at the chub on his cheeks. Still frowning, he relinquishes and tears off a slice of pizza, handing it to her. She takes it and rams the cold grease of it gratefully into her mouth.

He makes strange sounds with the next mouthful which it takes her a while to recognise, 'Thank you.'

'Thank you.' She concedes, wiping her lips and nodding.

His socks are wet and the permanent lump on his forehead is pinker than ever. He was smashing his head against the floor when she had gone out for a smoke, bent over himself as though in prayer smashing his small skull repeatedly on the lino. He wiggles his toes, taking another large mouthful of pizza. He seems calmer now, if tentative and sore. He is muttering to himself as he chews, the pizza gunk white in his small mouth. He wags a greasy finger in the air.

'No, no, no, stop Jack, no climbing Jack, bad, bad, bad, stop Jack.' He is using his 'bad-Mummy voice,' the one he uses to relive their arguments, with the few words he knows and has processed. He stops suddenly, frowning, his eyes wide. 'No school, Jack.'

She swallows what she has in her mouth.

He was excluded from school three days ago.

She had been called in from work to sit in the headteacher's office and sweat in her coat, which was the smartest thing she was wearing so not coming off. There was something so immoveable about the stern lines of the headteacher's face. She had wondered if this is how all headteachers looked or whether this one just looked especially like her old one. She had felt sick with longing to slouch in her chair, to pick at the loose bits of wood on the desk and kick at the carpet with her work shoes. She was polite, tried to nod along, but there was an inevitability about it all, she knew exactly what was coming. The head had said Jack was a danger to staff and pupils. He is five. He'd been suspended a few times, in Nursery as well as Reception, but this time it was worse. He hadn't been 'transitioning well' into Year 1. He threw a heavy wooden doorstopper at a TA, she had to go to A & E to get stitches.

Every morning since, he has put his trainers and backpack on and waited by the door. He doesn't seem able to understand that he isn't going back to school. The headteacher explained that Jack isn't allowed to be seen in public spaces during school time, so she can't even take him to the park to run around, or she could be fined two-hundred-and-something pounds. This has been the hardest part of it all, keeping him indoors for most of the day, but she doesn't want to risk the fine, or breaking any more of their rules. Tomorrow, she has to take him to a specialist doctor, the school has booked it, part of the panel review of his case. She hasn't decided yet whether the two buses will be worth the money saved on a taxi. Jack has been kicked off buses before.

She sighs and takes another bite of pizza.

'Spongebob.' He whines reaching out a hand to where the TV used to be.

'No more TV.'

'Broken,' he says dropping his hand.

'Yes, you broke it didn't you?'

'Broken,' he says again scrunching his face up into a forced sadness.

Today, Jack had his usual meltdown at realising there was no school in the morning, and then had tried again in the evening to put his shoes and backpack on. She feels the same way about work, when she glimpses her uniform, hung neatly in the wardrobe. They laid her off because she had left them suddenly understaffed, but there was no one else to be at home with Jack.

They finish the pizza without talking. She looks around at the shattered glass on the floor.

'Time for a bath, Jack.' She announces as he wipes the last of the grease from his mouth.

He makes to dart from the sofa, but she grabs his wrist just in time and hauls him up. He likes being carried so wraps his legs around her instead of struggling. He smells of sour milk and pizza grease and something else, something soft and lovely.

In the bathroom, he takes his clothes off hurriedly, almost tripping over his trousers as he steps out of them. He will only wash if he gets to sit in the tub as it fills with water. He positions himself staring at the tap the way cats sometimes stare at mice. While he is distracted with the flowing water, flicking at it with his hands, she inspects the soft pads of his feet, which are ashen with dirt and flour. She scoops water over them and can see no cuts or splinters of glass. He will have picked the TV up and stood on the sofa to lob it at the ground. He watches her touch his feet as though she is completely incomprehensible, as though it were she who acted suddenly and without explanation. She is never quite sure if he is on to something when he looks at her like this. She suspects he has studied other adults, other parents, and decided there is something off, something wrong and unexpected about her.

The ceiling and shower curtain are speckled with black mould and the grout around the bath is stained yellow-brown like spilt tea. There is no extraction fan. A chill cuts through the room as soon as she has the window open. She hears the slippery sounds of Jack trying to climb out of the tub. She darts back to him, holding out an arm to bar his way. He has climbed the bathtub and sink to close the window before, and has fallen, chipping a tooth.

He is barely upright when her arm knocks him backwards, and his skull connects with the bath in a dull clink. She is so struck by the sound it feels as though it were her head making contact. He is sitting up and laughing, this strange gasping laugh he makes when he is hurt – mouth open, eyes wet and wide – at the shock of it, the strength of the sensation. He puts a hand to the back of his head and laughs again.

'Ow!' He moves his head from side to side and kicks the water about his feet, wetting the arms of her dressing gown as she leans in over him to inspect the wet hair at the back of his head. There is no blood. She lets out a sigh of relief and sits back watching him as his laughter stills and he turns to meet her gaze.

The sound of the water rushing into the bath, the chill of the autumn evening prickling his skin into goosebumps, steam wetting his eyelashes. His hair is dripping, his chest still heaving. They watch one another. She could cry. She wants to hold him, to wrap him up in herself, to be able to mutter reassurances the way she has seen other mums do in the park, when a child trips over itself and scrapes the skin on their knees, 'There, there.' There is something about the way she and Jack connect, it's a collision, it's a bumping of heads, a pinching of skin and knocking of bones. They trade in pain. She doesn't know how to be fluffy enough to soften the blows for him. She doesn't know how to do any of this. She wets his flannel in the warm water and wrings it out before putting it to his head. He doesn't take his eyes off her until a few droplets escape the flannel and leak into them. He squeezes his eyes shut so tightly his eyebrows move over his eyelids. She moves the flannel down to his cheeks.

When Jack's dad was still around, she had tried to get him to bath Jack, knowing this was when Jack was at his sleepiest, his sweetest, but his dad had never engaged in the wrestling it took to get Jack to wash, to eat, to not blunder out into the road, or climb the guttering outside the flat. He would just turn blankly away. She had always had to work for his attention too, pinch his arm, push his hair back from his face, bite his lip. That used to get her what she wanted. They would fuck and she could scratch up his back, bite his ear, or he would shove her away, snarl at her, so she could shove him back, scream.

Sometimes she thought she knew why Jack slammed his head against the walls, there is something undeniable, something certain about the physicality of a wall, the pain of coming up against it.

'He's not mine, he's yours,' Jack's dad had retorted when asked to spend more time with *his* son.

And she knew what he had meant. Jack is hers. Jack is something of her concentrated, something of her anger, her otherness. She is why Jack is how he is. That is why, when his headteacher called her into the office, there was talk of how things are at home, of social workers and setting boundaries. Of good examples.

Jack's breathing has slowed, the heat of the bath slackening the tension wound through his tiny, angry body. He raises his arms up for her to lift him, wet and steaming, from the bath. Her own tension sings out as she bends over to lift him, that familiar twinge in her lower back. She tries not to think of how quickly Jack is getting bigger, tries not to envision the fully grown man he might become. As she towels him down, he winces when she touches his head. She carries him to their bed. She kisses his head as she tucks him in, his eyes already sliding shut. The warmth is still on his skin, the caustic smell of soap. She leaves the lamp on for him.

She enters the kitchen out of habit, to make herself a tea, and is greeted by floury chaos. She considers heading straight for the living room and just sitting down for a moment, then remembers the TV. She gets a bin bag from the cupboard and scoops the milky clumps of flour up with her hands. She wipes the remaining glistening streaks away with an old towel, wringing it out in the sink. She returns the jar of jam to the fridge and puts everything else in the bin. She feels strangely sick after, she doesn't feel like tea at all. She heads to the living room to bag and sweep up the mess that used to be the TV.

She takes out the bins. It is deeply dark, there are very few lights on in the estate. Curtains are drawn across all the windows. The skin on her legs and arms prickle with goosebumps. The night feels like a closed door.

When she was younger she was invited to dinner at other flats in the estate. It felt safe, the chatter, the chewing and clatter of cutlery, so proper and ordinary, but there would be this feeling that she wasn't quite there – that she was still alone in her dad's flat with only the buzz of the TV, the mould, and that feeling of dark nothingness all around. She slept mostly in the day, when she could hear her neighbours. Her bed was pushed against the wall, in half-sleep there was almost a conviction that if she pushed herself hard enough against it she might simply sink through.

There is a slug on the bathroom window. It curls itself into a small black ball as she picks it up, wet, mucus, cold. She puts it on an old toothpaste box and carries it to the door, then falters, unsure of herself. They're pests, like rats and pigeons, slugs. So maybe she shouldn't take it outside? She could put it in the bin, but she doesn't like the thought of it slimy and alive in there, being steadily buried by food waste and plastic wrap.

She is too tired to make this decision. She rests her back against the landing wall, lets her legs give way, puts the box with the slug, still curled into a ball, at her feet and turns on her phone. She googles *what to do with slugs*. The results are all ads or reviews of pesticides. She googles *what to do when my 5 year old has been expelled*, she googles *specialist doctor for expulsion panel*. She scrolls mummy support blogs where women talk about their children who have been given acronyms to explain their behaviour ADHD, ASD, ADD, GDD. The sleeves of her dressing gown are still damp.

The slug extends its antennae in the dark, undulates its soft body over the cardboard. It works its way onto the floor. She reaches out her cold foot, places it carefully over the slug, and presses down. The wet of it shocking at first. The resistance of skin, some tightly balled ache that is living, gives. A strange exhalation falls from her lips, like laughter, like relief. She wipes her foot with the bottom of her dressing gown and carries the slug's remains to the bin. It feels good having made the decision. She puts her dressing gown and underwear into the machine. The light from the hallway lifts her reflection, her scooped, tired body from the windowpane, a yellow apparition in the dark blues of the estate.

She showers with the window open. The tingling of numb toes returning to feeling. Breathing in the steam and night cold, the rotten smell of the rear of the flats where someone dumped a mattress a few years ago. She wonders how it would feel to be washed by your mother, to have someone bend over you and run a flannel over your face, your shoulders.

She dries and tugs on a tracksuit before getting into bed with Jack, the lamp still on. His eyes slip open just a crack, as the mattress shifts to accommodate her weight. He puts a leg over her, moves his small hand to stroke across her bare shoulder. His touch has the same softening mercy it did when he was a baby. His eyes are already closed again, his breath on her cheek. She closes her eyes. Only the foxes are there to see it, but from the dark of the street outside, the pair are visible from the window, the picture of love and ease.

Under Fire

NIGEL PROCTOR

Reg Miles ran. Ran through a world of black and orange. A world either burning or burnt. His chest hurt each time a boot struck the pavement, hobnails flinting on the stone, sparks swallowed by the maelstrom. With each stride, his Auxiliary Fire Service axe swung out from his belt and slapped back against his thigh.

Thumping his chest with a fist, he coughed and breathed in through his mouth. Tasted smoke and brick dust. Smelt scorched paint and smouldering timber.

He spat grit.

Coughed again.

Ran on.

Let them be safe, dear God, let them be alright. I don't ever ask for much, Lord, but I am asking for this.

Earlier, deep in the fire and dark, no thoughts, just instinct, he dug with his axe, his gloved hands wrapped tight around its rubber grip. Sixty crews, he reckoned, they were at least sixty crews strong now – some pumping water, tamping flames, others diving deep into the rubble, hoping to find survivors, expecting the worst.

Sixty crews, all getting nowhere. And he was separated from his. Working on his own. Schoolboy error. But this was his patch, his backyard.

And then.

'Over here,' Reg shouted to no one in particular. 'There's someone here.'

A voice shouted back: 'Who?'

'Does it matter?'

Reg recognised the voice and then the face: Arthur Shaw – Artie to his mates, styled after some American bandmaster – a man he knew to nod at, not a close friend. But any man was the right man to be here right now. And there was another man behind him, unknown to Reg but a useful pair of hands, no doubt.

'Come on, Arthur Shaw, give us a help here.'

'OK, Reggie,' Shaw said. 'What needs doing?'

Reggie.

No one called him Reggie – no one but Agnes.

'That. Can you hear that?'

'Hear what?'

'That,' Reg said, raising a hand and pointing.

A distant sound. A circular keening – rising, falling, repeating, shouting.

'There's someone in there,' Shaw said.

'There is.'

Reg bent down like a rugby prop forward going in for the ruck and scrabbled away at broken masonry.

The bombs had hit just before 11pm, falling onto the south side of the New Building. Nobody was sure how many bombs – nobody cared, not right now, the details could wait for later – but what they were sure of was the devastation: the broken concrete, the twisted steelwork, the incandescent flames, the black smoke rolling up and out of the impact crater, as if the explosion had opened a gateway to Hell.

And the people.

The crying, screaming, pleading people, shambling through

the murk, like so many shades walking the earth, not knowing where they were, not knowing they were already dead.

There was an explosion nearby and then another. The third man clambered down the rubble and slid in next to Reg and Shaw. He glanced up at the sky.

Reg smiled at him. 'Don't worry,' he said, 'that ain't the Jerries this time, that's just some of our stuff going up.'

The man looked puzzled. 'Our stuff?'

'Ammunition,' Reg said. 'They don't call us the Birmingham Small Arms Company for nothing, you know?'

Working away, the three men widened the gap in the fallen masonry. As if on cue, the keening stopped.

'Right,' Reg said, 'it's stable for the moment, let's see what we're dealing with.'

Unclipping his AFS lamp from his belt, Reg flicked open the blackout hood and rotated the on-switch. A faint yellow gleam lit up the rubble. He shoved the torch into the hole and pushed his head in as far in as he was able.

'Hello?'

'Hello.' A weak voice, a woman's voice, a young woman's voice.

'We're here,' Reg said. 'And we'll get you out. Is it just you in there?'

'No,' the girl said. 'Mrs Charles is here too but she's out cold. At least I think she's out cold. I don't know. I can't really see. She's breathing though. A bit ragged, it is. A bit of a snorer, actually.'

'Hold on,' Reg said. 'Just hold on. What's your name, bab?'

'Maureen,' the voice said. 'Maureen Unwin.'

'Well, you hang on in there, Maureen Unwin and we'll soon have you both out. You and Mrs Charles and you won't have to put up with her snoring no more. I'm Mr Miles, by the way.'

'Thank you, Mr Miles.'

Reg turned to face the other men, dropped his voice. 'It's not good,' he said, 'not good at all. The two of them are right at the back, behind a concrete lintel. The lintel, it's fallen across in a diagonal and is holding up a ton of bricks. One wrong move, it's all going to come down.'

'What you want to do, Reggie?'

'Someone's got to go in there and dig under it. It's the only way we're going to get them out.'

'You sure?'

'I'm sure,' Reg said, pulling off his jacket and rolling up his sleeves.

'You can't go in there,' the third man said, 'it's far too dangerous.'

'He's right, Reggie,' Arthur Shaw said. 'I mean look at the size of you. If anyone's going to bring that down, you are.'

'Like I say, someone's got to,' Reg said.

Arthur Shaw smiled. 'If you're crazy enough to go in there, we're definitely going to need a bigger hole.'

As soon as the gap was large enough, Reg bent double and waddled forward, lamp held out in front of him. He peered into the gloom. It was dustier now, particulates falling down from the roof like malevolent snow. It could only mean one thing: movement up top. And movement up top threatened further collapse.

And then there was the heat.

He couldn't see any flames but he could sense the fire was there – watching, waiting, biding its time. Reg would have to move fast, he'd known that all along but now he knew he'd have to work double-quick.

He could see the girl through a gap in the rubble. She had her knees up to her chest, her eyes closed. And he could hear the other woman, her breath heavy, rasping, uneven, fading.

'Maureen?'

The girl opened her eyes. 'Mr Miles?'

'I'm here.'

Reg looked back over his shoulder. 'Arthur Shaw?'

Shaw's face appeared in the gap. 'Yes?'

'You better get in here.'

'Me?'

'You.'

Reg went down onto his front and crawled forward until he was level with the lintel. Using his axe, he scraped away at the ground, pushing debris under and behind him. Inching forward, he coughed. The falling dust was thicker now and it wasn't just dust.

Smoke.

The hole was filling with smoke.

And it was hotter, too.

Much hotter.

The flames weren't far away.

'You alright in there?'

Reg glanced back. A voice he recognised. 'Who's that?'

'Ned. Ned Lucas. Is that you, Reg?'

'There's two women trapped in here,' Reg said. 'And there's a fire burning somewhere alongside us.'

'Understand. We're running a hose now,' Lucas said, 'water pressure's a bit down but let's see what we can do to get that fire out.'

'Ta,' Reg said, pulling aside a piece of masonry and pushing himself forward. 'Maureen, you still with me?'

The girl coughed. ' 'course I am, Mr Miles, where'd you think I'd be?'

Reg smiled at her tone, at her cheek. 'Good girl. How's Mrs Charles doing?'

'Not good. I can't hear her no more. I can't hear her, Mr Miles.'

'You hang on, Maureen,' Reg said, 'I'm almost with you.'

Reg reached forward and pulling with his hands and pushing with his feet, wriggled into the shallow dip beneath the lintel. It was a proper squeeze but with a deep breath and one final shove of his boots, Reg came up and out the other side.

Maureen Unwin watched as a dirt blackened and smoke shrouded shape appeared from the hole. 'Maureen?' the figure said.

'Mr Miles?'

'That's me.'

Reg looked around. He saw a pair of legs – one foot wearing a shoe, the other not – sticking out from behind a fall of bricks.

'Mrs Charles?'

Maureen nodded and Reg moved towards the older woman. But as he crawled closer, even in the gloom, he could see she was dead. Her eyes were open and staring, her jaw gaping, a loose denture on her lower lip. An iron rod pierced her left side and the ground beneath her was a blood-thickened shadow.

He pushed himself backwards towards Maureen.

'Is she dead?'

'She is.'

The girl gulped and dry sobbed.

'Now come on, Maureen,' Reg said, reaching out, patting a shoulder. 'Let's get you out of here.'

At the lintel, the girl looked down at the crawl space and shuddered. 'I can't go under there, I can't,' she said. 'It's tiny.'

The smoke was thicker now, the air hotter.

'I got through, didn't I? And look at me,' Reg said.

The girl nodded. 'You did.'

'And if I did…'

'I can.'

'That's right. Ned? You there?'

A face appeared in the gap above the beam: Ned Lucas. 'What can I do, Reg?'

'Ned, this is Maureen, Maureen, Mr Lucas.'

'Hello,' the girl said.

Lucas smiled. 'Alright.'

'He's going to help you through, aren't you, Mr Lucas?'

'I am, Mr Miles.'

'All you've got to do, Maureen, is lie down and crawl forward a bit. I'll be here pushing and Mr Lucas over there will grab your hands and pull. Easy. Alright?'

Maureen bit her lip and looked unconvinced. 'You say so.'

'I do,' Reg said.

'Can I close my eyes?'

'Best not,' Reg said.

The girl lay on her front and started to move forward into the gap under the lintel. Reg crouched over her, holding her by the waist and pushing.

Without warning, part of the wall to Reg's left cracked, bricks fell and flame spat. Reg felt the heat across his back, smelt cloth smoulder.

The girl screamed.

'Ned?'

'I've got her.'

'Then get a move on, will you?'

Reg loosed his grip and the girl slithered away, her feet disappearing from sight, pulled clear by Ned Lucas.

'Reg, you better get out now.'

'There's a dead woman in here, I'm not leaving her. She deserves better.'

'Just leave her, Reg.'

'No.'

Reg crawled down and around the rubble to where Mrs Charles lay. He twisted onto his side and as gently as he could, pulled her body free.

'Sorry,' he said, as if she were still capable of hearing. 'Sorry but I'm doing the best I can.'

He dragged the woman's body over to the lintel, easing her into the gap, head and shoulders first.

'Can you reach her, Ned?'

'Just about.'

'Then get her out 'cos I don't want to be in here much longer meself.'

Reg watched as the corpse's feet disappeared.

The lintel moved for a second time, more bricks fell, more flames, more smoke. And steam.

There was steam in the air now.

'Lord,' Reg said, 'don't let this be it.'

Throwing himself to the floor, he scrapped with the earth, a terrier at a rat hole, and twisted himself forward.

Something overhead moved and Reg felt whatever it was press down on the small of his back and then there were hands wrapped around his wrists, his arms, his shoulders, pulling, pulling, pulling and he was drawn free just as the lintel collapsed and the space behind him vanished forever, backfilled by fire and debris.

Minutes later, near midnight, Reg Miles stood on the street and looked back at the BSA works. Lit by flames, the southern end of New Building was entirely flattened but somehow, by some miracle, a large part of the structure appeared intact. Sides were missing but the interiors were untouched. It was almost as if a skilled doctor had taken a surgical saw to the place, removing damaged tissue and bone and nothing else.

Overhead and elsewhere bombs still fell, the air shuddering with each distant explosion. Other people's problem now, not his, not for the moment. He felt someone at his back.

'Reggie?'

'Arthur Shaw.'

'You like to cut things nice and tight then.'

'I was only doing my job. Doing what was right.'

'Maybe,' Shaw said. 'But the right thing for someone else is not always the right thing for yours truly.'

Reg nodded. 'Yeah, I almost found that out the hard way, didn't I?'

Shaw smirked. 'Made sense for me to give way to the professionals.'

A works lad, no more than fifteen, came racing towards them. 'Mr Miles!'

'Saul?'

'You live in Highgate Street, don't you?'

'I do.'

'It's been hit. Hit bad. Loads of houses is down.'

'Loads? How many?'

'I don't know. Just loads. Most maybe.'

Reg Miles ran on and turned the corner into his street. Into a scene he didn't recognise. Into someone else's life. He was anywhere but home.

To his left, a frontage torn away, a side collapsed, a bent chimney stack and a bedroom wall. An exposed fireplace below a wall-mounted mirror, the only wall left of what had been an upstairs bedroom.

To his right, water trickled from splintered pipes, dripping onto brick and timbers. It looked like a child's playset, stomped on in boredom and petulance.

He wiped smoke and dust from his eyes and bowed his head, not wanting to look at where his house had once been.

'Reggie?'

A voice in the gloom followed by a figure, a shape.

'Reggie.'

Running now, the figure leapt forward and wrapped its arms around him.

'Aggie?'

'Oh, Reggie,' Agnes Miles said, burying her head into his neck. 'Reggie.'

Reg pushed his wife away, put a hand on her left cheek. She looked up, smiled through the tears and smut that covered her face.

'Emmy?'

'She's at Phyllis's. We were in the shelter and now she's asleep on the settee in the front room. Well, got her eyes closed, at least.'

'She's alright then?'

'She's fine, Reggie. We're all fine. We're all safe. Our house too. Look at it, look at our little house.'

Through the dust, the ashes, the darkness, the flames, their house on the corner, still in one piece.

Reg raised his head to the heavens, said a silent thank you to whoever had been watching over Agnes and Emmy. And over the bricks and mortar he'd become so attached to. Sentimental, he knew, but he loved his house – their house – for what it meant to his family and the home it offered. He hoped whoever it was up there could see through the burning, smoke-filled sky and know just how grateful he was.

If there was anyone or anything up there, apart from the shadow of the Luftwaffe and the promise of more fire.

It's Birming-um

CHLOE SELL

The ship is quiet, and I feel fine, and everyone is cheerful as we eat our veal and drink red wine.

And then we hit the iceberg, and crew members are screaming, 'Women and children!' and ushering people to the lifeboats. But it is too late for me. I am drowning, and the water is pouring into my cabin. And everything becomes hazy –

I wake spluttering. Cold water running down my face, I look up. The damn cat is above me, and it doesn't take a scientist to realize she's knocked my water mug off the windowsill. She seems smug, though I know that really, I'm to blame.

My phone reads 3:39 in the morning.

Awake now, I rise from my bed. My husband's breath is heavy next to me. I hear scratching in the drywall. The rats are back. They love the bins outside the back alley. The alley I can barely walk through because of the skip, which I always get confused with the term 'tip.' I sigh.

Meandering to the living room, I turn on the light. If I peer outside our huge windows, I won't see my hometown of Indianapolis, Indiana. I'll see a dark road in Sheldon, outside Birmingham. Not Birming-*ham*, Alabama but Birming-*um*, England. I had to learn how to say it so British people don't laugh at me. I settle on the couch, about to doomscroll until I fall asleep.

When I moved to the West Midlands over three years ago, I was so excited to be away from home. In 2020, I thought England, with its history and literature and theatre, would make me happy, and I could really thrive. I stupidly thought every town was Stratford-upon-Avon, or Bath; I expected my life to be a Jane Austen novel. As soon as I moved to Birmingham, I realized how foolish, how naïve, how American I'd been.

Everything British people scoff at was at first a source of exhilaration. It was new and different and I loved it, until I learned that the locals had a point.

The trains, the buses, the tube! So many options for transport. Until there's a rail strike, or a bus strike, or a tube... well... strike.

And the weather. I actually liked the weather in England – you always knew what to expect. It's always jeans and hoodie weather. I liked not needing to look at the weather that much because it was always just bleh weather. But eventually the climate on the island got to me. When it gets a bit cold, i.e. 10 degrees for a Brit, the world stops. A Midwesterner will wear shorts in 50 degrees Fahrenheit. Once it snowed a few inches in Solihull and it took me two hours to get to work in Shirley, because the country just ceased to function. Whereas I drove through a literal blizzard one Christmas from Chicago to Indianapolis, and that's not uncommon in the States.

And the accents – Brits just had so many dialects. It's cool at first, until I realize that it is a two-way street, and people can hear *my* accent. Every time I get in an Uber, they hear me speak and think it's an invitation to ask me where I'm from. But in my mind, I'm not foreign. I'm just me. I even need subtitles for Sam, the man I live with, whom I've been in a relationship with as long as I've been in the UK.

Six weeks after meeting online, Sam picked me up from Heathrow the day I landed. I was just so happy to fall in love and be with someone who saw the good in me, that I decided to marry him. In my head, it was simple: love equals marriage.

It's harder to admit that three months after being married, I'm having doubts about our future. About us. I miss Indianapolis. I miss my family and friends. I miss feeling comfortable.

My phone lights up. *Why are you up*? My father texts me.

The phone rings twice and he answers.

'Isn't it... what time is it?'

'Three-something,' I respond. 'I keep waking up. My mind keeps going.'

'What are you thinking about?' Dad asks.

'Where to raise kids.'

'You keep obsessing about this,' he says. 'You just got married.'

It is true that I keep envisioning little baby cherubs named Margaret and Iris and Wilbur and Harry.

'I'm just upset,' I explain. 'Sam said if we stay in the UK, we might not even have kids because it's too hard without family support. And I told him what you said, that you'd help us if we moved back to the US to have a baby. But he thinks America is fascist.'

'I'm just concerned that you and Sam have such...' Dad hesitates. 'Such different opinions.'

I steel myself for what I am about to say. 'I'm worried too. I'm not saying I want to separate,' I whisper, trying to keep my voice low. 'I just feel so lost, and I don't know if I can go on like this... '

'What do you mean, separate?'

'It's not—I don't—'

'Chloe, what are you doing up?'

My husband is at the door in boxers and a band t-shirt that says, 'No one is an island,' looking quite bewildered and upset. Almost like he doesn't know where to look. Certainly not at me.

I ask Sam, 'Did I wake you up?'

'I don't know if you realize it, but your voice *carries*,' he responds.

Gulp. 'I'm sorry.'

Dad is still on the phone. 'Should we speak later?' my father asks.

'No, you don't have to go. I'm going back to bed,' Sam says pointedly, still at the floor, until he glances up at me.

His eyes shock me. I spy flashes of sadness, mixed with anger, and not a small amount of betrayal.

'I have to go, Dad.' I end the call.

I'm a little scared to speak, engulfed by the silence. Normally our silence is comfortable. It's a blanket that envelopes us when we make Tuscan salmon, or when he has his arm around me in Brueton Park and we wordlessly watch the ducks in the pond from a quaint bench. But this silence is disturbing.

I break it first. 'Are you okay?' I ask my husband.

'Just—stop.'

I frown. 'What do you mean?'

He laughs hopelessly. 'You only ask if people are okay when *you're* not okay. When you feel bad. Why don't you just be honest about how you feel?'

Shocked, then angry, I pivot. 'Are we really going to talk about honesty?' I ask.

'I told you from the beginning that I wasn't ready to have kids. Remember the beginning? When *you* were stressed because I said I'd never resent you if you didn't want children? Well now you want children and you act surprised when I have reservations.'

'I don't get it!' I exclaim. 'You always said you wanted kids, in an ideal world—'

'Yeah,' he interrupts. 'Ideally. Look around, is this ideal?'

As if on cue, the scratching in the walls starts again and someone's car alarm blares outside the Co-op. If I went outside, I'd see trash strewn around the alley and foxes peeking out from the neighbor's bins. I'd smell the chippy across the street, and if I were unlucky, rotting meat from a dumped freezer that the downstairs restaurant tipped when they went bust. Sometimes I imagine trying to have a child here. And like magic, the Soup Nazi from *Seinfeld* pops into my head and yells, 'No kids for you!'

The Indianapolis skyline, brimming with lights and skyscrapers and sky so blue that it hurts – I am sure that is the answer. I miss walking alongside the downtown canal. I miss biking on the Monon Trail, the old train line that was transformed to a walking and bicycling path that runs through multiple cities and towns. I miss my friends, whom I haven't seen in six months. If we move back, we can go to a local theater show once a month or stroll along Massachusetts Avenue on a night out. Sam can attend the Indy 500 motor race every year. Our kids can know my parents. That's important to me.

'Then why can't we go home?' I sat adamantly. 'To America?'

I am nostalgic for a time when people didn't say, 'You're not from around here.' I have the same accent as many people in the Midwest. At work yesterday, a man asked me what part of the States I was from and I said Indiana.

Indi-ana? he repeated, purposefully sounding nasally to mock me.

Yes, that's how I say it.

He proceeded to tell me he was from *Birming-um* (as if his accent was better than mine), then asked if I loved Trump. British people hear my American twang and think I'm a gun-toting, pro-life twat who hates healthcare and loves tweeting about free speech.

Sam is shocked at my suggestion. 'I'm not raising kids in a Nazi country.'

'It's not that bad!' I whine, and I sound desperate, even to my own ears.

'Chloe,' he says slowly, as if to get me to understand. 'You elected a fucking dictator in 2016.'

'And we voted him out,' I retort.

'I'm seriously worried you'll vote him back in,' he states.

'Would that... would that be the worst thing?' I see his face. 'No, I mean it would be terrible, he is literally the worst human being... but are we supposed to put our future on hold because of a president? There are going to be presidents we don't like. We're not going to have blue waves forever.'

Silence. Sam, bubbly, funny, nerdy, beautiful Sam, is suddenly silent, and I remember my dream about the Titanic, of hitting a big ball of ice and drowning, and waking up gasping for my life.

Sam's silence just sinks me.

'Why don't we talk about this tomorrow?' he says, clearly exasperated by the conversation, by me. He tries to smile. 'I'll see you in there.'

I say nothing, just watch him exit the living room.

The living room, which is normally my haven, feels cold, bitter. I don't know why, when I have so many books lining the shelves. Books used to be my home, my escape from my parents and their tumultuous relationship. I used to picture myself as the heroine, and I used to dream of meeting my soulmate.

My friend Angela once said, *I've known you since you were 19. If 19-year-old bookworm, goofy, serial dater Chloe could have what you have – a good man she married – she'd be happy. She'd be content.*

That is the problem. The crux of it all. I'm never content. I always want more and I don't know how to be happy with what I have.

I leave the couch after ten minutes and crawl into bed. Sam is still awake. He turns to me.

'What's wrong with us?' he asks, wide eyed. 'Why is it so hard now?'

I listen to the scratching and the cat mewling and the low hum of the city. 'I don't know.'

Eventually I fall asleep.

The dream begins with Sam interviewing for a nurse at what looks to be a hospital. He's busy chatting, selling himself. I'm impressed that he's doing so well.

Then suddenly, Sam collapses and crumples on the ground.

'Oh my god!' I yell. 'Sam! Sam!' I try to rush to him but can't touch him for some reason. I start yelling. Asking people for help. I call 999.

'We aren't an emergency service anymore,' the lady on the line says, annoyed at my audacity.

'But my husband could be dead,' I cry.

'Call someone else.' She hangs up.

Then I'm on a slow train to Coventry, asking for help, if anyone knows where my husband is. Everyone avoids me, as if I am asking for change. I know no one. I'm just a small being, all alone.

I wake up with great sobs wracking my body.

Sam's arm wraps around me. 'What's happening?'

I sob harder.

'Hey, hey, it's fine, you're okay,' he soothes.

'I just dreamt you'd fallen, collapsed. And you might have died.'

'I'm okay,' he whispers, stroking my hair. He's half asleep and still dazed.

'I'm just so sad. You're my world. Please don't go anywhere,' I say, sounding like an insecure child. 'I just miss home so much, sometimes I want to give up.'

'I won't go anywhere,' he promises. His lips are soft against mine. 'We're a team. You go, I go. We just have to wait a bit.'

'I don't want anything to happen to you.' I kiss him back

'Nothing will happen to me,' he assures me. 'Let's stay here, in bed for awhile. I'll hold you. Will you stay?'

I once said to Sam, 'We are such good friends at the heart of our relationship, that if we grew apart, we'd still support each other, have love for one another. There wouldn't be any animosity and we'd be okay.' I think I was trying to persuade myself that if he breaks up with me, it won't hurt that bad.

But now I don't know if that's true. I feel like Jane Eyre – so deeply attached to Sam that there is a cord connecting me to him, and if that cord is severed, I may never recover.

Sam's not my soulmate. He's part of my body. Something about us just works, and I can't explain it, but I'm grateful nonetheless. He is my right ventricle. He helps me function. I don't need blind love; I'm not a teenager anymore. I need someone who's honest, someone who genuinely likes and respects me. Someone who's funny and kind. Without Sam, I'm just in this industrial second city, on this island, floating. Pretending I don't need him.

But I do.

'I'll stay.'

And Deeds Need Doing February 1914

ELEANOR TRIGG

Esther opens the front door to February's icy breath. It rushes inwards, stinging the rounds of her cheeks as though it has been waiting in the dark to be let in. She pulls her shawl tight and replaces the key on the side table next to her father's chair. Her father had only taken to locking the door in the last year – now that they have *good things* – and it will only be unlocked for an hour or so. It can't take much longer than that, though she cannot be sure. She has never done this before.

It was her father who had brought them into the house, seeds of the rebellion tucked into the crook of his underarm. The stack of newspapers had seemed harmless to him when he picked them up from the side of the road. Their ink still bright, though dated several weeks ago. The masthead read: *The Suffragette*.

Coming home, he had found Esther crouched, knees to the floorboards at the fireplace, getting the ashes up. The weather had turned and the fire needed to be stacked anew.

'Waste not, want not', he said, handing the tattered papers to her, smiling as he took off his coat and walked into the kitchen. He continued talking from the other room, but Esther was not listening. She touched the front-page etching of a tall woman in a Grecian robe. The woman wore a blindfold, there was a sword in her hand, a homestead ablaze in the background. She opened the pages out and found the black newspaper print had rubbed off on to her fingers. The paper was telling her to have courage. The ink that the rebellion was now. The words to rise from the floor she found herself on.

Her father put his dinner plate down on the table, with one hand.

'Found them,' he said, gesturing with a fork. 'Woman on the street must've got moved on. Remembered we'd run out for the fire.'

Esther didn't reply and turned another page. Her father reached over and took the paper out of her hands.

'Alright now, Em-leen.'

She looked up at her father. She knew there had been rallies in Northfield where he had taken his evening classes, Emmeline Pankhurst had been there. He crumpled the paper in his palm and wedged it in between the firewood.

'Paper needs to be in tighter,' he said to her, as though she had not done it before. Crouching, he pushed it in further. She examined her fingertips in thought. He took the stack and crumpled another.

'If your mother was around, she wouldn't worry herself with things like that. Only good for the fire.' He righted himself using her shoulder and walked away into the kitchen again to wash his hands. 'The Libs don't like them. Asquith don't like them. I don't like them. Don't really want what they think they want.'

'Lots of girls at the factory wear the Votes for Women badges.'

'Any of them married?' he called around the doorway.

Esther is careful where she steps, but her boots are losing their grip on the frosted pavement. Through her own breath, she can see a tall woman standing at the corner of the road, waiting. The woman's dark clothing and hair camouflage her against the night as she approaches. They do not speak. Esther does not know her name.

She is older, and Esther wonders who she might have left sleeping – a husband, children – and what that means. The woman nods at her and they walk, Esther adjusting her own timid gait to match the woman's longer, stronger strides. She pushes her hands into her pockets to stop the spread of the frost prickling upwards. The other woman cannot do the same because her pockets are full of paraffin wax.

They pass Harry's house at the end of a neat terrace row. His windows are dark. Esther thinks of him sleeping. He is the brother of one of the girls she works with at the factory and she had feigned sickness when he called for her earlier, though her father always eagerly opens the door. He says Harry has prospects as a student of technical drawing, declares him willing to *put the work in*, use his mind to make better of himself in life. What thought had her father ever given to her own prospects, her own mind?

It wasn't that she didn't like seeing Harry. She had walked these same streets with him when they were warmer. In the summertime, he had picked wild lilacs and larkspur for her, brought violets and baby's breath to the house. In the autumn, he picked up horse chestnuts from the ground and pulling off their jackets, smiled at the smoothness under his thumb. He guided her hand to do the same, intent on her reaction, but she had looked away. He has an eye for beautiful things.

'When we marry,' he had said to her, 'you won't have to work. I don't want people to think that I'm not capable. You can stay home, look after the house. The children.'

She liked work at the factory, though the pay was low. She had found friends there, a feeling of independence. With Harry, she also found there was a language of unspoken understandings. By allowing his hand around the small of her waist, she was consenting to this life that he speaks of. That he assumes she wants. It is not a life that she doesn't want but even as she feels the blush on her cheeks, she knows she wants more – more than what is handed to women by the men around them, however gently it is done.

On the day they had walked Victoria Common together, a crowd had gathered by the gates. The people stood, captivated by a woman. A Suffragette who's face contorted as she spoke. Esther imagined an upraised sword in the woman's hand, just like the one from the papers that had stoked the fire. Harry put his lips close to her ear.

'I don't see what gives them the right,' he said. 'Surely they know not even all men have the vote?' His voice was soft, as was his grip when he pulled her away. 'Still just the rich. We need to get all men the vote. Then as wives, well, they can *influence* the way their husbands vote.'

'Not all women are wives.'

'No. I guess not.' He looked at her and kissed her hand. 'Not yet anyway.'

But all she could think of was: *what if the children are girls?*

The closer they get, the fewer houses there are to mark the way, and Esther can see it now, their destination: the Northfield Carnegie library. She looks backwards towards the last lit lamp-post and sees a second woman moving through the dark trees to find them. This one is a stranger too, but she joins the beat of their steps, and there are three of them now, accompanied by the rhythmic rattle of matches in a pocket.

All three women had attended the same rally where the plans were made, so each know that there are other women abroad tonight, on different street corners – other violence in mind. The crowd at the rally had been heightened and noisy when Esther got there. The speaker was stood, raised on a cast iron bandstand in the middle of the park.

'There has been little progress so far,' the woman spoke above the crowd, 'because the campaign has been led by middle class women! Prim women, who already lay claim to a voice through their privilege. *We* have achieved more than they have, in forty long years – and they call us violent women! What right have they to speak for us, to act for us? Almost as little as men. It'll still be votes only for the rich!'

The women roared back at the speaker, and the unity in their voices touched something in Esther that made her feel like sobbing.

'We must fight for ourselves,' the speaker concluded, 'through any means possible!'

Someone in the crowd screamed, 'Liberty or death!' and Esther felt it in her bones with the rising of the women around her. Emboldened by this braveness of others, she waited behind. She would volunteer. Find her conviction. Do what was needed.

She had hesitated when they told her it would be the library, knowing her father would disapprove. It had surprised her too that they would suggest it – these women of the people – because the library was built *for* the people, with donated money, donated land. She remembers the ribbon being cut.

But they had told her it had to be this way, because there will be uproar and the books will burn.

In the night, they will burn brightly.

The streets are still silent when she is ushered round the back of the library, through a gap in the iron fence where shrubs have been planted. There are no other buildings, no watching windows. Esther's woollen skirt snags on to the thorns and one of the women frees it while the other picks up a weighty stone from the ground. She wraps it in a piece of cloth and gives it to Esther, squeezing her hand around it, nodding towards the glass panes in the rear door.

'Put your force into it.'

Esther hesitates, thinking of Harry again. She remembers him pointing out the initials of George and Elizabeth Cadbury intertwined on the brickwork of the Village Institute. He said that when he made partner in a practice, he would do that: hide their initials on every building he drew. She wants them to understand – both Harry and her father, but she knows they can't, she knows she must choose. A woman can be many things at the same time. If only they would let her.

'I find it helps to remember that men were never asked to justify *why* they should be given the vote,' the woman whispers in her ear.

Esther breaks the window, and it is a thrill.

Inside of the library, they use the matches to light a candle. It illuminates rows of lettered spines and the grain on the wooden surfaces that surround them. Hot wax runs over and between the woman's fingers, but she does not flinch. She tells Esther to start piling up the books. The others leave with the candle to make sure that no one else is inside, while Esther rounds the counter. She scoops books from their shelves, trying not to read the titles, and drops them into the middle of the reading room floor, bending the covers backwards so the paper catches first.

'Not in the middle,' the two other women have returned and share a look. 'In the corner.' They begin to move the pile she has created. 'It'll go up faster. Just like building a fire in the hearth.'

At the meeting, the crowd had been told: *If you cannot speak, you can learn to speak. If you are heckled, you can learn to reply.*

She would learn how to set fire to things.

'Quickly.'

The first woman takes the paraffin wax out of her pockets, the second strikes a match, and the books are ablaze. Esther is surprised at the speed with which the fire takes hold. How the flames are already lapping at the ceiling, the walls cradling them, higher and higher. The three women stand frozen around the fire as the frost on the windows melts. Feeling returns to their toes. Water puddles at their feet. Esther can feel the full radiant heat of it now and understands what it must be like to work at a furnace. Her upswept hair slips. Strands of it are sticking to her neck and forehead, mingling with the sweat which drips underneath the cotton of her blouse. She watches the flames shift colour in the darkness – it must be the ink making it burn like that. The fire is not afraid to burn, it jumps from book to book and devours them. It breaks down the words and releases them into the night. They are heavy on the smoke as it circles the women, as it roils and hangs to the ceiling. Words written by men.

Esther licks the bow of her top lip and feels the ash on her tongue, tastes it bitter at the back of her throat. She feels the change as she sees it on the faces of the others, a strange cast that is hungry like the fire. Black shadows reach up the walls and seep into the texture and lines on the women's faces, around their eyes and forehead, in the extra folds that have formed at their jawlines. Their eyes burn.

What have the three of them summoned in the darkness?

One of the other women grabs another armful of books and throws them all together on to the fire. No one has considered what women are capable of, no one has considered women at all – only as givers of life, menders, soothers – and yet, this is how good it feels to destroy something. Would she still be beautiful to Harry? He has an eye for beautiful things. Can a violent woman be loved? She does not want to lose their love, *but is it love*, when they would give the same to a caged animal, or a little bird? They want her meek, they want her compliant.

He should have brought her oleanders.

He should have learnt to fear her.

The women are panting together in the heat. Sweat still drips down Esther's neck, the skin on her back and her thighs. It is herself she has summoned. The wild parts of herself. The fire demands more, so she removes her shawl, she doesn't need it, she does not feel the cold anymore. She wants to watch the dried baby's breath hiss in the flames and breathe in its fragrance. She wants to throw in everything she owns, all her *good things*.

The other women watch her and throw their own shawls to the fire.

She is as tall as her shadow: the fire, the other women, they have made her that way. She wants to feel this powerful all the time, this unpalatable. She knows they feel it too. The crackle has become a low roar. Wind enters through the open door, fanning the flames further. There is the smell of the bookcases burning. The crack of the varnish as it peels. The wood panelling is beginning to smoke. If it must be binary, then she picks this. She picks the roaring flame.

She wants to set fire to the world.

The world as men have made it.

DJ, MC, Banshee

TOM MAGUIRE

The Banshee finds me in the smoking area. I don't notice him at first. I'm too busy choking on a Marlboro, chatting with strangers about how the latest dance releases sound like shit. The basslines are too honking, too farty, the drums too anaemic. Nobody's listening to me but I don't mind. I'm half-cut on cheap ale and overpriced sniff, enough to keep my mouth going, whether I want it to or not.

'One sec,' I say, checking my phone for a message that isn't there. When I look up everyone's gone, scarpered in the lull. Except for him.

He's older than me, late fifties maybe. Bald head creased with wrinkles. Cheeks like bruised turnips, purplish-pinkish hues dancing on his white skin. Wire frame glasses hang over eyes reddened with burst blood vessels. He looks like he's about to cry.

'You're playing tonight.' His voice is all over the place, a bastard-child of Birmingham and Dublin.

'I'm on soon,' I say, my words fighting the ambient gallop of the drums. Behind me, the club's walls flex, unable to contain the noise. We're in a small venue nestled in the arse-end of the Jewellery Quarter. It's been around a while, hanging on by its fingernails. The residents of the new flats nearby have complained enough to enforce a curfew – nights that once went on until four are hard-capped at one. We'll most likely have to turn it down for my set.

'Maybe I could jump on vocals?' The Banshee smiles and I'm surprised to see all his teeth intact. He extends a hand. 'MC Banshee, AKA The Banshee, AKA Just Banshee AKA J to the B. Whichever you like.'

It's unexpected, I'll give him that. Most of the time it's kids in snapbacks and trackies blagging impromptu mic duties. The majority sound like coked-up horse-racing commentators, words tripping over themselves as they try to stay on beat.

'Sorry,' I say. 'I don't really know you, do I? And it's all a bit last minute.'

'Ah, come on mate,' he grips my arm a little too tight. I can feel the freeze of his skin through my jacket. 'You'd be surprised at the shit I conjure up.' A tear runs down his nose. His eyes are surreal, the pupils ulcerous, blood logged. The stare of an albino rabbit.

I don't reply. What am I meant to say? I look at my phone instead.

'No, don't worry. I understand,' he half-whispers. 'I see it now. Your head is full of death and you're scared of what might happen.'

'What are you on about?' My surroundings begin to churn. Beer and fags and filthy petrol-stained smog all congeal in me, a jellied knot.

He makes an imprecise shape with his mouth. A grin or a yawn. 'You don't have to hide it. You can't, not with me. All that loss. You stink of it.'

'Fuck off with the cold reading. You're not Derren Brown.' I want to get up and leave. I don't because that would be ceding ground.

'I didn't mean anything by it, like.' The Banshee leans towards me. 'I can see them, is all. Squatting on your shoulder. Quite a few, aren't there? And some are so fresh.' He looks briefly at his lap and his tone grows morose. 'Recent arrivals are always such a shame.'

I lay my hands flat on the table. I need something solid to hold onto. There must be a look on my face because he gets up, putting distance between us.

'Sorry,' he says. 'Don't want to get your back up. Just trying to understand. I dig deep on the mic and I spit pure truth. Not everyone can handle it.' He lights a fag and walks away, skirting the club and making straight for the outdoor exit.

He lingers at the threshold. From afar he seems impossibly tall, eyes vaguely luminous, a lamppost of a man. Behind him, the hodgepodge buildings of the Jewellery Quarter war with one another. Panels of yellowed light swarm through the dark, cast out by distant flats and houses.

My eyes are stinging. I blink, rub smoke from them. When I look up, the smoking area's empty. Beneath the shuttering gate lies the smouldering cherry of a dashed cigarette, little burning blood clot haemorrhaging at the night.

I'm at some afters in Selly Oak. My chest is a hollowed-out cavity. Heartbeat in my eyes, my ears, the back of my teeth like my organs have split into smithereens and gone travelling up and down my body. *Smithereens*. One of those words you only think of when you're spangled. I test it in my mouth, drop the serenity of the *serenes* so I'm left with *mither*. Mither, like your grandparents like to say. As in to worry, to have worries.

My head's full of electricity. I can feel it crackle, foil in my frontal cortex. What have I sniffed? Impossible to know, mouth doesn't work to ask. Sofa beneath me is hard. The springs press on me like they want to fuck me up the arse. Not a bad idea. Why do I only want to get fucked up the arse when I'm in a state? Does that make me gay when I'm off my head and straight when I'm not? If I'm always half off my head, does that make me half gay, or just bisexual?

Nonsense. Plughole-swirling-faecal-thoughts. I fold myself forward and use a blood-spackled note to hoover up crystalline remnants from the coffee table.

I must be the oldest person in this room. I bet none of this lot remember 9/11, or the loudness wars, or the birth of dubstep. Not sure I remember those things either, but at least I was around when they happened. Conversations soar and spiral, the words muffled by the percussive drone of techno. Everybody seems to be having one of those deep meaningful chats you always hope you'll have when you're fucked, moments you store like kindling inside yourself for when it gets too dark. Proof that you not only had fun, but that it was significant, worthwhile. Except I'm on the outside again.

Always somehow on the outside.

At least the set went well. Played a good mix of stuff. Snuck a bit of jungle in even though the promoters said not to – they never care in the end as long as people are dancing. Crowd was thin but that's the way these days. If you're still clinging to the scene at my age, it's never for recognition. Only the distracted regard of the other DJs and their mates and a few ketted-up kids near the front. I assume they were ketted-up tonight, anyway: their eyes were lidded, barely moving at all. They gripped the stage barrier like it was a cliff edge, the back of the club a yawning chasm.

The Banshee's words rattle inside me like broken bones. I try to shrink him in retrospect, make him diminutive and insignificant. His eyes were weird, granted, but it's not like I haven't been in a similar state before. I tell myself he's just some odd old stoner, though I'm not sure I believe it. I stare at the unlit nub of a spliff poking from between my fingers, grimace and dash it in the ashtray.

Beside me on the sofa, a pair of twenty-something lads sit with their foreheads pressed together. The taller one has his back to me. His over-sized, far-too-clean jacket hangs loose over his shoulders as he whispers to his mate. The exchange is strangely rhythmic, peaking and troughing like a muttered incantation.

'I just never expected it,' the taller one says, his words suddenly intelligible. 'He was so young. He seemed like the most together one. Thought he'd just gone away for the weekend, not told anyone. And then I woke up on Sunday and it was all over his Insta. His sister posted, saying he'd been found.'

The other lad just laughs. Why is he laughing?

Standing up is much harder than it has any right to be. The room warps and contracts around me, Alice in Wonderland. I try not to look anybody in the eye as I spacewalk to the bathroom. I vomit pink bile into the toilet and slip out the front door without a word.

My eyes rip again when I wake up. It's a bad one this time, hot needles spearing through my vision. I shake off the duvet, chest heaving against the pain, and fumble through the dark to the bathroom. No point turning the light on – it'll only make it worse. I run the tap as hot as I can, drench a facecloth in the scalding water and press it to my face. As soon as the heat becomes tolerable, I resoak and repeat until I can open my eyes without the needle-stab.

Turn on the light. Brow, cheeks, nose-bridge, nascent crow-lines – all have turned the colour of cooked lobster shell. Two not-quite symmetrical gashes are carved into the surface of each eye, red canyons running from the iris through the yellowing whites.

The doctors called it some long name I can never remember. The surfaces of my eyes aren't smooth, as they should be, but striated like the topographical lines on a map. Apparently, there are these hooks on the insides of everyone's eyelids. If your eyeballs are wrong like mine are, the hooks can catch. It's worse when you're sleeping: then, they have time to nestle deep, sit like barbed arrows. When you wake up to greet the day, they take a chunk of you with them.

It wasn't always like this. The rips only started a few months ago, around the time Emma left me and Sean left us all. Hard not to see the three things as related: the break-up and the funeral somehow altering my physiology. The doctors said that was impossible but they don't know everything. I've seen them get it wrong before. I'll never forget how they sent Sean home with bandaged wrists, a script for SSRI's and a CBT worksheet, thinking their job was done. Now, I suppose it is.

My head crackles like a spent fire. No time for this. No time, even, to eat. I have another set in forty minutes. I pop two Solpadol, have a quick puff on a spliff end and change into the first crumpled items of clothing I can find on the floor.

The venue's some swanky bullshit bar near Colmore Row. It's bolted to the base of a glass-fronted office tower which swats defiantly at the sky. It's all so sanitary, but I suppose that's the goal. The endpoint of development, the thing we're meant to strive for. Steel behemoths swaying above our heads while we serfs push our buttons in the basements, soundtracking the clink and splash of overpriced drinks down Botoxed necks.

I stumble through the crowd of bankers and asset managers, keeping my head down like I might catch affluenza. I'm late again but nobody cares. The bar manager's given up chastising me for it, just pipes whatever's on her Spotify through the speakers until I show up. Right now it's *There is a Light That Never Goes Out* by The Smiths. I slip behind the decks and unhook her phone from the aux so I can get on with the boilerplate stuff: top 40 remixes, 90s dance classics – what I overheard some kid call *dad house* the other day – and the blandest, most inoffensive tech house on my USB. Nobody is dancing and everybody is buying drinks.

Exactly how it's supposed to be.

My eyes start playing up about halfway through the night. It starts as a prickling sensation at the corners, followed by profuse weeping which warps my vision like raindrops on a camera lens. The lights above the bar blur, then shimmer. The screens on the CDJs become unreadable and I begin selecting songs blind, mashing Lana Del Rey into Shy FX into Joy Division.

I wipe my brow with my shirt, but the relief is short-lived. The feeling of debris prickling under the lids intensifies, layers into a lashing, searing pain. I check how I look in my phone camera. All I see is the discoloured impression of my face, dull crimson smears where my eyes should be like burnt-out LEDs.

Outside again.

Cold air only makes the weeping worse, but it feels right out here. More cathartic. I've left some pretentious overlong prog-house track playing on the decks. Hopefully the pain will be manageable by the time I have to go back in. Cigarettes help as long as I angle my head up and away from the smoke. Above, the moon bursts through the clouds with its fat jaundiced face.

Sean used to attend as many of my sets as he could – even the background music residencies like this one. He'd come out for fags with me or just stand and have a natter near the booth. We'd talk about the others we'd lost, most of them from the scene, all of them taken their own way out. Damien and Rae and Haz and Raheem. Names I still find hard to vocalise, though the scars they've left are well worn by now.

Across the smoking area, near the road, there's a bloke hunched over a concrete bollard. His bald head cricks to one side, neck contorted like a rung dishcloth. I can just about make out the bruises on his cheeks. The sharp glint of wire frame glasses angled towards me.

Is it him? I can't tell. Distortions ridge my sight like pleated clingfilm.

Something jerks at the back of his throat. He turns his head and wretches a jet of pink onto the pavement. I think of the blood streaking my own eyes. Sean, slipping in and out of consciousness in a waiting room. The blood-soaked kitchen roll.

I blink and pinpricks dance beneath my eyelids. Seething, I press the heels of my palms to my eyes. They're grubby, but cold. Soothing. When I remove them, he's gone.

I wake with a flinch, eyes bristling and acidic. If they've ripped, at least it's not a bad one. I forego my usual hot compress and shuffle through the flat, half-blind. In the hallway I see a brief snatch of a tall silhouette, an afterburn embossed on my vision. I enter the kitchen like a burglar in my own home. I suppose I'm worried The Banshee will turn up here, too. That I'll find him standing at the stove frying eggs for the pair of us, perhaps having climbed in through the seventh-floor window.

The flat's empty. Of course it is. Idiot.

The space between the weekends looms bloated and hungry, ready to drain what little money I've made. To top up my wages, I pick up a few night shifts from the cleaning agency, hoovering flats in Perry Barr and offices in Edgbaston.

I don't mean to start caning my stash. I usually keep it light on weekdays, try to give myself a break. Can hardly handle the comedowns nowadays. But there's a restlessness I can't seem to get rid of. An urgent itching beneath the skin, a new bite to the wounds littering my eyes.

Daylight becomes a myth, something glanced in snippets behind curtains. I empty every baggie and blister packet I can find. Codeine, Valium and liquor to help me sleep. Rails of speed with my coffee and fag during the night-mornings. Slugs of ketamine and nugs of weed after work to calm me down. One microdose of magic mushrooms that's very seriously misjudged because my scales are broken, so I see fractals of dust swarming at me while I wipe down a call centre.

Unable to rest. Heartbeat too fast and too slow, jerked between extremes in a chemical tug of war. A whirlpool, the world a pool, my eyesight split into whorls and pustules. I lose count of how many times they rip. I've grown used to the pink bloody sheen in my gaze.

I wake to rippled darkness. The alarm clock tells me I'm going to be late for my set if I don't leave in five minutes, but moving is so slow. Cold tattoos my arms and coils around my neck. My lips rub against each other like rough stones, gates to a mouth full of ulcers and sores. My eyes, old friends, remain lacerated.

Tonight, I'm on opening duties at Suki10c. Bass music, usual fare. Lights score the empty dancefloor and the beer taps wink at me seductively, but I'm ten minutes over so I go straight for the decks. Liquid DnB is already rolling from the speakers. It's a bit clean, but alright enough. Mournful samples and chopped-up vocals overlay the bass drone, all splintered snares and echoed ghosts of words. I elaborate on the theme, selecting dirgey tunes with wonky, minor-key hooks.

Not a soul on the floor. I keep mixing, adjusting, trying out blends that nobody will ever hear. I suppose it'll fill out for the headliner – or maybe not. Punters are fickle this time of year when the cold, wet nights settle over the city like a permanent hangover.

I'm not surprised to see The Banshee enter. I've come to expect him, crag-faced bad penny. Even across the gulf of the dancefloor, I can sense something has shifted between us, some tilt to the balance of power. He approaches in loping steps and clambers onto the stage. Stares down his purpled nose at me, expression flitting between what looks like hunger and apprehension.

There's a microphone in his hand. He fumbles with it a second before plugging it into the mixer.

'I never meant to upset you,' he says, shouting down my ear. 'Shame how it turned out, but maybe for the best. Some people can't quite get the rhythm right.' He winks and something thumps in my chest, a sucker-punch palpitation. His eyes are the colour of skinned flesh.

He turns away before I can reply. Just as well. My throat is tight, folded inwards like a disused tunnel about to collapse. Fleshy subsidence.

When he raises the mic, I expect machine-gun bars full of manic bravado. But The Banshee doesn't rap, or spit, or toast. Instead, the room fills with delicate, breathy singing. The vocals float over the grit and snap of the beat while the words drown in the melody, filling me with false memories of darkening skies and lost love. I try to pick a tune with a similar vibe but it clashes with his intonations. I mix out quickly, begin selecting stripped-back, pulsing songs which bubble beneath his lyrics, more infrastructure than architecture.

The crowd materialises from nowhere. Figures arrive through unseen doorways, melt upwards like stalagmites from the dancefloor. They move in stilted, hypnotic steps. Mouths slack, squinting eyes. Exaltation or discomfort, I can't quite tell. Maybe there's no difference between the two. Maybe they're on rhino ket.

The bodies simmer and roil, movements coloured by sound and light. They surge, press into one another until the front row is crammed against the barrier. A single mass reaching for The Banshee, trying to snatch his song from the air.

I scan for somebody I recognise, though I'm not sure who. It doesn't matter in the end. My eyes are too broken. All I can make out are smudged blurs, faces gnarled like tree burls. The songs begin to drift from one another, drums clashing and biting. I reach for the scorched iris of the CDJ but I can't find the beat.

Neon light strobes from behind the booth. It cuts into the crowd, into me, seeming to pass right through us.

About the authors

JOSH ALLEN

Josh Allen is a Birmingham based writer, journalist and contemporary historian. He produces Walk Midlands, a website of day walks across the English Midlands, doable without a car, and is writing a book about walking across the West Midlands.

ANJEM ANWAR

Anjem Anwar, a Brummie, grew up on books and Bollywood. Through his prose, he hopes to champion South Asian voices, joy, and culture. A lapsed scientist with an MSc in toxicology, Anjem is a teacher to little humans. He conjures up fantastical short stories while drinking copious amounts of coffee.

JAMILA BARRY

Jamila Barry is an Irish Brummie Muslim mother of grown sons who likes writing, cooking, and cluttering up the house with her own paintings. She writes for herself, mainly, about craving for belonging, stability and a sense of home.

ALAN BEARD

Alan Beard has published two story collections, *Taking Doreen Out of the Sky* (Picador, 1999) and *You Don't Have to Say* (Tindal Street Press, 2010). He has had numerous stories and flashes in magazines and anthologies, most recently in Leon Literary Magazine, trampset, Outside Left and Best Microfiction 2024.

PATRICK BOYDEN

Patrick Boyden's formative years were spent in the West Midlands. He has since led a peripatetic life and is currently happily settled in a remote part of Greece. *The Fox* is his second story to be accepted by Floodgate, and he wishes one of his unpublished novels could be similarly successful.

ESME BROWN
Esme Brown is a writer and carer living and working in Birmingham. She has never intentionally squashed a slug.

JAMES BROGDEN
James Brogden is a Birmingham-based author of horror and dark fiction, and occasional Australian. His stories have appeared in numerous anthologies and his novel *The Plague Stones* was short-listed for the August Derleth award in 2021. He is owned by three cats who do not approve of this nonsense.

TAYLOR BURNS
Taylor Burns's first novel is forthcoming from Zer0 Books in 2025. He also co-curates STORIE – a bi-monthly night of experimental prose – in conjunction with Voce Books. He lives in Birmingham and is working on a second novel, among other things.

SASHA BUTLER
Sasha Butler is a Birmingham-based writer. Her first novel *As Soft as Dreams* was shortlisted for the Cheshire Novel Prize 2022 and the Bath Novel Award 2022. She is represented by Bell Lomax Moreton literary agency and is currently working on her second novel.

LIZ CHURCHILL
Liz Churchill lives in Birmingham. She writes short stories and runs Mo Stories a live fiction night. She's part of Writing West Midlands Room 204 and The London Library Emerging Writers Programme. Her writing's been published online by *The Mechanics' Institute Review* and she won the Scratch Books A4 Competition.

HELEN CROSS
Helen Cross's stories are published in many magazines and anthologies, including most recently The Manchester Review, Popshot and *Digbeth Stories.* She is the author of four novels, including BAFTA-winning *My Summer of Love* and has written audio drama for twenty years, most recently two seasons of the acclaimed BBC podcast drama series *English Rose.*

R. M. FRANCIS

R. M. Francis is a Creative Writing lecturer at the University of Wolverhampton. He has produced novels, *Bella* and *The Wrenna,* poetry collection *Subsidence*, waybook *The Chain Coral Chorus*, and short fiction collection *Ameles / Currents of Unmindfulness*. His academic work has appeared in international journals and edited collections.

KIRSTEN HANDLEY

Kirsten Handley grew up in Worcestershire and went to Aston University, a big inspiration for this piece. She writes flash fiction and short stories and is delighted to feature in this anthology. Her short story *Body Count* featured in the *Digbeth Stories* collection and her flash fiction piece *Ice* appeared in the 2020 Flash Fiction Journal. She has also featured in Birmingham and Moseley Writers Group Anthologies. Kirsty works in finance with too many spreadsheets and PowerPoint presentations and therefore loves using writing as an outlet for her creativity.

ANDY HOWLETT

Andy Howlett is a Birmingham-based artist and filmmaker. He's interested in the power of collective walking to re-map and re-enchant our public spaces. His walks and films have been commissioned by Flatpack Festival, Ikon Gallery, Solihull Council, Creative Black Country and Voce Books/Influx Press. He is co-founder of walking-art collective Walkspace. If you do walk your own neighbourhood skull the collective would love to hear about it.

ALAN KANE FRASER

Alan Kane Fraser is a writer from Birmingham. His stage play *Random Acts of Malice* won the inaugural Derek Lomas New Writing Award. He had a short story included in *Digbeth Stories* (Floodgate Press, 2023) and his debut novel *The Muse of Hope Falls* was published by Lightning Books (2023).

SADIE KAYE

Sadie Kaye is a transgender woman, a poet, an artist and a feminist. She writes poetry and prose, much of it about her life as a trans woman. She runs a spoken word group called Birmingham VOICES and performs her works and exhibits her paintings in and about Birmingham, UK.

LIZ KERSHAW

Liz Kershaw is a prize-winning writer of short fiction. Publications include short stories and a novella (Mantle Lane Press), the Historical Writers' Association short story anthologies, and *Our Man in the Moone* (prose, drama and animation). She is a member of Writing West Midlands and Tindal Street Fiction Group.

RICHARD LAKIN

Richard Lakin is a former police officer and journalist now working in the civil service. His work has been published in the *Guardian*, *Daily Telegraph*, *Structo* and *Londonist* and others. He's based in Staffordshire.

ZAHIRA P. LATIF

Zahira P. Latif is a British Pakistani Muslim woman from a working-class background with a passion for writing. Her essays have been featured in national and international literary journals, as well as in various anthologies. She is currently working on her first book, a polemical critique of the implications of capitalism on well-being.

CATHERINE LOCKHART

Catherine Lockhart is a freelance writer, author and poet based in the West Midlands. Her poetry has been archived in Bishopsgate Institute as part of a Switchboard's 50th Anniversary competition, and her poem *Shrink* is published in Heroica's first anthology in September 2024.

TOM MAGUIRE

Tom Maguire is a writer and DJ who lives in North Birmingham with his partner, Alison. His fiction appears in *Digbeth Stories* by Floodgate Press, *Grim & Gilded* and *Crow & Cross Keys*. His non-fiction appears in *Blue Labyrinths*. He met The Banshee in a smoking area in November 2022.

SIOBHAN MAHER
After a decade designing jewellery (in Birmingham's Jewellery Quarter, natch), Siobhan Maher returned to her writing roots and now runs Authology, a brand storytelling studio. Halfway through an MA Creative Writing at the University of Birmingham, she is also tackling her first novel. Siobhan writes about art, motherhood and memory.

MEZ PACKER
Mez Packer is an Assistant Professor at Coventry University and teaches on various writing programmes. She has published two novels, numerous short stories and articles. Her debut, *Among Thieves*, was nominated for the Commonwealth Writers' Prize and Authors' Club First Novel Award. She also works as an editor and mentor.

CHERYL POWELL
Cheryl Powell is a Worcestershire writer published by *Coffin Bell, Litro, Spelk, Storgy*, Reflex Fiction, *The Bangalore Review,* Boudicca Press, *The Mechanics' Institute Review,* and Arachne Press, among others. Two of her stories have been performed by the Liars' League. She is a wannabe cold water swimmer.

CHLOE SELL
Chloe Sell is an American writer living in Solihull with her husband Ben and Bengal cat named Minnie. She dreams of lavender white mochas and world peace.

MATTHEW STORER
Matthew Storer was born in 1976 and spent his childhood in Rugby, Warwickshire. He read English Literature at the University of Sheffield before attending Nottingham Law School. For the last twenty years he has lived and worked in Birmingham. He is a big fan of trees in urban environments.

ELEANOR TRIGG
Eleanor Trigg is from Birmingham. She finds much more joy in writing stories driven by history, science, or myth, than she does writing about herself. She studied architecture and conservation at university and works as a Timber Frame Designer. Her words have been published in *Lucent Dreaming*. She is working on her first novel.

LYNNE VOYCE

Lynne Voyce's fiction and non-fiction has been widely published. She has won and been placed in many competitions, among them Legend, Flash 500 and the Calderdale Short Story Prize. In 2019, she was included in *Common People: An Anthology of Working Class Writers* (ed. Kit de Waal). Lynne teaches English and lives in Bearwood with her family.

BEN WADDINGTON

Ben Waddington is the author of *111 Places in Birmingham That You Shouldn't Miss,* now in its second edition. He is the director of Still Walking, a Birmingham-based festival of guided tours and walking events, and city organiser for Birmingham's PechaKucha nights. Tipping Point is an extract from his forthcoming novel *Material Girl.*

IAN WHATLEY

Ian Whatley was born in Hall Green and now lives in South Carolina. His fiction has appeared in *Lost and Found Times*, 6S Review and *The Legendary*. To support his writing habit, he has twenty-one patents on athletic footwear technologies and produces coaching videos for race walkers. His life is even stranger than his stories.

CHARLES WILKINSON

Charles Wilkinson was born in Digbeth and is a former full member of the Tindal Street Fiction Group. He has published five collections of short stories, four of them with Egaeus Press. His pamphlet *Ag & Au*, partly about the Jewellery Quarter, appeared from the Birmingham-based press Flarestack Poets.

Acknowledgements

GARRIE: Thanks again to my incredible family for supporting and encouraging me, Dan Ecclestone and Amber Fletcher for professional advice, the great writers whose support we received through attending STORIE and Old Mo Stories, run by Clive and Taylor, and Liz, respectively, to my fellow long-suffering editors for, again, not shooting me when a bullet would've made more sense, and to Juliet for always being there.

PETER: We are grateful to the following people for their help creating the Night Time Economy collection: Kit de Waal, Jonathan and everyone at Writing West Midlands, Clive and Maria at Voce Books & everyone at the Warehouse Café, Catherine and Claire at The Heath Bookshop, and everyone who spread the word on our behalf. Special thanks to those who bought a copy of *Digbeth Stories*, allowing us to carry on this venture.

NIGEL: As ever and always, thanks to Caroline, Rachel and Katy. Also, thanks to everyone who's ever taken Floodgate seriously by buying a copy of *Digbeth Stories*, stocking it on their bookshop's shelves, or trusting us with their prose. And a special thank you to Clive and Maria at Voce Books, whose kind support has been immeasurable and invaluable. Finally, to Pete and Garrie: blimey, only looks as if we've gone and done it again.